"I didn't say that we in the Islands aren't members of the human race. I said we aren't Earthlings. We're Lagrangists. You just came up from Earth-side. You know what it's like. It's a chaotic pigpen, polluted perhaps beyond recall, crime ridden, and governed by corrupt, venal incompetents who for half a century and more have been threatening to destroy the planet that saw the birth of our race with nuclear weapons. Well, they might destroy Mother Earth," there was a sneer in his voice, "but they're not going to destroy the human race. Because we Lagrangists are out here to carry on."

LAGRANGE FIVE
MACK REYNOLDS

BANTAM BOOKS · TORONTO · NEW YORK · LONDON

LAGRANGE FIVE
A Bantam Book / October 1979

ISBN 0–553–12806–X

Published simultaneously in the United States and Canada

Bantam Books are published by Bantam Books, Inc. Its trade-
mark, consisting of the words "Bantam Books" and the por-
trayal of a bantam, is Registered in U.S. Patent and Trademark
Office and in other countries. Marca Registrada. Bantam
Books, Inc., 666 Fifth Avenue, New York, New York 10019.

DEDICATED TO
Professor Gerard K. O'Neill, Space Pioneer

This story is laid approximately half a century in the future and thus the fictional characters are intended to have no resemblance to anyone living or dead.

Introduction

The Lagrange Five Project is developing so rapidly that it is all but impossible to keep up. New possibilities manifest themselves monthly, or even more often. There are even three newsletters devoted to space colonization and exploration. So it is that the reader must understand that this story is based upon the information available in the winter of 1976–1977. The present writer realizes that some of his background material will be antiquated before *Lagrange Five* can be rushed into print. For instance, as this is being written serious consideration is being made as to whether Lagrange Five or Lagrange Four are the best locations for Island One; there are other orbits that might prove more practical. Nor is it sure that the torus shape is the most suited for Island One. But this is, after all, only a story and space colonization is a reality that will be with us tomorrow and, possibly, the biggest "breakthrough" man has ever made.

Special thanks are due Professor Gerard K. O'Neill, of Princeton, and to his Research Aide Ginie Reynolds, for their cooperation beyond the call of duty in supplying my material. Professor O'Neill is especially thanked for granting permission to use quotes from his articles and papers directly.

ONE

Lance Holiday pedaled out of the town of Corcoran on a seventy-two hour leave of absence from his job. In the luggage rack behind him on the bike were his camping equipment and supplies for the whole period, plus fishing equipment and a small caliber pistol. He intended to supply most of his food with fishing and had gotten permission to shoot three rabbits.

He could use the camping trip. He had the feeling that he was going stale, that the job was getting on the monotonous side and life in general too much in the way of routine. Possibly he ought to swap Ruth for some different sleeping companion and possibly move to a different district. Corcoran was all right but he could probably use a change. It was kind of a suburbia of the type prevalent half a century ago, Earth-side. Now, little Mainz, up in the hills, might be the place. He'd never lived there but had passed through briefly more than once. Less built up than Corcoran, with its some 20,000 inhabitants, more trees around, mostly pine and very fragrant. The town had an Austrian motif complete to a *gasthaus* where they went heavy on dark Germanic-type beer. They even had a small volunteer band, complete with accordian and zither, which performed when the spirit moved them. As he recalled, about half of the resident men wore *ledderhosen* and the women *dirndls* after returning from their jobs.

Trouble with Mainz was it was further from the hydroponics tanks where he worked than Corcoran was.

1

From Corcoran he could commute by bike or even walk and he liked the exercise. From Mainz he'd usually have to take public transportation.

Well, he'd think about it later. For now, Lance Holiday wished to dwell upon his vacation. He was coming up on Lake New Bomoseen; heavier stands of trees were manifesting themselves and there were more bushes, shrubs and wild flowers. From one of the trees, a squirrel gave him hell.

He rode along the lakeside, savoring it. New Bomoseen was his favorite lake in Grissom. There was an even larger one, over in Komarov, with a charming, though somewhat primitive, Polynesian-type village on its edge. Lance had gone over several times for extended visits but he didn't think he'd want to live there. Komarov had a semitropical climate and he preferred the New England/European weather of Grissom.

Pumping away, he passed one of the Daniel Boone-type pseudo-log cabins tucked away in the woods atop a small hill. At this distance it looked as though it was constructed of real logs. He knew the place well enough. When he and Ruth had first taken up together, they'd spent several days there together on a sort of honeymoon. The trouble had been, Ruth didn't really like the wide open spaces, or, at least, Grissom's version of them. In actuality, she didn't even like the life in Corcoran too much. She was a city girl and would have preferred living in New Frisco at the end of the valley, which boasted almost 100,000 population and was the biggest city in Grissom or Komarov.

A rabbit broke cover and made a mad dash for thicker brush.

Lance Holiday swore inwardly. His target pistol was tucked away in his pack. Well, he'd have fish for his supper. Unless he was greatly mistaken, he'd wind up with all the landlocked salmon or trout he could possibly eat.

He was pleased at the fact that the wilderness didn't seem to be having much of a play today. In fact, he hadn't seen anyone for some ten minutes. Which was fine. He had deliberately chosen Tuesday as the first day of his outing. The weekends or holidays were another thing. There'd be thousands out picnicking, or sailing on the lake. As it was, the only other humanity he could spot was in two small sailboats out on the water.

On second thought, he looked up and, yes, there were three pedal-planes in toward the axis. It was a sport he'd never gone for. And, for that matter, the same applied to all low gravity activity. The feeling of zero-gravity, or even a quarter gravity, made him queasy. Which was one of the reasons he preferred to work in the hydroponic tanks, rather than in one of the zero-gravity factories.

The trees continued to grow more dense and he took a small side path and headed for a cove he knew of from trips past. For some reason the fishing at this point was the best he had discovered in the whole lake, either from shore or in a boat. And, yes, he could now see to his pleasure that if anyone else had stumbled on the spot, picnicing, or whatever, they had been as careful campers as he was himself. It was spotless.

He dismounted from his bike and unstrapped from the luggage rack his pack, small tent and sleeping bag. He got his pistol from the pack and attached the holster to his belt, on the off chance that another rabbit would appear. He'd applied for an okay on a couple of squirrels, in addition to his rabbit allotment, but it hadn't been forthcoming. It would seem that the rabbit population was a-booming, rabbit style, but that squirrels were in comparatively short supply, though he could hear several of them barking out in the woods. They had evidently detected his presence and weren't happy about it.

He got the tent up in short order and then, coffee addict that he was, brought forth his portable electric stove, his jar of instant coffee, a jar of condensed goat's milk, artificial sweetening—he was watching his weight —and a collapsible aluminum cup. He took up the small aluminium pot and carried it into the trees a few yards to where he knew was a spring and dipped up enough water for a couple of cups of his favorite brew.

Back at his little camp, he located the camouflaged outlet and plugged in the stove. In short order the coffee was on hand and he sat on a comfortable boulder and sipped away at it, looking more or less happily at the lake surface and the two sailing boats out there. There were three ducks as well about a hundred yards from the beach, mallards by the looks of them.

Yes, he could use this bit of ultrarelaxation.

Something came to him and he looked down into his coffee and, after a moment, he frowned. Why it had never occured to him before he didn't know, but the fact was he didn't particularly like the water of Grissom. What was the word? Possibly sterile. He had never liked bottled water, back in the States. It was flat, tasteless, though, Holy Zen knew, you had to drink it and cook with it, just about everywhere, of recent years. The days of his early youth, in Idaho, when you had hard water, and soft water, and some springs with a mineral content, and some actually with an effervescent quality, were long gone. These days, you got a mineral content in tap water all right, or, more likely, a detergent one, but for Lance Holiday's taste, it wasn't drinkable.

No, he didn't like the water supplied to the cities in the States and he didn't like the bottled product either. And now, he realized, he didn't particularly like the water of Grissom.

He sighed and put down his cup on the sand and looked about. What in the name of hell was wrong with him? He had been looking forward to this vacation of several days for a long time and here he was bitching.

Suddenly irritated by the taste of the coffee in his mouth, he unreasonably, since it was the taste of the water that had originally upset him, came to his feet and went into the tree grove and bent over to take a drink of the spring. And as his lips touched the water and sucked it in, he pulled his head back suddenly.

It wasn't a real spring, of course, no matter how well executed by those who had landscaped this whole area. There were pipes below, bringing in the recycled and sterile water.

He staggered to his feet and stumbled back toward his camp, a fear growing.

He stared accusingly at his little electric stove, plugged into the outlet. Outlets were everywhere in this supposed wilderness. The pollution of fire and smoke were taboo, the burning of wood was taboo. So, even in camping, you utilized the everywhere available electricity. No wonder so available. It cost all but nothing, the solar power stations took care of that—and the sun was good for a few billion more years, at least.

Breathing in short gasps, he stretched out on his sleeping bag and stared up.

Which was a mistake.

There were clouds above, yes, and "blue skies" but also above were the other two valleys and the three stretches of blue glass windows. At this distance, you couldn't see that the windows, each pane about twenty inches to the side, were not one. The titanium strips that bound them together were not visible. But, even worse, for his now twisting stomach, was the sight of the other two "valleys."

There, above him, in unhuman view, were the other two valleys which, with his, made up Grissom. Four miles away, so that individual features, smaller than towns, could not be made out, but there . . . there.

This was his universe. Closed in, closed in.

Here he was, 250,000 miles from the environment in which he had been born. And his parents before him. And the human race for a million or two years before them. He was in an artificial environment. Everything artificial. Everything *really* different from existence as he knew it. Everything *really* wrong. Such as springs that didn't actually bubble water, up from true soil, but were recycled water coming from pipes.

He knew now, he knew, why he had increasingly become repelled by the lesser gravity that you found as you ascended the artificial mountains at both ends of Grissom and particularly the complete free fall you found at the axis. He knew now why he didn't like to go watch the ballet performed in one-tenth gravity, by even such troupes as the Russians from Lagrange Four.

It was closing in on him.

He was 250,000 miles from where he was safe. He had to get away. He had to get back. It was closing in, it was closing in. This so-called valley, in which he lived, was two miles wide and about twenty long. No more. Above him, some four miles away, was the ultimate extent of his universe. And it was closing in, it was closing in!

He clawed at his pocket for his transceiver, finally got it out, panting, his eyes closed tightly.

He flicked the stud and screamed, "Emergency, emergency. Get a fix on me. I've got Island fever. I've got Wide Syndrome. I've got . . . space cafard . . ."

They came zeroing in on him within minutes. But by the time they arrived he was mewling, crouched in a fetal position behind the boulder on which he had been seated less than a quarter of an hour before.

Sucking in air themselves and even attempting to keep their eyes from him, the two medics leaped from the helio-jet, scooped him up and got him onto the cot in the rear of the aircraft ambulance. They jumped back into their own bucket seats and the pilot banged controls. The craft bounded up and headed desperately at full speed for New Frisco in the low hills at the end of the valley.

He was whimpering as they swooped in for the landing on the hospital roof.

Two others were waiting there with a straitjacket and a stretcher. The pilot had called ahead.

Within moments, the four of them had him secured and were rushing him below.

Doctor Poul Garmisch looked up wanly from his desk as they entered his office.

"Another one?" he protested. "Get him on the table. Nurse, the usual sedative. You men get out of here, unless you know that you're immune, and you probably aren't by that green look you've got around the gills."

The sedative was quick acting and Lance Holiday was completely out by the time the doctor bent over him. Nurse Edith Gribbin stood slightly back, breathing deeply. She thought she was immune, but you never knew.

The doctor, middle aged, which was an exception in Lagrangia, was heavy-set of build, which was another exception, and now tired of face though not through physical weariness. He shot a look up at Nurse Gribbin. "You all right, Edith?"

He seldom called her by her first name, though they had worked together ever since they'd come over from Island Two.

"I think so," she said. "Doctor, do you realize that this is the tenth case this week?"

"I know," he said. "Get on the phone immediately. On a medical crash priority, get him passage on the first available transport to Earth. We'll keep him in isolation here until he's ready to go. And, Nurse, don't let anyone else into the room."

"Yes, Doctor." She headed for her desk and for the phone screen there.

When she returned, it was to find him scowling down at the unconscious Lagrangist, perplexed.

"Space cafard," he muttered. "So-called Island fever. Sometimes it's named 'Wide Syndrome.' WAIDH, for 'What am I doing here?' "

"Aren't they getting anywhere at all toward a cure?" Edith Gribbin said, keeping her eyes away from the tragedy on the operating table.

He shook his head. "Not that I know of. Sit down, Nurse, we'll have a wait, at best. Space cafard is an unknown, compounded, we think, of claustrophobia, an unnatural environment, sometimes the fear of free fall, though that shouldn't apply when you live in a valley. Sometimes, perhaps, a feeling of the emptiness of space, even when looking toward Mother Earth. Sometimes, perhaps, an ingredient is what they used to call future shock, too fast a change in your basic way of life."

Just to be saying something while they waited, she

said, "Where did the name space cafard ever come from?"

"It means cockroach, in French," he told her. "A term that was symbolic of madness in the French Foreign Legion of a century ago. The men would go insane of the monotony, the boredom, the claustrophobia, in being assigned to tiny desert forts, which they dare not leave, in the mid-Sahara Desert."

She looked at him blankly. "But why were they there?"

The doctor was as glad to have something to talk about as she was. He said, "Because the French, in common with the English, the Belgians, the Dutch, the Germans and the Portugese, and finally the Americans when they went into such places as the Philippines, were anxious to bring the blessings of civilization to the backward, especially when it was profitable. Kipling put it:

> *Take up the white man's burden.*
> *Send forth the best ye breed.*

He grunted contempt. "Evidently, the best we bred was none too good. And evidently some of the supposedly backward cultures, such as the Chinese, who were actually far in advance of the Europeans in almost all aspects pertaining to culture—except warfare, if that's a part of human culture—went down like waterlogged trees. You know, to this day most people don't realize that both the Aztecs and the Incas, not to mention the Mayans, had a higher standard of living, including a better medicine, than did the Spanish who conquered them. They simply didn't have gunpowder, nor steel for swords."

There came a knock at the door and Nurse Gribbin went over and opened it a crack.

"Quarantined," she said. "Contagious."

A voice said, "We came for Lance Holiday. There's a mass-propulsion bus leaving for Island One in five minutes. We'll put him in with the luggage, where nobody

can see him. There, the *Tsiolkowsky* is heading in for
Earth within a couple of hours."

"Good," Doctor Garmisch said. "They've got a two
room sickbay on the *Tsiolkowsky*. They'll be able to
isolate him. Let them in, Nurse."

Two men entered with a stretcher and they, too,
were nervous and avoided looking directly at Lance
Holiday to the extent they could. They manhandled
the striken man onto the stretcher and left.

The doctor looked after them, unseeingly, and muttered, "Ten cases in the past week. I simply don't understand it. All of them here in the Grissom. Only a
few very mild cases of WAIDH syndrome anywhere
else, even in the Komarov, our sister cylinder. In all
the time I spent in Island One, in the old days, I never
saw a really bad case of space cafard. Why should it
pop up here, where it's so much larger than Island One
and so much more Earth like?"

She shook her head.

He came to his feet and said, "Nurse, I prescribe
that we both go over to Willy's Bar and get properly
drenched. We are not immune to the dangers of cafard,
the most contagious illness I've ever heard of. Once
when we were first colonizing the initial Island Two, a
transport carrying a hundred and fifty colonists developed a single case. The pilot hung on until the end
and reported how it swept through the ship. They all
went mad and killed each other, tore each other apart
with their hands and teeth. The pilot went last."

Nurse Gribbin shuddered. "I've heard about it," she
said. "But not in that grisly detail. I think they must
have suppressed the details."

"Yes," he said, as they headed for the door and
their much needed drinks. "Even hearing a news broad-
cast of that instant mental epidemic might have brought
on cafard symptoms in others."

TWO

Rex Bader had been out to Lagrange Five before, but that had been some ten years ago and there had been changes aplenty. Even before pulling into the docking area of Grissom, one of the two cylinders that made up Island Three, he was made aware of the changes. For one thing, the space shuttle which had taken them up to Space Station *Goddard* from Earth-side, had been larger than the earlier ones and was completely returnable, not even dropping the two boosters of the first models. Secondly, the *Goddard* had been considerably enlarged. With the growth of the number of Lagrangists, as they were calling the colonists now, the space station, in geosynchronous orbit above the Los Alamos spaceport, acted as a terminal for thousands of colonists rather than the scores of the early days. It seemed more like an orbiting hotel than the simple torus of yore.

Then there had been their means of transport from Earth orbit to Lagrange Five, that equidistant point in space from Earth and Luna. The Space Ship *Konstantin Tsiolkowsky* had been named after the Russian pioneer of space flight and colonization. On his first trip out, with Professor George R. Casey and his two Research Aides, Susie Hawkins and Nils Rykov, their vessel had been a space tug, a chemically-propelled ship derived from the original space shuttle but designed never to land in an atmosphere. The *Tsiolkowsky* was something different, with a vengence. Among

10

other little items, its mass-driver engines and solar-power plants extended a full fifty kilometers, which would obviously make no sense whatsoever to an Earth-bound ship, but was perfectly acceptable in deep space. It, along with several other similar craft, all built at Lagrange Five in space, plied continuously between Lagrange Five and the Space Station *Goddard,* taking twenty-one days for the inbound leg of the round trip and eight-and-a-half days for the outbound. The difference was due to the fact that the space ship carried 15,000 tons of reaction mass, industrial slag from the processing of lunar raw materials for further expansion of Lagrangia, the Islands of L5. Half of this had been used up by the return journey and the *Tsiolkowsky* consequently was considerably faster.

She rotated, too, which allowed for an artificial gravity; full Earth gravity in the public rooms, less in the bedrooms which were further in toward the axis.

On this trip, there were some two hundred fellow passengers, though the ship could have carried considerably more. Eight-and-a-half days weren't much more than would have been necessary to cross the Atlantic by liner and consequently Rex hadn't had the time to meet more than a handful of his fellow travelers.

Now, coming in, the address system suggested that everyone take chairs and buckle themselves down.

Rex Bader sat next to a black who had taken a place near one of the blue-tinted, small windows. He'd seen the chap around the past week, but had never come in contact with him. He seemed a little on the standoffish side, but then, being the only Black aboard he might have been ill at ease. There were a number of Orientals, including some that Rex took to be Indians but no other Africans, though the Indians were, if anything, darker of complexion than the Black. Old movie revival fan Rex Bader thought the other resembled Harry Belafonte, that handsome singer and actor of yesteryear.

Rex said, in an amiable way of making conversation, "First time up?"

The other eyed him, his face nearly expressionless but looking as though he didn't know whether to answer or not. Rex had assumed that he was an American but now he wondered. Perhaps the fellow was from Africa and didn't speak English.

But the Black said, "Yes."

Rex said, still friendly, "My name's Rex Bader. I'm no old hand myself but I was at Lagrange Five once before."

The other hesitated again before saying, "Whip Ford."

Rex Bader assumed that was his name. He tried once again, not really knowing why. "Going up to be a construction worker? I applied once and didn't make it."

This time, Whip Ford stared at Rex for a long, cold moment, before saying, flatly, "Tourist." He turned rudely and resumed his peering out the thick, dark glass porthole.

Rex said, "Excuse me for breathing."

The other turned back to him. "I don't appreciate your tone of voice," he said. "What's the matter, don't you like niggers?"

It was Rex's turn to look at him for a long moment before replying. "Darned if I know," he said. "I've never met one." And then he added, equally emptily, "Do you?"

The Black's eyes were cold, cold now. He said, "You aren't funny."

"Wizard. I wasn't trying to be, friend. It's not a very funny subject. I didn't bring it up."

"You're no friend of mine, Whitey."

Rex shrugged it off and stared beyond the other through the porthole into the area they were coming up upon. It reminded him of his first experience. Far from the beautiful paintings and color photos the publications came up with, the vicinity of a Lagrange Five Island looked like nothing so much as a spaceborne junkyard. Everything and its cousin was floating around. Zero-gravity factories, agricultural complexes, freight from Earth, Luna and the other Islands, stashed out in the biggest warehouse in the galaxy, space. Raw materials up from Luna, still to be processed. A gigantic radio telescope, off about twenty-five kilometers. Two large solar-power mirrors, kilometers in diameter. And this, that and the other thing, including space-suited individuals jetting around it all with what Rex knew were called Buck Rogers, small propulsion units strapped on the shoulders, with delicate controls, and named after that comic strip hero of the far past, who supposedly utilized the equivalent. Far off in the distance, about fifty miles, so he had read somewhere, was the Komarov, the sister cylinder of the Grissom at which they were landing. It looked quite impressive from this distance. You couldn't see all the debris cluttering up its vicinity.

He wondered about Whip Ford. Racism, he assumed, we would always have with us, or, at least, among some elements, for a long time. But you didn't expect to run into the more extreme types under these circumstances. If Ford was a tourist, it meant that he was in an income bracket far above Rex's own, since Rex was usually collecting Negative Income Tax, or Guaranteed Annual Stipend as they sometimes called it. Also, if the other had the intellectual curiosity to take a tourist trip to Lagrange Five it would indicate that his education was above par.

Inwardly, he shrugged again. It was of no importance.

There had been developments, too, in docking a space craft at an Island, since Rex Bader's last visit. The seemingly awkward, ugly *Tsiolkowsky* smoothed up to the Grissom so daintily that he felt nothing at all when contact was made.

The speaker system announced arrival and that passengers could begin disembarking. Without further words to Whip Ford, Rex unsnapped his safety belt, got up and headed for the hatch. It was already open and his fellow travelers streaming through, those whose destination was the Grissom cylinder.

He passed on through as well and found himself in a

sizeable lounge, much similar to an airport back Earthside though not so jam-packed.

He looked around, having no idea of what was in store. Rex Bader's instructions had been simply to come to Lagrangia and to the Grissom cylinder of Island Three. Grissom, he knew, had been named after an early space pioneer martyr, as Komarov, her sister cylinder, was after a Russian one. He wouldn't have dreamed of refusing. It was the first assignment he'd had in three months. Some years back he had spent considerable time and effort studying up on the Lagrange Five Project in hopes of being hired as a construction worker. Any job at all would have done but he had been turned down by the computers that had checked him out. Now he had given up hope. At the age of forty, he was passed the period where ordinary laborers were taken on, even had he fulfilled all the requirements. Had he been a name scientist or a highly-experienced technician, it might have been another thing, but he wasn't.

A voice from behind him said crisply, "Well, the last of the private eyes."

He winced and turned. It was, of course, Susie Hawkins, Research Aide, secretary, and Girl Friday of the renowned Professor George R. Casey, father of the Lagrange Five Project.

Susie Hawkins in her thirties was even more woman than she had been ten years earlier when he had first met her. A wee bit heavier, perhaps, but she could use the weight. She was small, perky and if she had gone to the trouble would have been prettier than average with such equipment as very blue eyes, a smallish though classical nose, very dark hair and the most perfectly shaped ears Rex had ever seen. However, as before, during working hours, at least, she obviously refrained from going to the trouble of projecting herself beauty-wise. She wore tweeds and looked very businesslike, very no-nonsense-like.

At one time, they'd had a bit of a thing going but it wasn't in the cards that Doctor Susie Hawkins, Physicist, and the right arm of Professor George Casey, could make a permanent relationship with the under-employed Rex Bader, private investigator by profession —when he could find work. However, there was a twinge on seeing her again, though he had known he would, of course. It had been her summons that brought him to Lagrangia.

"Susie!" he said, putting out his hand for a shake.

But she wasn't having any of that. She held up her face to him, and received his kiss with lips considerably softer than they looked.

He grinned and looked around at the milling space travelers and said, feeling inane even as he said it, "They'll think we're married and just getting back to-gether."

Susie gave a very un-Susie-like snort. "I doubt it. There's precious little marriage in Island Three. It's an institution we've largely left behind."

At another time he would have liked to go into that. But he said, "How's the professor?"

For the moment, at least, she didn't answer that but said, "I've already made arrangements to have your bag sent to the Space Ritz."

He eyed her, frowning puzzlement, "The what?"

She laughed briskly. "A joke. It's the largest hotel in Grissom. We don't have many hotels in Island Three. There aren't a good many transients, by Earth-side standards. But the so-called Space Ritz is usually where we conduct the VIPs. You'd be surprised how many VIPs we get in Lagrangia. Bunch of damned freeloaders, usually, on junkets, but that's the way the pickle squirts. We're actually making our own way, now, but from time to time we've got to deal with the powers that be, down Earth-side. But come along. You're not tired, are you?"

"How could I be? I've been sitting around doing nothing more physically demanding than staring out a porthole at space for over a week. How's the profes-sor?"

She looked at him from the side of her eyes, as they walked toward a staircase. She said, "That's what you're here to find out, Rex."

He almost stopped. He eyed her incredulously and got out, "What are you talking about?"

"We'll go into it a little later, before the Council."

"What council?"

"Come along, they're waiting for us."

Rex Bader gave it up. They approached a wide stairway, leading up.

He said, "What? No elevators, no escalators?"

Susie said, "For some reason, we make all but a fetish of getting as much physical exercise as possible. Nobody seems to know why. Perhaps because the median age here is about twenty-five. But we never ride if we can walk."

They started up the stairs, side by side. Which was a shame, Rex thought inwardly. He would have liked her to precede him so he could admire the sway of her hips. He tried to repress that thought. What was he, a sex-hungry teenager?

The steps weren't very long and they emerged shortly into a lobbylike room and then passed on through it and on through an entry onto a wide street.

"This is New Frisco," Susie said, now leading the way.

New Frisco was something else again. Except for the small town which was the center of Island One, Rex Bader had never been in a planned city.

This had been planned completely. Rex had seen enough Tri-Di shows about it and about Island Three in general not to be taken too far aback. But its absolute beauty was still impressive. He knew that it had a population of pushing 100,000 and that it nestled in the foothills at the end of the Grissom's three valleys, at the point where they connected. Beyond it, the mountains ascended toward the axis of the twenty-mile-long cylinder. Buildings shielded the view down one valley, but Rex Bader could look up and see the two other valleys and two of the equally-sized window strips, stretching away.

The city itself seemed to consist more of parks, gardens and plazas than it did of buildings and looked as though it had all been built the day before. Everything was modern, everything was new. No one building looked any older than any other, which, now that he thought about it, was reasonable. Island Three had only been in operation a couple of years or so. The buildings themselves were an architect's fondest dream. They each and all looked more like art objects than functional edifices and Rex couldn't tell hotel from office building, store from apartment building, cinema from restaurant.

The streets were moderately full of pedestrians and quite a few cyclists, but he could see only one vehicle and it was off a way down the street. By the looks of it, a small electro-hovercar of the type he had become acquainted with on Island One.

He said to Susie, "No parking problem so far, eh?"

"And there never will be, thank the Holy Jumping Zen. It's necessary to have some powered vehicles in town, but they're frowned upon. Cars in a city, not to speak of trucks, make it a horror. Have you ever seen Venice, in Italy?"

He shook his head.

"It's possibly the most beautiful city in Common Europe and there's not a car in it. The only transport is your feet, or the boats in the canals. There's public transportation in New Frisco but it's underground."

They had approached a sizeable bicycle rack and she pulled a woman's model out and began to mount it.

"Take one," she said.

He stared at her. "I can't swipe a bike."

Susie laughed at him. "They don't belong to anyone. We could walk to the Administration Building but it's a little far and the Council is in session and waiting."

"You mean they're free?"

"They're public property and available to anyone whenever needed. There are racks all over town. You pick one, ride it as long as you wish and leave it at the nearest rack when you're through."

Rex pulled out one of the bikes and mounted it. He couldn't remember having been on a bicycle since he'd been a kid.

"Socialism rears its ugly head," he said.

"Nonsense," she told him. "It makes for reason. If everybody owned his own bike, you'd clutter up the town with them. Can you imagine parking 100,000 bicycles all over the place?"

They got under way, Rex moderately pleased with himself at being able to still ride, after all these years.

He said, as they pedaled along, side by side, "What's this Council you mentioned?"

"What amounts to the government of Island Three."

"Oh," he said. "A Reunited Nations body, eh?"

She shook her head. "No, I mean the real government. The so called administrators that the RN sends up are simply figureheads. Politicians can't run technological projects such as Lagrangia. They wouldn't know where to begin."

THREE

Rex Bader looked over at her and said, "I labored under the impression that the Lagrange Five Project was in the hands of the Reunited Nations."

"Theoretically," she told him. "But in actuality the dizzards they send up haven't the vaguest idea of what's going on. I doubt if a single one has ever had the I.Q., the Ability Quotient, or the education and experience needed to get the simplest of jobs here. They're for show. They hold banquets for visiting firemen. They conduct VIPs around the Islands, showing them the sights. They pose around, looking distinguished for the Tri-Di cameramen who come up from Earth-side. They do a lot of drinking and eating in the best restaurants, bars and nightclubs. They do a lot of sleeping around, among themselves. A bunch of earthworms, actually. Their tour of duty is usually two years and few of them want to come back. Some do, but few wish another tour. Very seldom one will become enamored of Island Three and when his tour is up apply to become a colonist, a Lagrangist. So far, none of these have made it."

"Why not?"

She pointed at a beautiful round building, set in an extensive park, complete with trees, gardens, ponds, and swans.

"That's the opera house," she said. "The thing is, the Reunited Nations staff up here are all appointed. They're very good paying jobs by Earth-side standards and carry a lot of prestige, as well. Obviously, we

Lagrangists are in no position to refuse them entry. As you say, this is supposedly a Reunited Nations project. But they're political appointees. The more prestigious jobs are passed around from nation to nation, alternating. Right now, the head Administrator is Abou Zaki, of the Arab Union. His term has a year to go, and I have a sneaking suspicion that he hates Lagrange Five. I'm surprised that he doesn't come down with a case of space cafard, or fake one, so that he'd have an excuse to return to the Middle East."

"What's space cafard?"

"A mental illness a few people get up here. They say that it's mostly based on claustrophobia."

"Well, what's this Council? And what do they want with me?"

"I told you. The real government. It consists of a representative from each of the functions necessary in Island Three. It's more of a planning body than anything else. The professor is the honorary head of each of the Councils, on each of the Islands, but actually he doesn't always attend any except the more important meetings. They're really committees and alternate the chairmanship. Nobody has any more say than anybody else." She answered his second question. "They'll tell you all about it. No use going over it twice."

They rode past a playground which seemed little different than children's playgrounds Earth-side, other than possibly being somewhat neater. Rex had already noticed the rather large number of children in the parks and plazas. Most, but not all of them, were quite young, say, ten years of age or less.

As they pedaled along, he said, "You seem to be having quite a population explosion."

She looked over at him, saying, "Why not? We're not overpopulated in Lagrangia and probably never will be. The situation is perfect here for children. Practically diseaseless, good food, good air, clean, no poverty. You can't beat it, Rex."

"Wizard. Sounds like Utopia," Rex Bader said wryly.

"No," she said, shaking her head negatively. "Utopia

is perfection and there is no perfection. As soon as man has reached one goal, there is another beyond, and another beyond. If we reached perfection, then man would stagnate. I hope that never happens. But thus far Lagrangia is the nearest thing to Eden we've achieved."

Rex took in the kids some more and frowned. "How come so many of them look to be no more than ten? Where are the early teenagers and so forth?"

She said crisply, "Don't you see? Island One was colonized ten years ago, about. And that's when children started being born in space."

"Wizard. But how about the colonists bringing up their children from Earth-side?"

She nodded. "Some did. Some of those are the older ones you see. But the requirements for colonization include a minimum I.Q. of 130. If a couple applied for jobs in Lagrangia and they had a child, or more, the child, too, would have to have the I.Q. required."

He shot a glance over at her. "I didn't know that."

"Most people don't."

"But, listen. Suppose somebody has a baby here and . . ."

"I'll tell you more about it later, if you're interested," she said. "But here we are."

They were coming up on a building somewhat higher than the ones Rex had seen thus far, and possibly somewhat more staid. It was six stories in height. It would seem that the city planners didn't go in for skyscrapers.

There were extensive bike racks to each side of the main entry and they dismounted and found spaces for their two bicycles. Rex followed along behind her, for the moment, holding his peace. The lobby was moderately full of men and women, some papers in hand, some carrying attache cases or briefcases. A very standard looking governmental or business building, though the architecture was the most modernistic Rex could remember ever having seen. And there was more in the way of decoration than you expect a city hall, or whatever they called it, to have. There were two

Greek or Roman-type marble statues, both approximately twice life-size.

And then he came to a halt and stared. He said, "I'm no art connoisseur but isn't that a Rembrandt?"

She stopped and looked up at it appreciatively.

"Yes," she said. "We just acquired it last month."

"But a Rembrandt! Shouldn't it be in some museum, down Earth-side?"

"It was," she told him. "A private museum. You see, we're beginning to sell the Earth nations more and more energy, derived from our Satellite Solar Power Stations, our SSPSs. At first, when we were getting underway, we had to import a great deal from Earth-side but now that we're beginning to mine the asteroids, we need less and less. In fact, practically nothing. So our pseudo-dollar credits and other means of exchange are piling up. We don't want to precipitate some sort of money crisis down below, so we spend part of our earnings on such things as art objects. That isn't the only Rembrandt in Lagrangia. You must go through the city museum. But let's get along, the Council is waiting."

To his surprise, there were no elevators and they began to mount steps.

She could see what he was thinking and smiled at him before saying, "Two reasons. As I told you, we're exercise conscious. Besides that, we avoid mechicanization and automation whenever we can. We have so much of it in Lagrangia, particularly in industry and transportation on the outside, that we try to keep it out of our daily lives when we can. You see, we don't want to become appendages of machines."

"But six floors. How about older people?"

"We don't have much in the way of older people, and even if we did, it's unlikely they'd be working in this building. Later, as some of us grow more elderly, possibly we'll install some elevators in here. I don't know. Most of our buildings aren't this high. Most are two or three stories. People who can get around at all can usually take that many stairs. By the way, have you noticed the gravity?"

"No. What about it?"

"We're up in the foothills aways, so there's slightly less gravity. The closer you get to the Island's axis, the less the gravity. At the axis, it's zero. There's air there, but no gravity."

Their destination was on the sixth floor. Susie arrived without puffing, but Rex had been inactive for over a week and was by no means used to climbing stairs back Earth-side. Besides, he growled to himself inwardly, she was younger than he was.

They went down a corridor and all over again Rex realized how beautifully the building was done, how beautifully decorated.

He said, "All this material sent up from the Luna base?"

"Not quite," Susie told him. "We're beginning to mine the asteroid belt now and they have a wider range of raw materials including copper, nickel, even carbon and hydrogen. That last is going to be a relief from now on. We used to have to bring liquid hydrogen up from Earth-side to combine with oxygen for our water. We have all the oxygen we need from the moon oxides but there was no hydrogen to speak of."

They came to a double door and, without knocking, Susie pushed it open and led the way.

Inside was a typical conference room, with a heavy metal table in the center. It came to Rex Bader that lumber would be in short supply in Lagrangia. Maybe in years to come, as the forests had time to grow, it'd be available to some extent for furniture and such items but now, largely, the furniture he had seen, even the frames for paintings, including the Rembrandt, were metallic or plastic.

The table was circled by twenty persons, all of whom were taking in Rex and Susie as they entered. They seemed to average a little older than usual in Island Three. Rex would estimate the youngest at thirty, the oldest in his early fifties. They looked like top executives, top educators, top scientists or technicians. Eight were women.

There were two empty chairs, placed halfway down the table.

The fifty-year-old seated at the head of the table cleared his throat. "It's to be assumed that you are the private investigator come up from Earth-side, Rex Bader. Doctor Hawkins, will you do the honors?"

Rex and Susie remained standing while she introduced the Lagrangists. "Beginning with today's chairman, at the table's head, and going clockwise; Doctor Hans Ober, Medicine; Doctor Walt Hanse, Transportation; Doctor Fredric Economou, Education; Academician Alexis Ignatov, Power; Doctor Sal Sinatri, Manufacturing; Doctor Karl Kessinger, Communications; Doctor Abu Magumbo, Agriculture; Ms. Shirley Ann Kneedler, Distribution; Doctor Franz Zeigler, Research . . ."

Susie made the round of the table but Rex Bader had long since lost track of names and positions. He had refrained from going about the table and shaking hands. It would have been awkward. Instead, he settled for nodding to each, as his name was spoken.

At the end, Doctor Hans Ober said, "Please be seated Doctor Hawkins, Mr. Bader."

They sat and Rex Bader looked at the chairman, feeling slightly apprehensive. Whatever this was, he had a growing suspicion that he wasn't going to like it. There were no second-rate private detectives in the United States of the Americas any more. There weren't enough of them to have any second-raters. But if there had been, Rex Bader suspected he would have been listed as such. He had no delusions of grandeur.

They were all taking him in, sizing him up. For the nonce, nobody spoke.

Wizard. It was their ball; let them start bouncing it. But Rex cleared his throat and said, "Doctor Hawkins didn't tell me your purpose in bringing me to Lagrange Five."

Walt Hanse, who had been introduced as head of

transportation, and was the one who looked to be no more than thirty years of age, said, "We brought you here to investigate the disappearance of Professor George R. Casey, the father of the Lagrange Five Project."

FOUR

Rex Bader stared at him as though the other had gone completely around the corner. He finally got out, "What do you mean, he's disappeared?"

"Just that," the chairman said with a sigh. "Almost two weeks ago, George Casey disappeared."

Rex said indignantly, "How in the hell could you disappear in a place like Island Three?"

Doctor Ober looked to Walt Hanse and said, "You're our Transportation representative, Walt. Please elucidate for Mr. Bader's information."

Walt Hanse was a handsome young man in the Scandinavian tradition, very blond of hair, very blue of eye, and tall and stocky. In another era he would probably have gone far as a Viking chieftain. He had the look of a leader about him, and the aggressiveness. He also had a slightly sulky look about his wide mouth and didn't seem to be the type to do much laughing or even smiling.

He said to Rex, "Do you know anything about our methods of traveling between Islands?"

Rex Bader shook his head. "Some years ago, I took various courses pertaining to Lagrange Five in hopes of getting a construction job. But now I assume that you have gone far beyond the point that you were at then."

"Undoubtedly," the other nodded. "New technology develops fast in Lagrangia. We travel between communities with simple engineless vehicles, accelerated in a computed direction by a stationary, cable-pulling electric motor and decelerated by an arresting cable at the destination. The cable-car vehicles for such free flight need no fuel, no complex maintenance, nor a crew, and are quite inexpensive. With no need for aerodynamic design, they are more roomy and comfortable than a typical Earth-side commercial jet. The distance between the various Islands is about 200 kilometers, and at the speed with which the vehicles travel, the time involved in going between them is short."

"What's all this got to do with Professor Casey disappearing?" Rex said.

The younger man ignored him and went on. "There are various sizes of vehicles, and various types. Some are for freight, some for passengers. The passenger vehicles range in size from those that will carry as many as fifty persons in comfort, down to as few as four. Professor Casey was making a routine trip to Island One, in a four-passenger car, and he was alone."

Rex looked at him blankly.

Walt Hanse said, "He never arrived."

"What do you *mean*, he never arrived?"

"Just that. From what we have discovered, thus far, the dispatch crew at this end sent him off. It was strictly routine. But when the vehicle arrived at Island One, the professor was not in it. Since Casey had not called ahead to announce his coming, the receiving crew on Island One were only mildly suprised to pick up an empty vehicle. The crew chief there was in somewhat short supply of this size craft and figured that they'd sent it over from Island Three to augment his number of them. He simply parked the four-seater and for the time forgot about it."

Rex looked at Susie and said, "Where were you? You're his Number One Research Aide. I thought that you were supposedly always at his side."

She closed her eyes in pain. "He assigned me to do something else. His Island One trip was only for a few hours and he didn't need me. When he didn't return in the period I had expected him to, I didn't worry about it. The professor can get sidetracked with the greatest of ease and he might wind up spending a week on some detail he'd expected to cost him only an hour or two. But when he didn't arrive home the next day, I called Island One. He had never gotten there. I checked Transportation here and they reported that he had left alone in a four-seater for Island One. That's all we know."

She looked at him.

Rex turned abruptly to the chairman and snapped, "What did the police discover?"

"We have no police," Hans Ober said.

"Well, security, or whatever you call it."

Ober shook his head. "We have no police of any kind connected with the Lagrange Five Project, nor any of the other appurtenances of the State such as jails, or even courts in the ordinary sense of the word. We're civilized, Mr. Bader. Crime in the ordinary sense is unknown in Lagrangia."

Rex stared at him. "That makes no sense at all. You can't eliminate crime completely. Sure, I can see where you might get to the point where no one would steal. But you're not going to eliminate, say, crimes of passion. What happens if somebody kills somebody, over sex or something?"

The Council representative for Medicine nodded acceptance of the validity of that question. "The matter is turned over to my department. Obviously, he who did the killing was mentally unbalanced. He is treated as would be any other ill person."

Rex couldn't believe him. "And then he's turned loose, I suppose!"

"When cured," the other agreed. "What would you do, Mr. Bader, confine him to a barred cell, such as is not even utilized for wild animals in zoos any more? Or, would you execute him, because he is sick?"

Rex said sourly, "The fact that he had the excuse of being sick doesn't help the dead man any."

Doctor Fredric Economou, of Education, said mildly, "Nor would executing or imprisoning the mentally upset one help him. Revenge is not very highly regarded in ethics, Mr. Bader. But even if it was, the dead cannot enjoy it. Caesar was in no position to appreciate the death of Brutus."

Rex shook his head in lack of acceptance of their code, but said, "Then, what it amounts to is that you have no police of any kind in Lagrangia?"

Doctor Ober said, "There are four bodyguards, for some unknown reason, connected with the Reunited Nations staff. Even if we were interested in bringing the RN into this, I doubt if they are the type suitable for conducting an investigation into the disappearance of the professor."

Rex said in irritation, "Why didn't you notify them down Earth-side immediately? They would have sent up men from Interpol, the Inter-American Bureau of Investigation, Scotland Yard, the KGB, or whatever."

"Because we don't want the earthworms prying in our affairs," Walt Hanse blurted.

Rex didn't get that. Susie had used the term earlier, now that he recalled. "Earthworms?" he said.

"Earthlings," Hanse said sullenly.

"Holy Zen, man. You're an Earthling yourself."

"I'm a Lagrangist!"

Rex was staring again. He said, "Look, wizard, but moving into space a quarter of a million miles doesn't let you out of the human race."

"I didn't say that we in the Islands aren't members of the human race. I said we aren't Earthlings. We're Lagrangists. You just came up from Earth-side. You know what it's like. It's a chaotic pigpen, polluted perhaps beyond recall, crimeridden, and governed by corrupt, venal incompetents who for half a century and more have been threatening to destroy the planet that saw the birth of our race with nuclear weapons. Well, they might destroy Mother Earth . . ." there was a sneer in his voice ". . . but they're not going to destroy the human race. Because we Lagrangists are out here to carry on."

Doctor Ober sighed and said, "Walt. Walt. We've all, save for Mr. Bader, heard your diatribes before. They would seem to be out of order right now." He turned to Rex. "Without a police of our own, and undesirous of bringing Earth-side governments into it, we of the Council decided to hire a professional to seek an answer to the enigma of what happened to George Casey, our colleague and inspiration. Doctor Hawkins suggested you."

Rex looked at Susie. "Why?"

Susie said, "Because you are already partially knowledgeable. You acted for a time as the professor's bodyguard when he was in danger of assassination on the part of elements who wished to destroy the project by any means. You saved his life, at least once. You proved yourself trustworthy and he trusts you. So do I. We need you, Rex Bader."

Rex came to his feet and walked around the end of the table and stared through the large window which looked out over one of the three valleys. It had a strange, unearthly beauty. He could see almost the full length, which he knew as some twenty miles, but clouds obscured most of the further end. To each side of the valley were the strips of blue glass windows. Down its middle wandered a fairly wide river, which was fed, from time to time, by tributary streams coming down the side of the curving valley. There were various ponds and small lakes, and, down toward the middle, a fairly large lake, upon which, even at this distance, he could see sails. There were patches of forests, there were small towns and villages. Paths, not quite large enough to be called roads, wandered here and there. There were fields, pastures, orchards, and occasional single houses. Yes, Grissom had its beauties, strange though they might appear to one born and raised on the surface of a natural planet, rather than in the interior of an artificial one.

Rex turned back. They had all respected his thinking by remaining silent.

He took a deep breath and said, "I think that I'm still of the opinion that this matter should be brought to the attention of the Reunited Nations."

Susie Hawkins said softly, "Rex, the professor would

not think so. Though perhaps not quite so vitriolic as Walt Hanse, the professor is also of the opinion that Lagrangia must ultimately declare its independence of Earth. The whole present situation is very controversial. He would not like this matter to come to the attention of the Reunited Nations' supposed administrators of the Lagrange Five Project. If they could, they would like to eliminate him. Coming up with such a controversial thing as this might give them a lever with which to do it."

Hanse said darkly, "For all we know, some elements of the Reunited Nations might be behind this kidnapping, or whatever it is. I wouldn't put anything beyond, say, the Soviet Complex KGB. The Soviets might be having second thoughts about the building of Lagrangia. A hell of a lot of the scientists they've sent up here have defected and refuse to return Earth-side."

For the first time, Academician Alexis Ignatov spoke up. His English was only slightly accented. "Nor would I put anything beyond the American IABI, Colleague Hanse."

"Neither would I," Hanse growled to the older man.

Susie was looking at Rex Bader, appealingly. Appealingly, and there was something else there, he realized. Was she trying to get some other message through? Did she want to see him, away from the others, to tell him more?

All of a sudden, he decided that he was a businessman. Too often, when he did get one of his seldom assignments, a wheel came off and he was left barren of remuneration.

He said, "What's in it for me?"

A sigh went around the table.

Doctor Ober said, "We understand, Mr. Bader, that the last time you acted for Professor Casey you were put on the staff as a Research Aide of his, supposedly a socioeconomist. I suggest that we renew that position. When Island One was completed, it was assumed that the elements the professor had to be guarded against were thwarted and there was no further danger, so you were let go. But now, it would seem, your dismissal might have been premature. I suggest that you consider your dismissal rescinded."

"And where does my pay come from?"

Doctor Economou smiled wanly. "I assure you, Mr. Bader, the Reunited Nations staff now in Island One invariably rubber-stamps anything that the Council recommends. They are so far at sea that there is nothing else for them."

Rex took another deep breath. "Wizard," he said. "I'll do what I can."

FIVE

The meeting of the Council broke up and most of the members crowded around to shake hands with Rex Bader. It was obvious that they held Professor George R. Casey in the same regard as did Susie Hawkins and were highly concerned with his mysterious disappearance. When they had all met Rex, they gathered around in small groups discussing the matter, most of them were anxious.

Doctor Hans Ober came up with Susie and said to him, "In view of the fact that Doctor Hawkins is, temporarily, we ardently hope, without duties, I suggest that she assist you, Mr. Bader. The professor has a rather extensive apartment, since visiting scientists, and others important to the project, often stop with him. As good a base of operations as any would be there. Doctor Hawkins, as his secretary, has her quarters there. Why don't you move in? I understand that is what you did when you were his bodyguard some years ago."

Rex looked at Susie.

She laughed her brisk laugh and said, "Don't worry, Rex. Little of the old morality still pertains here. I won't be compromised. Why don't we go to the hotel and get your bag?"

"Sounds good to me," he said. "But just a moment."

Doctor Karl Kessinger, of Communications, was standing alone, staring pensively out the window. He was one of the older men present and looked the least of them all like a scientist. He was stocky, almost fat, had too much belly and furry brows. He hadn't raised his voice at all in the just-concluded meeting.

Rex said, "There was one thing I thought I ought to ask you about, Doctor."

"Why, of course. Though, frankly, Mr. Bader, I am not optimistic about the success of your efforts."

"Why not? I'm not either, but what are your reasons?"

"Professor Casey carried two transceivers with him at all times," the other said. "One was for use in Lagrangia and would reach anywhere here, including from within the vehicle in which he was traveling to within any of the Islands. The other was a tight beam with which he could communicate with Earth-side elements of the Lagrange Five Project, such as those at New Princeton with whom he still works. In fact, he is still on the faculty payroll there."

"So I understand. And?"

"He hasn't used either of those transceivers since his disappearance. Every message sent over a transceiver here in Lagrangia is recorded in our computer data banks. The last call we have on record of George Casey was a routine one from his home to the dispatch crew chief, at the dispatch terminal, ordering a four-seater for his trip. Nothing since. I submit that if he was confronted by violence, he should have had the time to flash a warning. We would have gotten a fix on him and sent immediate succor. No warning came, Mr. Bader. I am afraid that Professor Casey is dead."

"Can't you get a fix on his transceivers? Down Earth-side, the police can get a fix on anybody's transceiver at any time."

"We use the same type, but that is my point. We cannot get such a fix on either of George Casey's pocket communicators. Which would indicate them destroyed. What did you want to ask me about?"

Rex shook his head negatively. "That was it. About his transceivers. Thanks."

He turned to rejoin Susie but on his way, Walt Hanse stopped him momentarily to say, "If there's anything possible I can do, including anything pertaining to physical violence, let me know. I'm an amateur pugilist and wrestler. There's something funny going on around here."

"Yeah. I'm dying laughing," Rex said bitterly. "But thanks. I'll remember, if I need help to sock somebody."

"I wasn't trying to be funny," the other said sullenly.

He was obviously miffed. Rex said, "Sorry. I know you weren't. Thanks again."

He turned back to Susie, who was waiting at the door for him. They left and wound down the stairs to the lobby and then out into the street. The bike racks were nearly empty, but there were two remaining. Rex was forced to take a woman's model.

He said, "What happens when you run out of these self-serve bicycles?"

She said reasonably, "You either walk down to another rack that has some or take the metro, down below. We have the most beautiful metro I've ever seen save perhaps in Moscow, Earth-side."

Just as they were mounting, a child walked by. She was a lovely youngster, beautiful of posture, blonde of hair and obviously in sparkling health. She looked to be about eleven.

Susie smiled and spoke to her in some language Rex couldn't remember ever having heard before. The child stopped and smiled back and answered in the same tongue. They exchanged a few words, the girl sounding very adult and looking very possessed indeed, and then she walked on.

As they pedaled away, Susie said, "Do you know who that was?"

"Why, no. Nice looking kid."

Susie said, "Well, that's Virginia Dare Robbins, the first child born in space."

"Holy Zen, that old already?"

"Her mother was pregnant when she came up. Virginia was born at Island One, shortly after it was opened to the first colonists. She has already passed her La-grangist examinations. Came through flying with an I.Q. of 143."

Rex didn't quite get that and would have liked to go further into it, but there were more important things on hand.

As they pedaled along, he realized that he was going to have to sort out his thoughts before getting to the professor but he said, absently, "What was that language you were speaking to the Robbins child?"

"Interlingua, the official language of Lagrangia."

He looked over at her questioningly.

She said, "When you were on Island One, we were still working on it and, since at that time the Lagrange Five Project was under NASA, we all spoke English. But since the project is now international we had to have an international language. Practically every nationality of Earth is represented in Lagrangia. One of the requirements, before you can become a colonist, is to learn Interlingua. It's sort of a cross between Esperanto and the original Interlingua, but with some refinements. It's very easy to learn. There are only half a dozen or so grammatical rules, for instance, while for other languages you have to wade through whole volumes to learn the grammar. Sometimes with such languages as German I wonder if anybody ever learns it, save a few college professors."

"What's wrong with English for an international language?" Rex said. "It's spoken just about anywhere you go Earth-side by about anybody who is educated."

"It's a bastard language composed of Celtic, Latin, German, Scandinavian, French, and various others to lesser degree. And it has some of the most fantastic grammatical rules going. It isn't even phonetic, as are the Latin languages and German, and the spelling is consequently ridiculous. A child has to learn to spell each word in his vocabulary. And the meaning of words. Take the word *can*. It means that you are able to do something. It means a tin container for food. It means your boss fires you. It also means a resort city on the French Riviera, but then it's spelled Cannes.

At any rate, colonists must learn Interlingua and the children born here are taught it from infancy. They can learn other languages as well, if they wish, but they must have Interlingua."

"We spoke English back at the Council meeting."

She smiled. "There was no alternative. You don't speak Interlingua. A good many educated people of all countries speak English. However, you'll note that some of the Council members didn't enter into the discussion. Doctor Zeigler, for instance, and Doctor Abu Magumbo, the black who sat next to her. They had to be briefed later, in Interlingua. But, here's the hotel."

The Space Ritz, as Susie had dubbed it, was as pleasant a building as any of the rest, with wide sweeps of very green lawn and gardens. These people, Rex found, certainly went in for flowers. But, why not? With year round perfect weather, sun every day, no pests or parasites, flowers were an obvious thing. He suspected that you merely buried a seed and then jumped back to get out of the way of the growing plant.

They entered the somewhat ornate lobby and walked toward the reception desk, Susie explaining the ultraluxurious qualities of the room by saying that this hotel was largely for Earth-side VIPs, whose taste was often solely in their mouths, thus the lobby was a duplication of luxury hotels down below.

To Rex's surprise, there was a live reception clerk. You seldom saw one in Earth hotels any more. Hotels, like everything else, were largely automated. You could spend a week in one without ever seeing an employee. No wonder some ninety percent of the work force in the advanced countries were unemployed and on Negative Income Tax, or the equivalent.

Susie caught his surprise and told him it was something like stairs instead of elevators. To the extent they could, in their day-by-day living, off the job, they avoided automation. They didn't want life to become sterile.

It turned out that the reception clerk had not sent

the bag upstairs as yet. He had been waiting to find what kind of accomodations Rex required.

They retrieved the suitcase and took it out to the bicycle racks where they had parked their bikes. Rex slung it into the luggage rack behind his seat.

"What would happen if I had three or four bags to carry?" he said.

"Why, we'd summon a cab, or go down to the hotel's vehicle pool and get a car. I didn't say we had no vehicles save bicycles in New Frisco, only that we frowned on them and avoided them as much as possible."

They climbed back on the bikes and took off again.

Rex said, "That reminds me. How do I pay for something, such as renting a car? Can I get an advance on my salary?"

"You won't need it," she told him. "For all practical purposes, you, along with all Lagrangists, are on an unlimited expense account."

He almost stopped the bike to stare at her. "Unlimited expense account!" he said. "You mean that I don't have to pay for *anything?*"

"That's right. Neither does any Lagrangist. Tourists and others, up from Earth-side, are another thing. But they can pay at the hotels for rooms and meals, or renting cars, or whatever, with their ordinary International Credit Cards. It's all kept track of in our account in Switzerland."

"Now look here," he said. "You mean that I can just walk into, say, a bar, order a drink, knock it back, and walk out again without paying?"

"Yes. It's the most sensible thing we could work out. Imagine the man-hours we save on accounting."

"But, look. Every lush in Grissom would be drenched on a full time basis."

"There aren't many lushes in Grissom. Alcoholism is a disease and our health is checked out all ways from Tuesday before we ever are allowed to become Lagrangists. We're all but disease free. But if you were a lush who had to pay for his drinks, you'd get them anyway. Pay is high here."

"What do you mean high?" he said indignantly. "You just said there wasn't any."

She looked over at him and laughed her brisk laugh. "No I didn't. Not exactly. I simply said that all expenses in Lagrangia are now on the house. Saves bookkeeping. But all workers in Lagrangia have deposited to their credit ten thousand pseudo-dollars—or the equivalent in whatever other currency they want it—a year, in any bank they wish down on Earth."

"But how do they spend it?"

"On vacations, Earth-side. Or they let it accumulate until they retire and go back to Earth. Or, which is more usual, if they don't wish to return to Earth, on retirement, possibly they give it to some relative, or friend, or whoever, who lives Earth-side." She added, rather quietly, "Or perhaps they use it to support one of their children who lives down below."

Rex Bader shook his head in continuing disbelief. "But, look, what keeps everybody from, say, going into a restaurant and ordering all of the most expensive dishes on the menu, over and over again?"

"Some do, for awhile. But you'd be surprised how soon most people get tired of fancy food. Most of us prefer simpler, basic foods well prepared. It's hard to beat a good slice of roast, a baked potato, a fresh vegetable, and a salad, accompanied by wine or beer and followed by a good dessert."

"I'd think the clothes horses, both men and women, would go into the shops and gather up all the most expensive clothes and shoes there and take off."

Susie was still amused. She said, "In the first place, there aren't any shops. In the second place, there aren't any clothes that are more expensive than any other clothes. Remember, they're all free. When all the clothes and shoes you wish are always available, why store large amounts of them in your home?"

"You're throwing these curves too fast," Rex told her. "First of all, what do you mean, there aren't any shops?"

"Well, let's say there's one big shop. You have ultra-markets down Earth-side. We have one big ultra-ultra-market. It's located underground, under New Frisco. It's automated, of course. The vacuum delivery chutes are also underground, put down when the Island was being constructed. Every house, every apartment, has its delivery box. If the item is too large for the delivery chutes, it is sent out by vehicle."

"But if you can't see the item . . ."

"You can dial the catalog."

"But some things you have to feel, try on, or whatever."

She was being patient. "Such items you can dial, try on, and if you don't like them, send them back."

"What's this about there being no clothes more expensive than others?" he said.

"We simply don't make inferior products. Everything manufactured is of the best quality we can produce."

Rex was confused by so much of this coming at him at once. He said, "Well, suppose you wanted something cheaper?" That question didn't seem to make much sense even to him, even as he asked it.

Susie said, "Rex, there is no such thing as something cheaper. We make only the best, there is no such thing as a cheaper quality. Actually, there probably never has been. Take a man down Earth-side who's on Negative Income Tax and knows he has to watch his pseudo-dollars. He shops around and buys a pair of shoes for six dollars. They last about six months. But a better-to-do man goes out and pays fifty dollars for a pair of shoes made with the best leather and by the best methods. They last him for ten years, with suitable cobbling. What were the cheaper pair of shoes?"

She thought of something and added, "I don't mean that we don't produce a variety of goods, for instance, different colors, different styles in clothing. That is, you could get yourself a pair of attractive-looking slacks meant for nice wear, parties and so forth, or you could get yourself a pair of hard-wearing work pants for working. But your slacks would be the best quality produceable, and the work pants would be the best possible in that category."

"All right, wizard. I give up," Rex said.

"Here we are," she told him, pulling up before a three story high apartment building. They had left the public buildings of the downtown area and this was obviously a residential section, once again, parks, plazas, and gardens predominating.

The building in which the professor was housed was similar to the others in the vicinity, so far as quality was concerned. Rex got the feeling that the same thing applied to housing as Susie had told him about clothing and other consumer goods. There was no such thing as inferior and superior. All housing was the best they could produce. Oh, he assumed that there were such differences as size. A larger family would want more bedrooms and so on. Or a scholar, such as Professor Casey, would want a study-library, while a construction worker with children might not have that requirement, but might wish a playroom. Or some might wish to live in the country, or a smaller town, and some might prefer a private house to an apartment. But all would be of the best quality possible to build. It was a new way of thinking for Rex Bader, but he supposed it made sense in a place like Lagrangia. If these people made *all* of their expenses plus ten thousand pseudo-dollars a year, deposited down Earth-side, then they must be the highest paid group of workers in history. The power they were beaming down to Earth must be really paying off.

There was a small bike rack before the building and they parked their bicycles in it, Rex taking up his single bag. He followed her into the building, saying, "I still don't get the feeling of nobody being able to buy anything at all."

She said, "Oh, each larger town has what you might call a shop. It's for luxury items we haven't gotten around to producing as yet up here. Things from Earth. Suppose your fancy led you to wanting some exotic food, or, say, a bottle of vintage champagne from

France. You could buy it, using your regular International Credit Card ,and having the amount deducted from your Earth-side account. But these places don't handle much traffic."

"Why not?" Rex said. "I can see where a lot of things would be available on Earth and not here."

She looked at him from the sides of her eyes, as they mounted the steps and said crisply, "Because we're not particularly stupid. Can you imagine what it costs to ship up a case of champagne from Earth-side? It makes the prices of especially bulky and heavy items astronomical. We can stick to our own champagne, which isn't at all bad."

SIX

The professor's apartment was as Rex Bader had expected it to be, similar though larger than the one Casey had had in Island One, ten years before. In spite of the fact that Susie Hawkins lived in, it was a bachelor's home, the furniture for comfort, not for show, with no attempt at interior decorating. The paintings, for instance, were not of any one school but were obviously a collection built up over the years for no reason other than that Professor Casey liked them. He even had a print of that classic of yesteryear, Marilyn Monroe being blonde all over. There was a well-stocked bar. There were books, books, books; hardcovers and paperbacks, many of them technical but not all. The professor was obviously of the old school. He liked real books, the type you could mark and make notations in; not for him the sterile library booster screen attached to the data banks. There was even a gun rack.

Rex turned to look at Susie. "Guns?" he said.

She nodded. "There's a certain amount of hunting in Island Three."

"There is?" He was surprised.

"Yes, of course. We have areas in both Grissom and Komarov which we call wildernesses, about 25 square miles apiece, and we make them just as similar to untouched primitive wilds, virgin forests, as we can. They are for hiking, camping, picnicing, fishing, and even hunting. We've brought up not only domesticated animals from Earth but game animals as well. You

43

know, deer, antelope, gazelle, rabbits, wild boar, partridges, hare, pigeons, squirrels, and fox squirrels, even turtles. But only animals that are edible and useful to man. We have no predatory animals save for dogs and house cats, if you can count them."

Rex said, "It seems a hell of a long way to bring something just to shoot."

"They're not just to shoot. They're like the fish in our streams and lakes, a very valuable source of protein. Since there are no carnivorous animals to keep them down, we have to hunt them to prevent their number increasing to the point where they would be overly dangerous to the crops. So they're kept track of and from time to time those who like to hunt are allowed a certain quota."

Rex said, "This reminds me of something. I knew better than to bring a gun with me. They search through everything you're bringing up, there at the hospital at the Los Alamos spaceport when they're sterilizing everything that goes into space. Is it possible for me to get one? Zen only knows what I'll run into before this is all over."

She thought about it. "I don't know much about guns, but the professor likes to hunt. I believe he's got a target pistol which he keeps back in his bedroom. I'll get it."

She left him in the living room and he went over to the French windows that led onto a rather extensive terrace, and looked out over the town. He breathed deeply in appreciation. There was something about the air that he had noticed before as they were bicycling. He hadn't been able to put his finger on it but now it came to him. Not only was it clean and fresh beyond anything he had ever known Earth-side but it had a slight perfumed quality. And it came to him. There were so many flowers, everywhere, that their odor permeated the air. It must apply to all of Grissom, not just this residential area of New Frisco. It was almost like living in a perfume store.

From this point, nearly at the end of the cylinder and three stories high, he could see all three of the valleys and all three of the stretches of windows as well. It came to him that if he had a pair of strong binoculars he could probably pick out individuals on all three of the valleys, those above, seemingly walking upside down. The very thought brought home to him how really alien this all was.

He got the damnedest feeling that he was living in a gigantic submarine, which, in a way, was what he was doing, of course. It was as Earth-like as they could make it, well enough. But who was kidding whom? Here they were, some half a million Earthlings, living in a gigantic submarine. The thought unnerved him a little and he went back into the living room.

Susie was there, an automatic pistol in her hand. She was holding it gingerly.

Rex took it from her. It was a six-inch barreled, .22 Long Rifle caliber and meant for plinking or very small game. It wasn't much of a gun for serious work. You'd have to hit a man rather selectively, say between the eyes, or plumb center in the heart to do much more than dent him. He flicked the stud and dropped the magazine into a side pocket and jacked the slide. There was no cartridge in the firing chamber. He left the receiver back and stuck his thumb at the end of the barrel and peered into the front. The barrel was spotlessly clean and had obviously been fired very little.

"No holster?" he said.

She shook her head. "If he has one, I don't know where it is."

He returned the magazine to the butt of the gun and said, "Wizard. I'll have to stick it in my belt. Where's my room?"

She showed him down a hall leading off the living room, giving him a conducted tour as they went. Dining room, kitchen, the professor's study, her room. She said, "Down here are three guest rooms. You can take your pick."

He took his pick, finding it to be a small suite, rather than just a room. There were bedroom, bath and a small sitting room cum study, complete with desk on

which was both a TV phone and a library booster.
It was in keeping with the rest of the apartment and
very comfortable indeed. Two Impressionist-type paintings on the walls, wall-to-wall carpeting.

He put his suitcase on the bed for the time and
didn't open it. She had remained standing in the doorway while he looked his new quarters over.

He said, "Well, I suppose we should get to the nitty
gritty. Let's go to the living room and you can tell me
everything you know about this whole thing."

She led the way, but rather than seating herself went
over to the bar, saying, "We should toast your new
job—grim though it is."

She reached down, opened the small refrigerator door
and brought forth a heavy bottle. She twisted the top
expertly, after setting out two champagne glasses, and
there was a satisfying pop. She poured quickly, before
the sparkling wine could foam up over the neck of
the bottle. She put the two glasses and the bottle on a
serving tray and brought them over to where Rex had
settled down on a couch. She put the tray on the
cocktail table before him and seated herself in an arm-
chair across the way.

Rex took up one of the glasses and handed it to her,
and then one for himself. "Well," he said. "Champagne.
I thought that it was too expensive to bring up from
Earth-side."

Susie held up her glass. "To your new job."

"Cheers." He sipped along with her and then
looked down into the glass. He said, "I'm no expert
on champagne, but this is great."

"Domestic champagne," she told him. "Lagrangia
brand."

He took another drink. "I'll be damned. You mean
you make it right here in Grissom?"

"Not exactly. This is made over in one of the Island
Twos. You see, we have division of labor. It would be
silly, in four Islands, with a total population of less
than a million, thus far, to duplicate each other's efforts. So far as potables are concerned, they specialize

in sparkling wines. We specialize in brewed beverages such as beer, ale, stout, and hard cider. Island one goes in for distilled guzzle. The same applies to everything else. One Island will specialize, say, in tools, another in bicycles and other vehicles, another in ceramics, and so forth. And then we trade. As the Islands increase in number, we'll continue the policy and branch out into industries we haven't developed thus far."

"Makes sense," Rex said. He sighed and put down his glass. "Wizard. Why was the professor going to Island One?"

She frowned and said unhappily, "We don't know."

"I mean, who was he going to see?"

"We don't know. Nobody over there seemed to be aware of the fact that he was coming, or what it was he planned to do, or who he was going to see."

Rex looked at her in surprise. "Did he often make such surprise visits? Kind of spotchecking?"

"No. If that's what he was up to. I've never known him to do it before."

Rex Bader thought about it for awhile. He took up his wine and finished it and raised eyebrows at her. When she had acquiesced, he refilled both of their glasses.

He sighed again and said, "Look. Would it be possible for Casey to have opened the door of that four-seater from inside and have gone out into space?"

"Yes," she nodded. "The hatch can be opened from either side."

"Then it would have been possible for someone else to have opened the vehicle from outside and taken the professor out?"

She admitted that hesitantly, saying, "Yes. But if that had happened surely he would have used one of his transceivers to give an alarm."

"Could some other craft have pulled up alongside his four-seater and its occupants gotten into the professor's spacecraft? Not necessarily someone unfriendly, who would provoke him into giving an alarm."

She said, "Why, yes. We have various small chemically propelled craft, used in construction about the Islands, in maintenace outside, and so forth. But it seems an unlikely thing to happen."

"If the professor had gone out into space, on his own initiative, would he have died?"

Susie scowled at that one but said, "There are light, emergency spacesuits in each vehicle. He could have put one of these on."

"And if he didn't?"

"Then, of course, he would die. Contrary to popular belief, space is neither hot nor cold. Things in it are hot or cold but not space. Without a spacesuit, he would immediately die of lack of air. But even if he had one of those light emergency suits he would eventually radiate away his body heat . . . and die."

Rex mulled it over some more, taking another pull at his drink. He said, "What would happen to his body, in that case?"

"It would drift away into space. Eventually, probably, to be blown by solar winds completely out of the solar system, in spite of the fact that we are at Lagrange Five and supposedly indefinitely stable."

"No way of finding him?"

"Not unless he had his transceivers with him. Then we could get a fix."

He thought some more, drank some more. Finally he said, "Look, Susie, could there have been any possible reason for George Casey to have committed suicide?"

She shook her head emphatically. "I saw him roughly fifteen minutes before he left. He was perfectly normal. Besides, he's simply not the type. I've never seen anyone with such a lust for life, such enthusiasms."

But then she hesitated for a moment. "It would seem very unlikely. I'd say he was immune to space cafard, as I am. But no one is completely immune and it can hit unbelievably quickly. If there had been someone else in the four-seater with him, who was suddenly hit by cafard, then the professor might have been stricken as well. It's terribly contagious, especially in a confined space."

"What's space cafard again? You mentioned it briefly before."

Susie said, "It's always been rather rare, actually, but it's the most dangerous thing in space. We know very little about it, but it's thought to be largely based on extreme claustrophobia and the sudden realization that you are in an environment other than that into which you were born. When it strikes, and it can do that out of a clear sky, you become hysterical, violent, and can attack others . . . or suicide. But Professor Casey loved space, loved living here in the Islands. He is the last person in Lagrangia I would expect to contract cafard. The only possibility I can think of is his being exposed to someone else in the throes of it, and we know that he was alone in that four-seater."

"Besides," Rex said gloomily. "There are other strange aspects to the whole thing. Why didn't he take you? Why didn't he even tell you why he was going to Island One? Who was he going to see there and why? What was he going to do?"

She shook her head in rejection of his questions.

The TV phone screen sounded and Susie got up and went over to it. When she returned she was frowning.

She said, "It's a chap named Whip Ford. He wants to see the professor."

"Whip Ford!"

"You know him?"

"Very slightly. He was a fellow passenger coming up. Kind of a chip on the shoulder type. I can't imagine him wanting to see Casey. He said he was a tourist."

"Yes. We have a certain number of them now. They're allowed to stay for a limited length of time, since they usually don't fulfill the requirements to stay permanently in Lagrangia. However, they're good publicity for us when they return Earth-side. They're almost always ecstatic about their visit. Comes under the head of public relations."

"What does he want?"

"I don't know, but I'll have to see him. The professor invariably sees to such things. He might be a reporter wanting an interview and George Casey never refuses. It wouldn't do to just brush this Whip Ford off. I'll see him and tell him that the professor is off on a tour of the other Islands and see if there's anything I can do for him, as the professor's private secretary."

She added, "See here, Rex, you must be famished. Across the street and a hundred yards or so to the right is a small British type bar called The Pub. Neighborhood kind of place and very nice. They have excellent meat pies. Why don't you go over and have a bite while I'm seeing Ford? By the time you return, I'll have finished with him and we can continue with the professor's problem."

"Sounds like a good idea," he said, coming to his feet. "You sure you don't mind being alone with him? He's a little on the hard-to-take side."

She scoffed. "No, certainly not. Nothing untoward ever happens in Lagrangia."

He looked at her sceptically and said, "The professor disappeared, didn't he?"

When he had gone, she put away the empty bottle and the glasses, and sat down at the desk for a time, checking out some routine matters.

Finally, there came a knock at the door and she went to answer it. Door identity screens were an unknown in Lagrangia, another rebellion against the tyranny of the machine.

The man who confronted her was as handsome a black as Susie Hawkins had ever seen, though this was somewhat balanced by the fact that he wore a scowl, rather than a smile.

He said, his face sullen, "I'm Whip Ford. You say that Professor Casey isn't around?"

"I'm afraid that's right. I'm his secretary. Perhaps I can help you. Won't you come in?"

He looked at her suspiciously. "You're sure that he's not just giving me the brush-off?"

"I'm very sure of it, Mr. Ford. Come in." She led the way, saying over her shoulder. "Just what is it that you wished to see Professor Casey about?"

"I want him to tell us how to go about building one of these Islands."

SEVEN

Rex Bader had no difficulty in finding The Pub and was mildly surprised at how pleasantly it had been done. Somebody had gone to a great deal of trouble duplicating a real British type pub. There was even a sign outside duplicating an Elizabethan sign, complete with a rampant lion.

Inside, the motif was continued with a vengeance. A very typical English pub. Rex Bader had been in several once when one of his few and far between private investigator jobs had taken him to London. The interior was moderately dim, as behooved a bar, so at first sight the rafters, the furniture, the bar itself seemed of heavy dark wood. It was only after he had climbed upon a stool and leaned on the bar that he realized that it wasn't truly wood but some sort of plastic done up in such wise as to resemble it remarkably. The Pub had ten tables and half-a-dozen booths along one wall. On the walls were faded posters going back to World War One days; scenes in London music halls, complete with dancing girls, war propaganda posters, including Huns cutting the hands off little children and nuns, that sort of thing.

It was the bar itself that was the height of pub authenticity. It had British-type beer spigots, a somewhat beat-up mirror, deliberately beat-up in appearance, undoubtedly, to add to the atmosphere, and a wide selection of bottles, some of the labels of which Rex recognized; scotch, rum, gin, cognac, sherry.

There were only three occupants of the room when

Rex entered. Two customers, man and woman, were in a booth leaning confidentially across the table, holding hands and whispering, over two tall glasses of beer. It had been a long time since Rex had seen such magnificent glasses of beer. You got a poor portion for your money in the auto-bars down Earth-side these days.

The other occupant was the bartender. He looked more British than John Bull. Rounded of face, with a walrus mustache, red hands, and a semi-clean apron tied around his waist. It had been years since Rex Bader had been in a bar that boasted a live bartender. The class of drinkery he could afford was invariably automated. Swanker restaurants, he knew, often sported live waiters and bartenders but such were not for citizens on Negative Income Tax or Guaranteed Annual Stipend, GAS, as it was sometimes called.

Rex climbed up on a stool and looked up and down the bar appreciatively. Now, here was the sort of place to drink in. Susie had been correct in recommending it.

"Wot'll it be, Mate?" the bartender said. He even affected a slight British accent.

Rex said, "The Pub was recommended to me for its brews and its meat pies. I think I'll just have a beer first and then a pie with my second glass. What's your best dark beer?"

"Well, Mate, my own favorite is Russian Imperial Stout. But it's on the strong side."

"Never heard of it."

"Well, sir, it was originally brewed to order for Catherine the Great of Russia by one of the English breweries. It's the strongest stout made. And the only one that carries a vintage label. It has to be aged at least one year before being consumed."

"Wizard," Rex said. "I'll have one."

Russian Imperial Stout, it turned out, wasn't on draft. It came in a dark bottle, with an impressive looking lable. And it was the darkest looking brew and bore the heaviest collar that Rex had ever seen.

The bartender watched him with concern as he took

his first sip. Rex stared down into the glass. "Holy Jumping Zen," he said, in protest. "The poor man's whiskey."

"Good, eh?" the bartender said in satisfaction. "Rich and strong."

"That it is," Rex told him, venturing another cautious sip. "You mean to tell me you ship this up all the way from Earth?"

The other looked at him as though he was out of his mind. "No, of course not, Mate. We brew it right here in Grissom. We just do the best we can to duplicate the original, even down to the appearance of the bottles and labels."

Rex frowned and pointed a finger at the bottles of spirits lining the shelf under the mirror. "But those. Black and White Scotch, for instance. That has to come up from Earth."

The other grinned at him. "You must be new in Lagrangia, Mate. The only thing that came up was a few labels to be copied. We make all our guzzle up here, in one Island or the other. Most are pretty good copies of the real stuff down Earth-side, but we haven't got some of them down pat. The heavy Jamaica type rum they make over in Komarov, for instance. It doesn't have quite the body."

Rex took another gulp. The stuff was growing on him and its strength, on top of the champagne Susie had served, was beginning to warm his food-empty stomach.

He said, "You know, I'm surprised to find a bartender in a little pub like this. With all the fancy requirements to get a job in Lagrangia, and the high pay everybody gets, I'm surprised at utilizing such labor."

The other laughed, reached up and pulled off his false mustache. "This isn't a job," he said. "Actually, I'm an electrical engineer."

Rex looked at him, puzzled. "How do you mean?"

"We've got a club we call The Pub Crawlers. Composed of folk here in New Frisco who like bars. It's a hobby. All the work is volunteer. I get to act as bartender, here in The Pub, for four hours, twice a week. We've got several other bars in town. One's a French sidewalk café type. One's a Wild West saloon. One's a duplicate of a speakeasy of Prohibition days. We have a lot of fun. Some of the women members have even organized a dance troupe and they do the Can-Can and so forth at the French cafe and the Wild West saloon, in 19th Century costume."

"Holy Zen," Rex said. "What a hobby."

The other grinned and stuck his mustache back on. He said, "Oh, everybody's got hobbies in Lagrangia. When you work only a thirty-hour week, you've got a lot of time on your hands. Glider clubs, sailing clubs, low gravity swimming and diving clubs, low gravity ballet troupes. I happen to like bars. When I'm not allowed to tend one, because there are more volunteers than part time jobs, I just spend quite a bit of time hanging around in them. I'm not really much of a drinker, most people aren't up here, but I like the gregariousness, the atmosphere, especially here in The Pub."

Rex Bader looked around again. "It's nice, all right. What's this about the meat pies?"

The bartender indicated a large, obviously heated, glass container sitting at one end of the bar. "Our specialty," he said. "Real British type meat pies, meat pastry they call it. Pork, chicken, rabbit . . ."

"No beef?" Rex said. "I had a beef pie in London once. It was delicious."

The other shook his head. "You *are* new to Lagrangia. We don't have any beef in Island Three. Maybe when we finish Island Four. Hell, they're even talking about importing a small herd of buffalo for the king-size wilderness they're going to have there. But up to now, we only keep the most efficient animals in the four Islands we've already built. Cows aren't one of them. It takes tons of fodder to fatten up a steer to butchering size. Chickens are different. Raised scientifically, you can get a pound of chicken meat from two pounds of feed. Pigs aren't quite that good but they're awfully efficient compared to cattle. Turkey's aren't

bad and the protein content of their meat is twice that
of cows but they aren't very good layers, don't turn
out many eggs per year."

"No cows?" Rex said. "How about milk for all these
kids I see running around?"

"Goats. Goat's milk is as good as, possibly better
than, cow's. It's naturally homogenized, for one thing.
And a good milk goat, such as the Toggenbergs we
have, will out-produce a cow two to one by weight and
by food consumed. And it's not true that a goat will
eat tin cans but they'll thrive on a diet that a cow
would starve on, things like corn husks. There are other angles. A female goat is ready to breed at six months
and they almost always throw two kids, sometimes
three. The males you castrate and in three to six
months they're ready to be eaten as cabrito, or kid.
More delicate in taste than lamb."

Rex said, "I understand the milk tastes strong. Goat
smell."

The bartender shook his head. "Female goats have
no odor. It's the buck. You have to keep the buck away
from the does, especially in breeding season. Then
there's no odor in the milk."

Rex looked at him sceptically. "Your herd wouldn't
increase very fast with those tactics, would it?"

The other laughed, even as he polished the bar with
his bar rag. He said, "Artificial insemination. We have
the sperm sent up from Earth-side, from the best Toggenbergs in Switzerland. We started, originally, with the
best prize does we could buy. Our herds are being
bred up at a helluva rate and in size too. A doe goat
throws two sets of kids a year. Compare that to a
cow. Would you like a kid's meat pie?"

Rex got down from his stool and took up his half
empty glass. He said, "Thanks. Not for the moment.
I'll finish this, first."

He took the glass over to one of the tables on the
far side of the pub and sat down. He wanted to do
some recapitulating, to mull over what he'd learned so
far about the disappearance of Professor George Casey.

He had barely noticed when the three new customers had entered, too immersed in remembering all that Susie Hawkins had told him. They had gone over to the bar, got themselves draft beers and then two had sat down at a table and the third had approached Rex's.

Rex had finished his beer and was about to come to his feet to refresh it and to get his meat pastry, when the other sat down across from him. He was a man of about thirty, well built, clean-cut, as the expression goes, but with a somewhat sardonic something about both eyes and mouth.

Rex Bader said, "There are other tables—unoccupied."

"What spins, Rex?" the other said easily.

Rex's eyes narrowed. "All right, now we've established that you know my name. Let's go on."

"Bowman. Mark Bowman," the newcomer said, twisting his mouth. "At your service, Rex Bader, last of the private eyes."

"Wizard. What in the hell do you want, Bowman?" Inwardly, Rex was thinking, *Who in the name of Zen can this be? Nobody but Susie and the Council know I'm here and that I'm a private investigator. And I just arrived this morning.*

"The chief wants to see you," Bowman said.

"Wizard. Who's the chief and why does he want to see me?"

The other looked at him, a bit mockingly and drawled, "You'll undoubtedly find that out when you see him."

"Great," Rex said, irritation mounting. "You tell the chief that I'm having my lunch. If he wants to talk to me, bring him around."

"I'm afraid that's not his orders, Rex, old chum-pal."

"Well, great. What am I, under arrest, or something?"

"In a way, if that's how you want it."

Rex stared at him. "Under what charge?"

"Oh, rape, or molesting small children, or something like that. Or maybe homosexuality. I understand they screen out homosexuals in Lagrangia. Which is a hell-uva thing in this day and age. What are they, pre-gay age?"

If the other had intended it or not, that was a new angle. Perhaps, in his attempt to be smartassed the other had made a mistake. He had revealed the fact that the selfnamed Mark Bowman was obviously not a Lagrangist. Then, what in the hell was he? Rex Bader became increasingly more cautious. He unobtrusively unbuttoned his jacket, on the possibility that a quick draw would be called for.

"Let's stop kidding around," Bowman said. "Don't be a dizzard. If the chief wants to see you, he'll see you. Why cause any trouble? Come along."

"I think I'm staying," Rex said. "I smell Denmark." He began to come to his feet.

Mark Bowman made a slight gesture with his hand and two men stood up from a nearby table and approached. Rex was an old hand. He noted the bulges under their left arms. He sighed, and sank back into his chair.

There were three of them and one of him and all looked in good trim and some ten years younger than he was.

He said bitterly to Bowman, "Your elequence convinces me. Let's go see the chief."

"You're an easy lay, Bader," the other grinned at him. "Why didn't you just start yelling bloody blue murder and see what developed?"

"Because I didn't want to run the chance of getting the other two customers, or the bartender, winged," Rex said. "Nor, particularly, myself."

"Let's go, then," Bowman said, standing.

Rex Bader didn't mind as much as all that. This intrigued him. He wanted to see what was going to develop. It had to apply in one manner or the other to the professor.

He said, as they walked to the door, the two silent gunmen bringing up the rear, "I thought that there were no cops in Lagrangia."

Bowman said, airily, "Oh, there are police and police, you know."

In front of the pub was parked one of the small electro-hover four-seaters.

"And I thought that these were almost taboo, too," Rex said.

"Oh, we've got a lot of pull," his captor told him. "You'd be surprised how much weight the chief throws around."

They crowded into the small vehicle, Rex and Bowman into the back, the two goons into the front. Control was manual. Automated vehicles were another unwanted, evidently, in Grissom. The one behind the controls dropped the lift lever, tread on the accelerator, and they were off.

"How'd you know where I was?" Rex said to Mark Bowman.

"We followed you, chum-pal," the other said, and suddenly reached over and snatched the pistol from Rex Bader's belt, under his jacket.

"Hey!" Rex snapped and reached for it.

The other held it away, grinning mockingly. "You won't be needing this," he said. He looked at the gun before sticking it in his belt. "A twenty-two," he marveled. "What were you going to do with it, pot at tin cans? Now, here's a *gun*." He pulled back his jacket far enough that Rex could see a Gyro-jet automatic snuggled in its shoulder holster.

So, our Mark Bowman and his companions had had some method of getting heavy calibered weapons past Earth-side customs. That was something interesting. Rex Bader had left his own Gyro-jet in New Princeton, knowing full well that he'd never get past all the inspection points with it. In actuality, they went through the triple check largely to be sure you didn't bring in any agricultural, or any other kind of pests, including bacteria, but that didn't mean that they wouldn't find a gun and ask difficult questions about it.

To Rex's surprise, their destination was the Space Ritz. They drove down an entry ramp and into what he assumed was the vehicle pool Susie had mentioned. Here were parked various cars and what amounted to small buses; most were of the same size as that in which they were riding.

"Home again," Bowman said and they got out.

Instead of the main staircase, they ascended what Rex assumed was a service stairway. It bypassed the lobby. They reached the second floor, went down the corridor a way and came up to the door of Suite D. Bowman gave a brief knock but then reached down, twisted the knob, and opened the door before receiving a response.

"After you, chum-pal," he said.

Rex entered a fairly large living room.

At the room's desk was seated John Mickoff, of the Inter-American Bureau of Investigation, the amalgamated police and espionage-counter-espionage forces of the United States of the Americas. He looked up at the entry of Rex and his captor.

He said, "Well, younger brother, are your eggs completely scrambled? What are you up to this time?"

EIGHT

Susie Hawkins looked at Whip Ford in complete surprise. "Build an Island?" she said. "You want to build an Island?"

"That's what I said," Ford told her. "Or, at least, find out if and how it could be done."

Susie said, "Sit down, Mr. Ford. Could I get you a drink?"

He said, "No," but sat down on the same couch that Rex Bader had occupied earlier.

Susie Hawkins took the chair across from him, at the other side of the cocktail table.

She said, "I don't understand."

"What is there to understand?" he said, a touch of impatience in his voice. "I represent a group that wants to build an Island of their own and live in space."

Susie was bewildered. "But why not just apply to the Lagrange Five Project to become colonists?"

"We're all Blacks, Doctor Hawkins. And we're fed up with how our race gets pushed around. As the old joke had it, we're tired of the world and want off."

She said, "You being black has nothing to do with it, Mr. Ford. Colonists are selected for their abilities, their education and experience and their mental and physical make-ups."

He sneered at that. "This Lagrange Five is primarily a Whitey project. Oh, you let a few Blacks in, Uncle Toms, just to show how democratic the whole thing is. But largely you're whites."

"That simply isn't true, Mr. Ford."

"Like Zen, it isn't. Those computers that check out your qualifications are rigged against us."

Susie shook her head definitely. "No. There are more than just a few Blacks in Lagrangia. And even more Orientals. All races go to make up our population."

"Then why are so many of us turned down when we apply?"

"A good many Caucasians are turned down too, literally millions of them.''

"Then how come whites predominate so much?"

"Probably because more of them have the qualifications."

"Oh, we're not as smart as you are."

Susie was becoming a little impatient, but she hid it. She said crisply, "I'll be brutally frank, Mr. Ford. It has nothing to do with the color of your skin. I have worked on the computers that do the selecting of our colonists. They are not programmed to check your race, or color or creed, only your Ability Quotient, your I.Q., your education and experience, and your physical attributes and health. It's true that there are more whites than the other races, but that's because the average white is more apt to have the qualifications, as I've already said.

"I am not defending the situation Earth-side which has led the so-called colored races to be surpassed. Mr. Ford, a child's brain is developed in the first seven years of its life. If it has too low a protein diet, the child's brain suffers, in comparison to the child on the type of diet we find in Europe and North America especially. There are also, in the more backward areas of Earth, such diseases of poverty as pellagra, which effect both brain and body. A child raised in areas of the Sudan, for instance, will very unlikely make it to Lagrangia. Even if it survives the handicaps, there is little chance it will secure the education and skills required. How many universities are there in Sudan? For that matter, how many high schools? The same applies to India and Pakistan and other Oriental countries. Not so much to China, but it would seem that few Chinese *wish* to become Lagrangists. Some we have, of course, but few, considering the population of the People's Republic."

"So," he said coldly. "Africa, which gave birth to civilization, now takes second place to the Whities. We had a high civilization in Egypt, Doctor Hawkins, when your own ancestors were running around in animal skins and knawing their meat off bones while they were squatting around campfires."

She put a damper on her irritation again. "The Egyptians weren't exactly Blacks, Mr. Ford."

"What do you think they were, Englishmen? Hawkins is an English name, isn't it? The Egyptians were Africans. The first indications of their civilization came down the Nile from Nubia, from western Ethiopia. I know, some of your historians and anthropologists like to call them Hamitic, squirming to admit that they were and are Blacks. Take a look at the head of the Sphinx, or such statues of the pharaohs as that of Rameses the Second, all Negro features. Or go to Egypt today. Except for a few comparatively recently arrived Arabs, the Egyptians are black in color. I don't know why it is that you Caucasians can have groups as diverse as the tall blond Swedes to the north, and the short, very dark Greeks and Sicilians to the south, and still call them all whites, but won't accept the Blacks as Blacks, unless they're Bantus."

Susie closed her eyes in pain. She opened them again and said, "See here, sir. I'm sure you didn't come here to argue the relative merits of the races. I'm sure we've all contributed to the development of the human race."

But Whip Ford wasn't having any. He was well into his pet peeve. He said coldly, "Yes, we've all contributed, haven't we? But to varying degrees. Off hand, I can't think of a major breakthrough in the development of man that came from Europe. You were still primitives when the Africans and Asiatics were discovering such things as ceramics, agriculture, the domestication of animals, the use of metals, writing. Did you know that a system of writing was worked out in Africa, various parts of Asia, including far China, and even in Mexico by the Mayans and other Indians, but never in Europe? Europe had to import a system of writing from Asia Minor. We also first developed mathematics, including the use of the zero in India, and astronomy and various other sciences while you were still not much above the level of the animals you hunted. It's unlikely that today's European and North American art surpasses that of Egypt of four thousand years ago."

Susie sighed and said, "The Caucasians, too, have made contributions to progress, Mr. Ford."

"Yes, from the military use of gunpowder to the atom bomb. Oh, I'll admit that you've made *developments* in the sciences that we originated, and you instigated the industrial revolution. But you never would have gotten underway if we hadn't given you such little items as the wheel. And now, as a result of your military prowess, we of Africa and Asia are second- or third-class citizens. That's why we want off the world."

She could see that the man was all but trembling with anger.

Susie Hawkins said, "See here, Mr. Ford. We have gotten far off the track. You originally said that you had come to see the professor about the possibility of building an Island for yourselves."

He pulled himself together and said, "That's right."

"I'm sorry that he's not available. However, I've been with him from the very first and I'll give the same answer I am sure he would. Yes, it's possible."

His eyes narrowed.

Susie said, "However, it would not be a cheap thing to do and I doubt that, under the circumstances, the Reunited Nations would help financially."

"We didn't expect them to," he said belligerently. "They're dominated by the whities."

Susie sighed again.

Ford said, "All Blacks are not as poor as those you described in the Sudan, Doctor. We even have multi-millionaires among us, and many with good paying positions in industry, the sciences, the professions, and the arts."

"I'm sure you have."

He pressed on. "Our organization numbers a little over ten thousand persons and we're of the opinion that others will join up if and when we get underway."

"Then I would say that you could probably undertake it, Mr. Ford. The largest costs were in the early days of the project, building the mines and the mass-driver on Luna, building the construction shack here at Lagrange Five to house two thousand workers, and building Island One. The material for all this had to be lifted off Earth at great expense. It cost many billions of pseudo-dollars. But now we're under way and those costs are behind us. The building of new Islands is comparatively inexpensive, especially now that we're tapping the asteroids. Your group could assemble here and with expert help build a construction shack and have it pushed out to the asteroids. Once there, still utilizing trained experts, you could begin your Island. I would imagine that you would aim at one similar to our Island One, for a population of ten thousand or so. If your numbers increased, you could always build a larger one. Possibly as large as our Island Three, here."

He told her coldly, "We wouldn't want to depend on Whitey experts."

She wanted to roll her eyes upward in exasperation, but refrained. She said, "We have quite a few Black ones out here, or any other color or flavor, for that matter. We have no ghettos in Lagrangia, Mr. Ford. See here, it's obvious that I antagonize you. By coincidence, we have, a few houses down from here, one of our top construction engineers, a Mr. Washington Carver Smith."

"With a name like that, I assume he's a fellow Black. You mean he lives in a white neighborhood?"

"This isn't a white neighborhood. I told you, we have no ghettos in Lagrangia. The thing is, perhaps Wash is the one to talk to. Short of the professor himself, he's probably the most well-informed person on the subject available. I couldn't say whether or not the Council would give Wash leave of absence from the Lagrange Five Project to be one of your needed experts, but certainly he could fill you in with what you'd need and what it would approximately cost. He's on the same side of the street as this house, and four houses down. He's probably home at this time of day. Give him my regards."

Susie came to her feet.

Whip Ford stood as well. For a moment, he looked at her as though to apologize, at least a bit. But he wasn't quite up to it.

He said, "Thanks," and turned and headed for the door.

Susie Hawkins shook her head, after he had gone, and turned and headed for the bar. "Give me strength," she muttered. "I should have told him that one of my grandmothers was a Creole."

A figure entered the room through a door behind her. The newcomer said, "I'll have a drink, too. Where's Bader?"

Susie turned and smiled welcome and said, "Over at The Pub getting a snack, while I interviewed a Black who represents an organization that wants to build an Island as a refuge from racial discrimination Earth-side."

"Did you tell Bader anything?"

"No, of course not."

NINE

Rex Bader sank into a chair. Mark Bowman, looking sardonically amused, stationed himself near the door.

Rex said, "What I'm up to is classified information. I've got a client."

John Mickoff, in his early fifties, was going slightly to weight, however, he was still handsome in the square-faced Slavic manner. He looked considerably like Marshal Tito, when that revolutionist was in the same age group. He was stockier than Rex and shorter. He held some high, but by Rex unknown, office in the IABI, some sort of troubleshooter position, and was reputed to be the hatchetman of the present director of the police and espionage agency. On a couple of occasions, he and Rex had had contact before.

"I know you have," he said now. "Your client is George R. Casey, younger brother."

Rex was mildly surprised at that. He said, covering, "How did you know?"

"We've been monitoring all messages emanating, from Lagrangia. Doctor Susie Hawkins called you and asked you to come up for a possible job. Susie Hawkins is Casey's right arm. Obviously, she was calling for him. So, what did he want you for, Bader?"

"I'll never tell," Rex said. "You can twist my arm and shine bright lights in my eyes while you give me the third degree, but I'm iron."

"Stop it, stop it, your wit is killing me," Mickoff told him.

Mark Bowman said conversationally, "He was carrying a shooter when we picked him up."

Mickoff said in disgust, "Well, give it back to him. He's on our side now."

Bowman shrugged and pulled Rex's pistol from his belt, walked over and handed it to him. "It's only a popgun, anyway," he said.

Rex Bader tucked the small calibered gun back into his belt, looked across the desk at Mickoff and said, "Where'd you recruit this clown? I've been trying to get a job in the IABI for years, so I could get off Negative Income Tax, and the job computers have always turned me down. And you wind up with a character like this. He must watch the old movie revivals. He thinks he's Humphrey Bogart."

"Why, you dizzard," Bowman said.

"Shut up," Mickoff told him, "and get out into the hall with Jim and Marty. Sometimes I think Bader's right. You watch too many of those espionage Tri-Di shows. What'd you do, strongarm him? No, don't bother to answer."

Bowman, his face registering resentment, left.

Rex said, "What in the name of Zen do you mean, I'm on your side now? I've got a client."

"You've got two clients."

"Wizard. I didn't know," Rex said. "All right. It's your glue, start sticking it."

Mickoff leaned forward. "Look, younger brother, we need somebody in Professor Casey's camp. Something queer is going on and it's something the United States of the Americas doesn't like. You're an American."

Rex said, "That's great, but I've got a client. How do you get a drink around this pad?"

Mickoff stood and went to a bar set in one corner. He said, "Did anyone ever tell you you drank too much?"

"Yes, my sainted mother, when I was ten years old. What in the hell are you doing up here, Mickoff?"

The other took up a bottle at the bar and stared at the label and said, "Here we are in Island Three and they don't even have automated bars."

Rex said, "They try and escape from automation every time they can in Lagrangia. And what's your big mission, Mickoff?"

The IABI man turned back to him, two glasses in hand. "I'm here to find out what's going on. And, more important, what's *going* to be going on."

"Well, it's your top, let's see you spin it," Rex said, taking the proffered glass. "What *is* going on?"

"Among other things, the brain drain," Mickoff said, reseating himself.

"What's a brain drain?" So far, Rex was getting nothing.

Mickoff said, "Listen, have you ever eaten a wild strawberry up here?"

"I haven't eaten anything up here. I haven't had the time. And I'm starved."

"All right, listen. I've eaten wild strawberries. My mother was a great one to go out and pick wild strawberries. There's nothing more delicious than wild strawberries."

"What in the name of Holy Blue Zen are you talking about, Mickoff?"

"The wild strawberries in Upstate New York that she used to pick are nothing like, I mean nothing like, the wild strawberries they have here in Grissom."

Rex looked at him as though he was completely around the bend. He said, "What in the hell's that got to do with what?"

The other leaned forward. "That's what I'm telling you about. Do you like corn on the cob?"

"The real thing's my favorite vegetable. I haven't really had it for years. What you've got to do is pick roastin' ears a few minutes before you stick them in the pot of already boiling water and they can't be in for more than, say, three minutes and then . . ."

"Yeah, yeah, yeah. That's what I'm saying, younger brother. You haven't eaten here even once. Listen, there's no food like they've got here."

He seemed to switch subjects completely, to Rex's confusion.

"Look, suppose you were going down the street

and you met the most attractive curve you ever saw in your life—of course, different curves appeal to different guys. You could walk up to her and just tell her so, and most likely she'd give you a date . . . I mean in her bed."

"Oh, come on now. They aren't that far out. These Lagrangists have only been up here ten years or so."

"And that's evidently been enough and they're upgrading, if that's what you could call it, by the minute."

"But what would her husband say?"

"She hasn't got a husband and she doesn't want one."

Rex stared at him blankly.

Mickoff said, "Maybe I'm not putting this over right, but what I'm saying is that anybody who wouldn't want to live in Island Three is out of his ever living mind. And the corollary of that is—everybody wants to live in Island Three, if they've got a mind. Have you breathed the air, drunk the water, walked or bicycled around in their villages or wildernesses? Holy Zen, have you gone fishing?"

Rex was still goggling him.

Mickoff said, "Which brings us to the mind drain."

"Wizard," Rex told him bitterly. "I thought we were talking about wild strawberries, corn on the cob, and the easy availability of nooky in Lagrangia."

Mickoff ignored him and went on, after slugging back half of his drink.

"The big requirement for becoming a Lagrangist is an I.Q. of a minimum of 130 and a high-rating Ability Quotient. Oh, they have other requirements such as health and a good education. You know what the average education is up here?" He didn't wait for an answer. "A master's degree. That's average. Even construction workers, laborers, usually have an engineer's degree. There are more doctors and academicians in Lagrangia, per square foot, than have ever before been seen."

"Come on, come on," Rex said. "The brain drain."

"That's it. Every scientist, every technician, every

engineer worth his salt on Earth, wants to become a Lagrangist. The British and Germans used to complain in the old days of the brain drain to the United States, the high pay and the superior working conditions. The hundreds of millions of dollars spent on research by government, industry, and foundations made for wonderful opportunities if you liked your work, and most of these types do. So the best brains of England and Germany were going to America. Obviously, the British and German governments were bitter. Well, it's happening to the whole world today."

Rex was beginning to get the drift.

Mickoff pressed on. "It's bad enough now, when the three already completed Islands have a population of less than a million, but when that Island Four opens up do you realize it's going to have room for a population of millions? And that's only the first Island Four. They plan to build more than one, and there's even talk already of an Island Five. Zen only knows how big it'd be. There doesn't seem to be much in the way of a limit."

Rex said, "It'd take forever to build."

"Not with automation it wouldn't, and almost all of the basic work is already automated, computerized. And with automation, the Chinese could have built the Great Wall of China in a few years. And another angle here. It's not just scientists that are being drained away to Lagrangia. They're already letting in such types as artists and writers, just so they have that necessary I.Q. The Lagrangists have a real bug in their bonnet about that. They wouldn't let a Picasso in, if he didn't have all of the qualifications."

Rex finished his drink and got up and snagged Mickoff's glass as well, and, without invitation, went over to the bar and poured two more. They were drinking the Lagrangist version of Scotch, which was near enough to the original that Rex couldn't tell the difference. He returned with the drinks and sat down again.

He said, "Well, what are you building up to?"

"This. With a Lagrangist population of less than a

million, we're already feeling the drain. What's going to happen when there's room for a few dozen millions?"

Rex eyed him, uncomprehending.

Mickoff said, "Do you know how many persons there are on Earth with an I.Q. of over 130? Damn few, comparatively. The average intelligence quotient is 100 and the overwhelming percentage of us lie between 90 and 110. As you get above that, the number falls off drastically, and almost in a reverse geometric progression. When you get up to 140, which they call 'gifted,' there are damn few left, in the whole world. That means genius and there are precious few geniuses in any one generation."

Rex said, less than happy, "Well . . ."

Mickoff was waggling a forefinger negatively. "Rex, everybody, for all practical purposes, wants to become a Lagrangist and get out of the cesspool the world has become; get out of the ever present fear that a new war will develop. Rex, they're going to drain away the cream of Earth, and leave the dregs. At least, that's what it looks like. Professor Casey and his gang haven't said so, as yet. They haven't said anything on the subject. But that's what they *are* doing."

Rex thought about it and said slowly, "Maybe, later, they'll lower the requirements and even such dizzards as you and I can be colonists."

"Don't kid yourself. From their viewpoint, why should they? Why take in second-rate citizens when they can have the best? Why let the stupid, the lazy, the bums, the criminals become Lagrangists? Why let the diseased, the cripples, the uneducated into their Islands?"

"Maybe it's the best thing for the race," Rex Bader said slowly. "We've made a mess of our world, maybe they'll do better."

John Mickoff looked at him in disgust. "With that kind of an outlook, why don't you just go and shoot yourself? You've already applied to become a Lagrangist, from what your Dossier Complete in the data banks tells me, and they turned you down. I have a sneaking suspicion that they'd turn me down, too. What it means is, we've knocked on the door of paradise and St. Peter won't let us in."

Rex Bader could think of nothing to say to that, so he took another pull at his drink.

Mickoff said in disgust, "What's going to happen to those who are left behind, all three billion plus of us? Drained of our best elements, not just the scientists but the best technicians, engineers, educators, and even the artists. What's going to happen to Earth?"

"I don't know," Rex said. "But I've had the Lagrange Five Project dream for years."

"So have I, fifteen years ago. But now that dream's turned into a nightmare. Professor Casey and his team have created a Frankenstein monster that's not going to destroy them but will destroy all of the race that can't get into space."

"Wizard," Rex said wearily. "So why are you up here and what's it got to do with me?"

"I've been sent up to case the situation, to try to come up with some answer, if what I've been telling you is true, and I'm already largely of the opinion that it is."

"Why don't you just shoot them out of the sky? It wouldn't take much to bring one of these Islands down. And I understand that secretly both the United States of the Americas and the Soviet Complex have military space cruisers. Oh, they call them scientific craft, but they're armed, all right, all right."

The other glared at him before knocking back the balance of his drink. He said, "Your eggs must be scrambled, younger brother. In the first place, the world is dependent on the solar derived power that they beam down. And, secondly, every cloddy on Earth has the space dream, just as you say you have. The public wouldn't stand for an attack. Most of them fondly believe that when there's more room for colonists in the Islands, they'll have their chance. They won't but they'll never believe it. A jerk never knows that he's a jerk. He thinks that he's at least as good as the next man. He'll continue to dream that one day he'll be allowed to become a Lagrangist, even though his I.Q. is less than a hundred."

"Where am I supposed to come in?" Rex said wearily.

"You're right next to the professor and Doctor Hawkins. We want you to keep us informed."

Rex stood, shaking his head. "I'll think about it, but I suspect the answer is no. In spite of what you've said, I still have the . . . the dream."

Mickoff roared at him, "You damn dizzard! Don't you realize that you're one of the underprivileged? You're like a kid with his nose pressed up against the window watching a party going on inside to which he wasn't invited. He's too square to resent it; he still thinks it's a beautiful party."

"It is," Rex said softly.

"Well, I'll tell you this, younger brother. I'm going to blow the whistle on you. They put you on the payroll as a Research Aide to Casey. Yes, yes, I already know about it. But the only qualifications you've got are as a private eye. I'll take steps to have you fired."

"Why bother?" Rex shrugged. "They'd just get somebody else. And possibly you won't have a line on the next one. I'm a known quantity."

"Just what in the name of Zen does the professor want with you?" Mickoff growled.

"I'll never tell."

Rex Bader turned and left the room, the IABI man glaring after him.

He found Mickoff's three agents posted outside in the hall.

Mark Bowman evidently guessed, from Rex's expression, that the interview hadn't been a success from his chief's viewpoint.

He said softly to Rex, "Maybe I'll be seeing you again, buster."

"Maybe. I can't wait," Rex told him, heading for the stairs.

Down on the street, he went over to the inevitable bicycle rack and selected a bike. He mounted it and began trying to remember the route Susie had led him over earlier. It wasn't especially important. He could either call Susie on his pocket transceiver for directions, or ask some pedestrian. He assumed that everyone in New Frisco knew where the professor lived.

What Mickoff had said was disquieting. It had never occured to Rex that as the Islands became larger and larger, and more numerous, that the restrictions wouldn't be dropped and everyone that wanted to could migrate from Earth-side to Lagrange Five. Certainly, he had always looked forward to the day when he could.

But then the question came to him: if there was so limited a number of those eligible to become Lagrangists, with requirements of a high I.Q. and all the rest, where were the professor and the Councils going to get their millions to populate the coming Islands?

He swerved to avoid two ten-year-olds who had darted out from the sidewalk, laughing shrilly, before his bike. He had never seen so many children. But then, the day of the large family, Earth-side, had passed. Zero population growth was the goal everywhere and had been attained in at least all of the more advanced countries. Indeed, at least ten of them now had falling populations. Even married couples seldom had more than one child and practically never more than two. Some, none at all. Children didn't fit into the present way of life. They didn't even build housing for large families any more.

Something came to him as he pedaled and he worked it around in his head.

Somewhat to his surprise, he had no difficulty retracing the route to where Casey and Susie Hawkins lived. He pulled up before the apartment building, pushed his bike over to the rack, and parked it, then entered and ascended the stairs, his face thoughtful.

Susie was in the living room, working at the desk. She looked up at his entry and smiled and said briskly, "You've been gone for a long time. How was the meat pie?"

"I didn't have any," he told her. "I was picked up by three of John Mickoff's agents and taken to see him."

Susie stood quickly, as though distressed. She said, "I'll fix you something in the kitchen." She led the way and he followed. "What did Mickoff want? We knew he was here, of course," she said over her shoulder.

"He wanted to know what I was up to."

She began looking into the refrigerator, and said, "And did you tell him?"

"No," Rex said. "I didn't. He didn't seem to know that the professor has disappeared."

She brought forth various dishes. "He doesn't. Mickoff's been trying to get in touch with him for the past week."

In no time at all, Susie had fixed up a lusty looking cold spread on the kitchen table. She told him that she had already eaten but she took a chair across the way.

Rex said, between bites, "Remember when we were talking about that Virginia Dare Robbins child?"

"Certainly. She's a real darling and bright as the proverbial button."

"Ummm. That's what you said. You said that she had already passed her Lagrangist examinations and had come through with an I.Q. of 143, I think you mentioned."

"That's right. She was the first of the spaceborn children to take them. We were all sitting on the edges of our chairs, waiting to see how she would do."

Rex took a sip of the beer she had provided, along with ham, cheese, some cold fried chicken, pickles, and very dark bread."

He said, "What goes into the tests besides I.Q.?"

"Oh, the medical and physical tests. Ability Quotient isn't so easily tested at that age. And, of course, education is up to us. We check out children from the earliest ages for their particular bents. You know, if they seem inclined toward the sciences, a profession, a skill, art, or whatever, and then direct their educations in that direction."

"I see." Rex Bader asked the question he was building up to. "What if she hadn't passed?"

Susie bit her lower lip slightly before saying, "She would be returned Earth-side."

"And what would happen to her there?"

"She'd go to live with relatives, or be put up for adoption."

"Or be sent to an orphan institution, eh?"

"Possibly, in some rare cases."

"Suppose the parents object to giving her up?"

"Either, or both, of them are free to accompany her back to Earth."

"Have to give up their jobs, eh?"

"They'd usually find jobs with the Lagrange Five Project on Earth. Many of our employees are down there. After the child has grown up and is on its own, they can return to Lagrange Five, of course."

"It seems a little rough."

She nodded to that. "It is."

"I never heard about this element of Lagrange Five, back Earth-side."

"No," she admitted. "It hasn't been publicized. It's a fairly recent ruling of a meeting of the Grand Council which consists of the Councils on all Islands, to coordinate their efforts. This decision was made shortly before Virginia reached the age of ten. There can be no permanent residents of Lagrangia with an I.Q. of less than 130, or any who fail to meet physical standards."

"And more kids are hitting age ten daily, eh?" he added. "And some of them don't make the grade."

"That's correct." She could see his direction. "Rex, the fact that parents might have I.Q.s even much higher than 130 is no guarantee that their children will have. Most likely they will, but there is no guarantee. Their children might be born morons or physically defective."

"I see. And in another ten years these children, passing the age ten point, will be old enough to be colonists in the new Islands you're building, won't they?"

"Yes. In eight years, to be exact. We consider eighteen to be full maturity."

"This population explosion I commented upon. It's a deliberate policy of the Grand Council, I suspect."

"Yes, it is."

"Eventually, you expect your new Lagrangist to be recruited from the children of the earlier colonists, eh, rather than coming from Earth-side?"

"That's about it."

"And then you won't recruit anymore from Earth?"

She bit her lip again. "That remains to be seen. The consensus among members of the Councils is that we'll continue to accept anyone who can meet the requirements. However, some, such as Walt Hanse, are of the opinion that the day should come when we'll no longer recruit from Earth at all. Our growth in population will be internal. But we'll make that decision when its need is upon us." She ended with somewhat of a plea in her voice. "Rex, it has been decided that we do not wish second-class citizens in Lagrangia."

"I get it," he said. "Take the cream and leave the dregs behind. Well, thanks for the lunch. Perfect. Everything perfect. Shame there weren't any wild strawberries, or corn on the cob."

She looked at him in lack of understanding. "What?"

"Never mind," he said. "Look, we've got to get started. Let's take a look at the professor's study and then his bedroom. Possibly, there's some clue as to what happened to him."

"I doubt it," she said. "I've gone through both with a fine-toothed comb."

"Well, let's see."

He followed her into the study and looked about, wondering where to begin. Finally, he went over to the cluttered desk and thumbed through the papers there. Most of them were technical and he didn't have an idea as to their meaning. He started in on the drawers. Susie had taken a chair and was watching him, as though doubtful of his success.

In the third drawer, he came up with a steel strongbox. It was locked. He turned to Susie, the box in hand.

"What's this?"

"I don't know. His most personal things, I assume."

"You don't have a key?"

"No. It's about the only thing George Casey kept from me. I've never seen the contents, never seen it open."

"Wizard," Rex said. "So we'll pry into the professor's deepest secrets."

He sat down at the desk, put the strongbox before him, brought out his leather folder of picklocks and began experimenting. It took him less than five minutes to have the lid back.

Susie had come up to stand beside him, curiously.

They both stared down. Most of the contents of the box were papers. The whole interior of it was lead lined, and fairly thick lead at that.

Lying on top of the papers were two transceivers.

Susie took one up and ogled it.

"The Professor's?" Rex said.

"Yes."

TEN

Rex took the two transceivers and went over to a chair and sat down. He looked at them for a long time, in silence.

Finally, he said, "Would the lead in that strong box so shield these that Communications wouldn't be able to get a fix on them?"

"I would think so," Susie said. "I don't know the professor's original reason for having it so shielded. Perhaps in the past he had some experiments going with radioactives and wanted some place to hide them. I don't know."

"That representative from Communications on the Council . . ."

"Karl Kessinger."

"Yes. He said that the last record that data banks had of Casey using his transceiver was to call for a four-passenger vehicle to take him to Island One. That would mean he could have made the call from here, then put the transceivers in the strongbox and taken off."

"But why? In this day and age, not carrying your transceiver with you is almost like going around naked. You're continually using it."

"There's another possibility," Rex said thoughtfully. "How difficult is it to get into this apartment?"

"Why, it's not difficult at all. There are no door locks in Lagrangia. There's no need for any."

"Then, if someone has done the professor in, either kidnapped or killed him, that someone could have taken the transceivers and returned with them here and stuck them in the box."

Susie scowled at him saying, "But the box was locked when you found it."

"Wizard. But the someone could have taken Casey's keys at the same time he lifted the pocket phones."

"But *why?* If your someone wanted to destroy them, all he'd have to do is grind them under his heel."

"I don't know," Rex said glumly. "Look, how does this space cafard work? Could the professor have gotten a case of it, decided on suicide, ordered the four-seater, put his transceivers in the strongbox and then, when he got into space, simply stepped out of the craft to his death?"

She shook her head. "It's not the way it works, Rex. A case bad enough to bring you to suicide hits suddenly. You don't have the time to plan anything complicated."

The TV phone buzzed and Susie went over to the desk and sat and answered it. At the angle she was sitting, Rex Bader couldn't hear what was being said, but her face went wan. She talked for a few minutes and then clicked the phone off and turned back to him.

She said, "That's a coincidence. That was Doctor Poul Garmisch, over at the main hospital. He's our specialist in space cafard, though Zen knows, nobody knows enough about it to make any difference."

"What did he want?"

"He wanted to report to the professor that there have been two more cases today. Bad cases."

Rex said, "What's the cure for this space cafard?"

"The only cure is to put the victim under heavy sedative and rush him back to Earth. Usually, they make it. Once on Earth, the patient snaps out of it within twenty-four hours and is quite normal, though he can never return to space."

"Wow," Rex said. "Some disease."

Susie said, "Thus far, it has never struck a child born in space who has never lived on the Earth's surface. They seem to be immune. Even when in the presence of the most contagious of cases, real raving maniacs, they aren't affected. Only persons Earth-born."

She looked worried. "In the past, there were very few cases. And usually fairly mild ones. But this is starting to become a regular epidemic."

The phone rang again and Susie sighed and went over to it. This time Rex, for some reason or other, came along and stood behind her.

The face that faded in was that of Doctor Walt Hanse, of the Council. He was excited. "Doctor Hawkins, Bader! I'm over here with Karl Kessinger at Communications. On a twenty-four-hour-a-day basis, he's been trying to get a fix on Professor Casey. And now, we've got him!"

Rex said, "Where is he?" his face sceptical.

"Why, surprisingly enough, somewhere in the immediate vicinity of where you are now. His apartment, perhaps. Is he with you?"

Susie said, "No, he's not here, Walt. I assume that you got your fix on his transceivers. Mr. Bader found them in a lead-lined strongbox in his desk. As soon as we got them out of the lead shielding, you got a cross on them, obviously. But no, the professor isn't here."

Walt Hanse looked blank, momentarily, and then stormy. "You mean to tell me that the professor left his transceivers at home, before taking off for Island One?"

"Yes," Susie said. "That's the way it looks."

"I don't believe it! It's ridiculous. There's dirty work going on somewhere. It's the goddamned earthworms. They hate the professor. They hate us! They know damned well that we're superior to them and they're jealous to the point where they'd do anything to foul us up, and especially the professor. I tell you, Susie, it's long past time that we declare our independence, expel that silly Reunited Nations staff and the Earth be damned!"

Susie sighed. "In time, in time, Walt. You and your group of hotheads are in too much of a hurry. To a certain extent, we still need Earth, and they certainly need us."

"Why do we need them?" he said heatedly.

And she replied patiently, "Walt, there are quite a few things that we don't produce up here as yet."

"We can continue trade. In return for energy they'll gladly send up such things as we need. But we don't have to be connected to those birdbrain politicians for that!"

She said, "There's also the fact that it will be eight years before any of our young people begin to come of age. Meanwhile, we need competent colonists to fill the living space we're creating. Suppose we declared our independence and as a counter they banned all immigration to Lagrangia?"

"Let them!" Walt Hanse all but shouted. "We don't need any more of them. Our own natural increase will soon be providing all the population we want."

"Not even if we bred like minks," she said flatly. "It's not quite as fast as all that. Your radical section of the independence movement is too hotheaded, Walt. I heard a talk by your Herman Klein, the other night. He rather darkly hinted that it was our manifest destiny not only to colonize the solar system but eventually, and in the not too distant future, to set Earth right. He was of the opinion that the masses on Earth would follow wherever we led and he was all gung ho to overthrow every existing government Earth-side."

"And he's probably right," Hanse said, his voice still hot.

Susie said patiently, "Walt, it's the professor's opinion that if the people Earth-side want to overthrow their socioeconomic systems it's their right and they'll possibly do it. But they don't need any leadership from us."

"I don't know if the professor feels that way or not!"

"But I know it. Good-bye, Walt. Mr. Bader and I have plenty to do."

The other's face was still angry as it faded out.

Susie shook her head, got up, and went over to sink back on the couch. Rex joined her and looked at her strangely.

He said, "What's this radical section of the independence movement all about? What's the independence movement, for that matter?"

For a moment she looked as though she was considering whether or not to answer his question.

Rex said, "For all I know, there might be some tie-in with the professor's disappearance."

She considered that and then nodded. "It seems unlikely, but we don't have anything else to work on. Yes, there's an independence movement among the Lagrangists. It calls itself the Sons of Liberty. There are two wings, the Radicals and the Conservatives. When heated, the Conservatives call the Radicals Bolsheviks, and the Radicals call the Conservatives Fascists. Actually, I believe that the professor considers the whole movement premature. I think he believes that eventually the Islands will have to free themselves of any remnants of Earth-side domination, but that's for the future."

"Why complete independence?" Rex asked. "We're all members of the human race. Through the Reunited Nations, why not keep up the closest of relationships?"

She looked at him and made of gesture of rejection. "The lowest I.Q. in Lagrangia, Rex, is 130, save for tourists and the Reunited Nations staff. The average Earth-side I.Q. is 100. But there are over three billion of them and just slightly less than a million of us. We're intolerant of their domination."

He said in argument, "You wouldn't be here except for the sacrifices the Earth made to finance the beginnings of the Lagrange Five Project."

"That's true," she admitted, "but it makes no difference to history. The Thirteen Colonies wouldn't have been there in North America if it hadn't been for the efforts made by England and the expenses gone to by the British people. But events marched on and eventually the Colonies had to sever their relations with England and face their own destiny. The same applied to Latin America. The Spanish went to a good deal of expense in both money and lives to, ah, liberate, I believe is usually the term, Mexico from the

Aztecs, Peru from the Incas. But in a few hundred years the citizens of Mexico and Peru expelled them."

Rex said, slowly, as he thought it through, "There's something of a difference, though. The Spanish Conquistadores were adventurers financed by the wealthy and motivated by the gold and silver of the Indians. The British colonies were financed by such business ventures as the East India Company, which were motivated by profit. But the Lagrange Five Project was financed with the taxes of hundreds of millions of persons of all lands. Through the Reunited Nations, just about everybody kicked in to some extent or other. And there was precious little protest, among the common people, at least. Billions of pseudo-dollars and other currencies went into the Lagrange Five Project. Not just the wealth of Spanish aristocrats or British businessmen. And they contributed willingly because they, too, had the space colonization dream. They, too, wanted to leave a plundered, polluted, dangerous, and sad Earth and go out into space. But now you plan to withhold the dream from them."

Susie said, "Well stated, Rex, and possibly I, as well as Professor Casey, largely agree with you. But I'm afraid that history has no sentiment."

He nodded. "Perhaps, though it still seems a dirty trick. But we've got to get back to the professor. Where's this terminal, or whatever you call it, where he disappeared?"

"At the far end of the cylinder."

"We have to ride there on bicycles?"

She laughed. "Of course not. Come along."

She stood and Rex followed her out of the apartment and down the steps.

On the street they picked up two of the inevitable bikes, mounted them, and were on their way.

"Where are we going?" Rex said.

"To the Maglev Station."

"Oh, fine," he said. "Now I know just as much as I did before I asked."

She laughed again, her brisk, clipped little laugh. "We usually use bicycles for short trips but obviously if longer ones are called for we need fast public transportation. We utilize the dynamic magnetic levitation system, maglev for short, in underground, vacuum tubes. The technology of high-field superconductors make it possible for a vehicle to sustain a strong constant magnetic field without the expenditure of power. Actually, they're capable of speeds up to three hundred miles an hour, but since the furthest point to which you can go, the other end of the cylinder, is only twenty miles, we're not usually in that much of a hurry."

"Wizard," Rex said sourly. "Dynamic magnetic levitation. I still know just about as much as I did before."

It turned out that the Maglev Station was just across the way from the exit of the space docking port. They racked their bicycles and descended stairs to an area that resembled an Earth-side subway station, though admittedly more spick-and-span. Shortly, a streamlined vehicle smoothed up before them and Susie and Rex joined the other passengers in entering airline type doors.

It still looked like a subway to Rex Bader. He and Susie found seats. The doors closed, a diaphragm closed to seal off the entrance, and the wheelless vehicle began to accelerate.

"How long will it take to get there?" he said.

"Only a few minutes. This is an express going all the way to the other end of the cyclinder. There are locals that stop at every village and town along the way. There's not a town in Grissom that's further than a half mile from a Maglev Station."

Rex said, "This dispatch crew that shot off Professor Casey to Island One. Do any of them know that he never arrived?"

"No. Only the Council and I, here in Island Three, know about it. We've kept it just as quiet as we could."

"Only the Council, eh? Tell me more about this Council."

"Such as what?"

"Well, you said that they were the real government of Island Three. How do they get to that position?

From what you've said, they obviously aren't appointed by the Reunited Nations staff."

"Why, they're democratically elected."

He looked over at her. "But they represent different functions, as you called them, transportation, medicine, education, manufacture, and so forth, not towns or cities, or whatever. They're scientists and technicians, not politicians."

"Yes, certainly. Take Transportation. It's divided into several subdivisions. Lagrange Five to Earth, inter-Island, between cylinders, and inner-Island, such as this transport system we're utilizing now. Suppose that you work in an inner-Island system. You and your immediate fellow workers vote for your foreman. The foremen get together and vote for a supervisor of the subdivision. The supervisors get together and vote for a Councilman to represent the Transportation function on the Council. The Council of Grissom cooperates with the Council in our sister cylinder, Komarov. And both of them represent Island Three when there's a Grand Council meeting with representatives from all Islands, to coordinate all Lagrangia activities."

"I'll be darned. How long are they elected for?"

"No set period. Certainly not for four years or anything like that. Any function official can be removed immediately by the majority of those who elected him, from foreman right up to Councilman."

"How much more pay do they get?"

She seemed surprised. "Why, none. All Lagrangists get all expenses, if you can call it that. And all get their ten thousand pseudo-dollars, or the equivalent of any other currency, deposited down Earth-side."

"Then, what *do* they get out of it?"

"The honor of serving. The honor and respect granted them by their fellow Lagrangists."

"To each according to his needs and from each according to his abilities, eh?"

"Why, I suppose so," Susie said, not recognizing the quotation.

"Syndicalism," Rex said, surprised in his turn. "An updated form of 19th Century syndicalism. My father used to teach off-beat socioeconomics, and some of it rubbed off on me."

"Syndicalism?" she said. "Never heard of it. We thought we'd stumbled on the idea on our own. It was the only thing that seemed to make much sense. We figured that true democracy was difficult as practiced Earth-side, where you vote for people you don't really know, or know anything about, in spite of all the political speeches, the press agents, the Tri-Di shows, and all the rest of a political campaign. But where a person works, he is knowledgeable about the abilities of the people who work next to him. For instance, I'm a physicist and can evaluate the others here in Lagrangia who are also in physics. But I wouldn't have the vaguest idea of who to vote for for a senator or president who's reached me only through the news media and speeches."

"It's syndicalism, all right," Rex said, marveling. "I'm surprised that a howl hasn't gone up Earth-side. You can't get much more radical than syndicalism."

Susie said, "They don't know much Earth-side about what goes on here. The common belief is that the Reunited Nations is in charge in Lagrangia. Well, here's our station."

It hadn't occurred to Rex Bader that they were going to be in free-fall at the dispatch station, but he should have figured that out. At the very end of the cylinder, they were right on the axis where there was zero-gravity.

There were rails to pull themselves along and Susie led the way, obviously an old hand at this means of getting around.

The dispatch compartment was large and as Walt Hanse had described it at the meeting Rex had had with the Council. There were various-sized vehicles around, some obviously for passengers and some for freight.

Right at present, there seemed no vehicles about to be either launched or received. From the far end of the compartment, a man wearing a Buck Rogers rocket-belt came jetting over, gracefully. Rex Bader had been introduced to the device on his first visit to Island One, a decade before. Once you got the knack of them, they were fun, even in open space.

When the other came up, Susie said, in her usual clipped way, "Hello, Lon, what spins?"

The other smiled his welcome. "Well, Doctor Hawkins. How are you doing, Susie?"

"Fine. Lon Karloff, meet Doctor Rex Bader. He's George Casey's latest Research Aide. Lon is the dispatch crew chief on this shift, Rex."

The men shook.

Susie said, "I promised the professor that I'd give Rex the usual conducted tour, Lon. If you don't mind, I'd like to show him around."

He said, "Sure, Susie. I'll come with you. We don't have anything assigned for an hour or so."

He led the way, not utilizing his Buck Rogers rig now. He gave them the sightseeing tour with pride. It was something that Rex was already getting used to. These people in Lagrangia liked, and were proud of, their work.

Lon showed them, though Susie was already well acquainted with it, obviously, the largest of the passenger vehicles. It was a sphere of about thirty feet in diameter, protected from cosmic rays by a dense outer shell of some fifteen inch thickness and, Rex was told, had a total mass of about two hundred tons. It contained seating on three different levels and could be entered into by three different airliner-type doors. There was plenty of elbow room and leg room for each passenger, something like that of first class seating on a long-distance airliner, Earth-side, and could accommodate as many as 100 passengers. Rex was suitably impressed.

He said, "This is where Professor Casey took off for Island One, isn't it?"

"That's right," Lon said, and looked over to Susie. "Is George back yet? Possibly he came in on a different shift than mine."

"No, not yet," she said. "Zen only knows where he is."

Rex said, "Is this the kind of spacecraft he took?"

The crew chief said, "No. He was all alone in one of the little four-seaters, this one over here. They're the smallest of all the vehicles we shoot back and forth between the Islands." He led the way.

The four-seaters were, internally, at least, surprisingly similar to an Earth-side limousine. Very comfortably done. Rex displayed true interest. He got in and sank down into one of the well-upholstered chairs.

"Completely automated, eh?" he said. "The passenger doesn't have to do anything? You fire him off and at the other end they catch him?"

"That's right," Lon said. "As a matter of fact, this is the very four-seater that the professor took on his last trip. It brought over some tourists from Island One a few days ago."

"It is, eh?" Rex said, projecting interest. He looked at the hatch. "What in Zen would happen if somebody opened this when he was out there between Islands, in space?"

Lon grinned. "He'd get sick awfully fast. But not for long. He'd be dead."

"I imagine," Rex said. "But don't you have some kind of a, well, lifebelt, in case of emergency?"

"Oh, sure. Each vehicle carries emergency spacesuits. They'll last for quite a few hours—until somebody can get to you."

"I'll be darned. Could I see one? Can an ordinary person, not a trained spaceman, get into one?"

"Sure," Lon said. "In this locker, here." He opened the locker in question and dragged one forth to display it. There were three other remaining spacesuits.

Rex said casually, "A four-place vehicle and four spacesuits, eh?"

"Oh course," the crew chief laughed. "You wouldn't want anybody left out in the cold."

Rex was shown the whole thing. How the vehicle was locked into the driver. Where the crew chief sat before the computer, waiting for the split-second to fire. Where the crew proper stood, shielded and out of the way. He asked after every detail and his guide was obviously pleased at the keen interest.

When they had left and were on their way back to New Frisco, Rex said to Susie Hawkins, "What do you think?"

"I don't think anything that I didn't think before. I've been through that a hundred times. What do *you* think?"

Rex said, "I don't know. Something occurs to me, but I'll have to worry it around."

Largely, they remained quiet on the return trip, deep in their own thoughts, but at one point Rex said, "Lon told us that the four-seater the professor disappeared in was the same one that he showed us."

She looked over at him, questioningly.

Rex said, "There were four spacesuits in it. That means that Casey didn't use one of them. Had he there would have been only three left and Lon Karloff, or someone else, would have noted the fact and immediately become suspicious."

"Yes," she said. "I hadn't thought of that. It would mean, then, that he didn't, on his own, leave the vehicle." She paused, before adding, "Unless he deliberately suicided, and I can't accept that."

Rex Bader considered it. "Unless he was intercepted by some other spacecraft and whoever occupied it brought over another spacesuit and got the professor into it before removing him. They might possibly have done that, knowing that if someone found only three suits remained he might smell a rat."

It didn't seem very likely and they lapsed back into silence.

By the time they arrived back in New Frisco it was dark.

Rex had read that it was the policy of the Islands to duplicate the night and day of Earth. The more Earthlike the life in the Islands could be made, the better, had been the reasoning, for psychological purposes. Indeed, when inside an apartment or other building, it was so Earth-like that Rex sometimes forgot that he

was off the world by some quarter-of-a-million miles.
It was when you were outside and could see, seemingly
in the sky, the other valleys and the strips of windows
that you realized how really alien the interior of the
Grissom was. How had he thought of it earlier? A
tremendous submarine, in space rather than in the
ocean.

The night and day effect, he knew, was achieved by
warping the aluminum mirrors which reflected the
sun's beams into the Island. As yet, he hadn't witnessed
either dawn or sunset but he knew that they had both.
It was quite a technological achievement.

They pedaled back to the professor's apartment, still
largely taken by their own thoughts. Rex, at least, feeling sour. Susie's face was expressionless.

At the apartment, Susie silently went to the bar.
"Martini, before dinner?" she said.

"Thanks. Do you even have vermouth up here?"

She was busy with the tools of the bartender's trade.
She said, "Yes, why not? There's no reason why we
shouldn't be able to duplicate any Earth-side potable.
Sometimes, ours come out better than the original."

"And olives?" he said, just to be saying something.

"They have groves of olive trees over in Komarov,"
she told him, stirring vigorously.

"I thought it took seven years before an olive tree
began to bear."

"You'd be surprised at how the agronomists have
been able to speed up the growing of trees. But actually these olive trees were originally planted in Island
One and then, when Island Three was completed, trans-
planted here."

She brought his drink over to him and seated herself,
tucking her long legs under her. She took a small sip
and said, "Rex, what do we do now?"

He, too, sipped at the cold cocktail and found that,
yes indeed, they were able to duplicate dry vermouth
in Lagrangia.

He shook his head and said, "I don't know, Susie. I
haven't the vaguest idea of where to begin. We don't

seem to have any clues on just where he might be, assuming that he's still alive, and until we get evidence to the contrary, we're going to have to go on that assumption."

"Yes," she said softly, her voice much less clipped that was her wont. "We'll definitely go on that assumption."

"Let's take it from another angle. Who has a motive for wanting George Casey out of the way?"

"That's obvious," she told him, sipping again. "The energy people Earth-side. They can't compete with the power that we microwave down from our SSPSs, the Satellite Solar Power Stations. Now that we've got four Islands in full operation, we're really beginning to turn them out, on a mass production basis. And when Island Four is completed, you'll truly see something. In a few years, for all practical purposes, all energy needed Earth-side will by provided by Lagrangia."

"The oil people must love you."

"They always have, and the coal people too. And the shipping interests with hundreds of millions of pseudo-dollars tied up in their supertankers. Not even to mention the mining and oil workers unions who are already beginning to be thrown out of their jobs."

"Who else?" Rex said, relishing the martini again. It had come to him how tired he was. He'd been underway since early morning, having new strangenesses thrown at him.

She said thoughtfully, "One new element, perhaps. Politicians from just about every nation, Earth-side. They're not blind. News of Lagrangia filters down to Earth through the news media, through Lagrangists who go down on vacation, or who leave the Islands permanently because they can't hack it, for whatever reason. And through the Reunited Nations staff and through junketing politicians who come up to see for themselves. So some elements Earth-side become aware of our high standards of living and also of our socio-economic system, which you called an updated syndicalism. They see the handwriting on the wall. There are a lot of people on Earth who look up to Lagrangia, no play on words intended. Suppose they begin to consider this upgraded syndicalism themselves?"

"That's an angle. It'd give politicians the willies," Rex said, finishing the cocktail. "And the Soviet Complex would be in just as much danger as the United States of the Americas or Common Europe."

"Let's sleep on it, Rex," Susie said, coming to her feet. "Usually, the professor and I do our own cooking. We're both avid amateur chefs. But I don't feel up to it tonight. We can dial our dinner from the automated kitchens."

"Wizard," Rex told her and they went on into the kitchen.

They ate at the small table there, rather than going to the dining room and Rex was surprised at the quality of the food and wine. They had automated kitchens in the high-rise apartment building in which he had his mini-apartment in New Princeton, but the meals were nothing like this. He asked Susie about it and she told him that it was a combination of factors. For one thing, everything was fresh here, all year around. They used no canned foods, nor frozen, nor any prepared dinners and such. For another thing, scientists and technicians weren't the only ones attracted to Lagrangia. Some of the world's best chefs from French to Chinese, had also zeroed in on the Islands. A surprising number of them had the qualifications to become colonists. Evidently, haute cuisine was not just a matter of inspiration, it took intelligence, ability, and there were few undereducated among them. They had taken over the setting up of the automated kitchens on each of the Islands. Others among them presided at the restaurants that abounded not only in Grissom and Komarov but all the other Islands as well. The Lagrangists had become gourmets almost to a man.

Following dinner, they made their goodnights and went to their respective rooms.

Rex Bader's bag was still on the bed. Yawning, he opened it and began reaching for his pajamas, but then he scowled and stared down. As a bachelor, he was picky about some things, a bit on the fuddy-duddy side, if anything, overly neat and a creature of habit. His toothbrush and shaving equipment occupied just-so places on the shelf above the washbowl in his bathroom. His comfort chair hadn't been moved a fraction of an inch from its given place for years. And when he packed a bag, it was always done in the same manner.

In short, he realized that his suitcase had been searched.

It only took him moments to see that nothing had been taken, but it had been searched.

He scowled down into it for long moments, then turned to the door and made his way to Susie Hawkins's room. He knocked.

The door opened and there was Susie in a diaphanous white shorty nightgown, a comb in her right hand.

"Why, Rex," she said, a mocking quality in her voice. "I had no idea that you were so impetuous. Come in."

Rex swallowed and followed her into the room.

She turned to him. This was a different Susie than the efficient Doctor Susie Hawkins, top Research Aide of the father of the Lagrange Five Project. No tweeds, no air of briskness, no crisp, clipped way of speaking. No, this was a different Susie.

She stepped closer and smiled up into his eyes. "I know what you like," she whispered, all sultry.

ELEVEN
A Flashback

It had been approximately a year before the above events that a small convoy, which had come out from the airport at Riyadh, approached the palace of Prince Jabir Riad. It consisted of a leading hover-jeep containing four neatly uniformed troopers and a mounted laser rifle, two old-fashioned wheeled limousines beautifully maintained, and the rear was brought up by another hover-jeep identical to the first.

The palace could have been taken for a medium-sized town, and even from a distance looked like a Hollywood set of Baghdad in the days of Harun-al-Rashid and Scheherazade. It was stonewalled with battlements and towers periodically spaced. Sentries paced the walls, and the towers were topped with gun emplacements.

The convoy pulled up before a gate which pierced through a large square tower that measured about fifty feet on each of its four sides and about twenty feet in height. The gate was a beautiful horseshoe arch, on the keystone of which were a white marble slab, a carved hand of Fatima, and a carved key. None of the visitors realized that the five fingers of the hand symbolized the five fundamental principles of Moslem law, the oneness of God, prayer, alms giving, fasting, and the pilgrimage to Mecca. The key was the chief symbol of that same law and denoted the powers invested by

Allah in the Prophet to open and close the gates of heaven.

The heavy iron gate swung open, obviously electrically powered, and seven issued forth, six soldiers, identically uniformed to those in the hover-jeeps, and assault rifle armed, and another dressed in traditional Arab wear, a ghutra, the agalas headdress of braided ropes worn over a white kaffiyeh, and soft red leather boots.

They strode some ten feet from the gate in the direction of the convoy and the six soldiers came to the salute. The civilian waited, smiling.

The two limousines contained six men and a woman, who emerged. The men, who were in their middle years or beyond, stared up at the impressive gate. They were all impeccably dressed in conservative European suits and all looked as though they had stepped from a barber's chair but moments ago. The six were darkish in complexion, and obviously of Latin background.

Sophia Anastasis, though now pushing fifty, was a striking brunette in the beauty tradition of the Mediterranean. She wore faultlessly the products of the dressing houses of Paris, Rome, or, perhaps, Budapest, the fashion center of the Soviet Complex. She turned her dark eyes to the Arab.

He approached, bowed slightly, touched forehead, lips, and heart and said, "*Salaam*. You are bid welcome to the home of Prince Jabir. May your lives be as long and flowing as the tail of the horse of the Prophet." His English was perfect.

"Thanks," Sophia Anastasis said, one side of her mouth turning down slightly.

The Arab said, "The Prince has sent me to greet you. Would you wish to be shown to the apartments so that you may refresh yourselves?"

One of the men said, "That won't be necessary. Our aircraft is quite comfortable." His features were on the rugged side, but his accent was that of one of the Ivy League colleges.

"Then, if you will, I shall conduct you immediately to the conference." The Arab made a flowing gesture toward the gate and the seven newcomers followed him.

They passed the soldiers, still holding their salute, and through the gate to emerge into a court some 140 feet long by 75 feet broad. In the center was a large pond set in the marble pavement. As they passed it, the newcomers could note very large, very exotic looking goldfish. There were myrtles growing along the pond's side. There were galleries on the north and south sides; that on the south was about twenty-five feet high and supported by a marble colonnade. Underneath it to the right was what Sophia Anastasis assumed was the principle entrance to the building proper. Over it were three elegant windows with highly decorated arches and miniature pillars.

Their guide continued to lead the way and they passed through the entrance. The room beyond was a perfect square, about 25 feet to the side and with a lofty dome and trellised windows at its base. The room was exquisite. The ceiling was decorated with blue, brown, red, and gold tiles and the columns supporting it sprang out into the arch form in a remarkably beautiful manner.

"Hah, not bad, eh?" the oldest of the newcomers wheezed.

"Quite impressive, Uncle Caesar," Sophia Anastasis murmured.

They passed on into another patio, one even more elaborate than the first. It seemed to be some 100 feet in length by about 65 in width and was surrounded by a low gallery supported by a good many white marble columns. A pavilion projected into the court at each extremity, with filigree walls and light-domed roofs, elaborately decorated with openwork. The square was paved with colored tiles, and the colonnade with white marble, while the walls were covered five feet up from the ground with blue and yellow tiles, with a border above and below of enameled blue and gold. In the center of the court was a fountain with a magnificent alabaster basin.

They passed down a corridor elaborately hung with tapestries, done in the Moslem geometric designs, and approached a heavy wooden door flanked by two more assault rifle armed guards, who stiffened to salute upon their appearance and then flung open the door.

They entered a library of majestic proportions, which was centered with a large square table whose surface was designed as a chessboard, the squares defined in an inlay of mother-of-pearl. There were pots of mint tea and cigarettes, cigars and ashtrays on the table. The lower casements of the library's tall, narrow windows were almost eight feet from the floor. The effect was not oppressive because of the proportions of the room, and an elevation created by a soaring ceiling and arched beams gave it a sense of cool isolation. The size of the library was not deflating; on the contrary, the great space enclosed by tiled floors and vaulted ceilings seemed relaxingly intimate, which was an effect achieved by cleverly outsized rugs and furniture. The heavily-fringed ends of the glowing Persian carpets were separated by almost eight feet of casual designs in blues, greens, and tans, while the ottomans, ornate in red and green leather, were almost as large as comfortable beds.

Around the table were seated eight men, almost as dark as Negroes in complexion, and Semitic of features. They ranged in age from perhaps forty to as much as seventy and all were in burnooses and wore, as did the guide, agalas, the braided headdress over snow white kaffiyehs.

All stood as the Caucasians entered.

The guide bowed and said to the visitors, "May I introduce Prince Jabir Riad, Prince Samir Al Fay, Emir Abu Bernaoui, Emir Ahmad Yasfir, Sheik Feiyad Shakhashir, Baydr Saad, Sheik Ali Youssef Ziad, and Abou Zaki?" All had bowed their heads as their names were recited.

Sophia Anastasis took over the honors. "I am Sophia

Anastasis. These are Giovanni Luciano, Caesar Montini, Achille Lauro, Pier Storti, Luigi Morin, and Al Ghiberti. Each of us represents one of the families which control International Diversified Industries, Incorporated, through our syndicate."

The one who had been introduced as Prince Jabir Riad and who was hence the host, gestured gracefully to the table and he himself held the heavy chair for Sophia Anastasis.

He was seemingly in his late forties, was tall and deceptively slim, with an alertness and neatness in his bearing. His hair was black and his skin was darkly tanned; his eyes were warm and brown under luxuriant, slightly arched eyebrows; his nose, which had been broken, looked like a rugged scimitar, his lips were delicate and almost feminine.

When all were seated, the youngest of the newcomers, who had been introduced as Achille Lauro, said apologetically, "Sorry we're late, Your Highness. Our pilot had some minor trouble."

The prince smiled and said, "To delay a pleasure is only to increase it. May I offer you refreshment? Mint tea? Perhaps a sherbert?"

"Mint tea?" Caesar Montini said blankly.

Luigi Morin cleared his throat and said, "You haven't got a drink around here, have you? Even with airconditioning, this desert air is dry."

The Sheik Ali Youssef Ziad looked shocked, but he alone. The prince clapped his hands and a score of servants materialized bearing golden ice buckets and glasses on trays also of gold.

All were served save Ali Youssef Ziad, who poured himself more mint tea.

The prince toasted, "To our common enterprise."

After all had sipped the bubbling champagne, the prince said, "As you have possibly known, wine is forbidden the faithful, however, in my case, Allah has performed a great miracle. When I put a glass to my lips, if there is alcohol present it turns to water."

"By a great coincidence, the same miracle has been wrought with me," the Emir Ahmad Yasfir said. His

English was as perfect as that of his host, but there was an Oxford accent.

The balance of the Arabs didn't bother to comment but gulped appreciatively, burped politely, and immediately their glasses were refilled to the brim.

Sophia Anastasis said to the Prince, "Shall we get to our subject? If possible, our party would like to finalize this operation and return to our plane before the day is out."

The prince bowed to her. "I had planned an entertainment and for you to spend the night, however, *Sitt* Anastasis, as you Americans say, business is business and if time presses you . . ." He let the sentence fade away.

Giovanni Luciano said, "The way I see it, we've put things off too long already. You people probably know our families started off almost a century ago during what they called Prohibition. It wasn't long before we cornered the guzzle market, cooking alky, brewing Near Beer and then needling it, that sort of thing. But when Repeal came along, we had to get into other fields, labor unions, gambling, that sort of thing. More legit, as they used to say, than alky, but still on the edge. But by that time we were heavy enough to send the kids coming up to the better schools."

"Heavy enough?" Baydr Saad said. His English didn't seem quite as good as that of the other Arabs who had thus far spoken.

"Wealthy enough," the prince told him. "American idiom, you know."

Luciano went on. "So step-by-step we branched out into other fields, especially entertainment, restaurants, resorts, casinos, in areas where gambling was legal, retirement centers, and allied investments. After we bought the Bahama Islands, we also went into banking, the biggest con game since some ancient grifter invented religion and put nine tenths of the human race on the sucker list."

"Bought the Bahama Islands?" Emir Ahmad Yasfir said emptily.

Sophia Anastasis took another sip of her wine and

murmured, "Yes, and Malta and Macao, for that matter. As the families became more and more affluent, the godfathers decided to become increasingly legitimate, until today all of our enterprises are as above board as any multinational corporation. But as Cousin Luciano mentioned, our resources are tied up almost exclusively in resort centers, retirement centers, casinos, and other such lucrative fields. Now we are faced with an unprecedented rival. It is bad enough with their present islands, already tourists are being attracted to them in increasing numbers. But we can see the trend. When their Island Four is completed, can you imagine what it will offer in the way of resorts, health spas, retirement centers, sports centers? Perfect weather, year around, sun every day, hospitals and health hotels in partial gravity for those with anything from heart trouble to bed sores." She shook her head. "Even casinos, if they choose to open them. But, above all, economy. It will be cheaper to go up to Lagrangia, in short order, than it is to fly across the Atlantic. And once there, why should prices be high? Practically free power, practically free raw materials, food grown on a year around basis, such as we have never seen here on Earth."

"All right, all right, Cousin Sophia," one of the men said gruffly.

Sophia wound it up, saying, "At any rate, the success of the Lagrange Five Project means disaster for us."

The prince nodded. "In some respects, your history duplicates our own. We were largely poverty-stricken nomad tribesmen a century ago. But as the years passed, more and more oil was found under the sands of our deserts. We, too, became all but a monopoly. *Al-humdu li-llah.*" He translated for the Westerners. "Praise be to Allah."

"But already our control of the world's energy is threatened," the Sheik Feiyad Shakhashir said darkly, as a servant hastened to top his glass.

Prince Jabir nodded and said, "Before, we two organizations acted unilaterally in our attempt to foil the devilish project of the accursed Professor George Casey, both hoping that his elimination would forestall the Lagrange Five Project. But we failed."

He smiled politely at the representatives of International Diversified Industries. "But now we unite, in the knowledge that if Lagrangia continues to expand, both your resorts, casinos, and retirement centers, and our markets for petroleum will be dealt death blows."

Caesar Montini wheezed, "Hah, we shoulda hit this fink Casey a long time ago."

"We tried to, Uncle Caesar, remember?" Sophia Anastasis told him soothingly. "And it didn't work. Now it's too late to merely eliminate Professor Casey. It wouldn't stop the expansion of Lagrangia. It would be a blow to them but the rest would carry on. No, our only answer now is to completely destroy the whole project and end forever the idea of space colonization."

The prince said, "Which brings us to the purpose of our meeting." He clapped his hands and when the Arab who had escorted the family heads to the library came hurrying up, said, "Summon Doctor Gerhard Johannisberger."

Doctor Johannisberger need never fear unemployment. If all else failed, he could without difficulty have gotten a job portraying a German scientist on Tri-Di shows. He was a stereotype to end all stereotypes. He would have particularly been good as one of Adolf the Aryan's devoted experimenters on subjects pertaining to the final solution to the Jewish problem.

He stood before them and beamed.

Prince Jabir said, "For the sake of those who are not completely acquainted with the subject, will you give us a brief recapitulation, Doctor?"

The portly, middleaged doctor beamed. "Zertainly, Your Highness."

He removed his pince-nez glasses from his nose with the thumb and forefinger of his right hand, looked about the assembly, then returned them. He said, "The broblem bresented to myself and my colleagues vas to find a disease that vould decimate the Lagrange Vive

Islands. It vould not be detectable, zo far as the means uf invection vas concerned."

He put his fingertips together and beamed again. "The broblem vas vasinating."

Sophia Anastasis said from the side of her mouth to Luciano, "That accent. He has to be kidding."

And he murmured back, "That character doesn't kid. We checked him out, all ways from Tuesday. In the old days, he would have made a top hit man."

Doctor Johannisberger continued. "Now, zen, ze requirement you set us, *ja?* That the method of admineresting the disease without detection vas grucial, *nicht?*"

He beamed, still once again.

The prince said, "Go on, Doctor," accepting more of the champagne. He sipped it. Evidently, he found it less than adequately cold and his eyebrows raised. The waiter blanched and left, carrying the golden ice bucket with him. The other waiters grabbed up theirs and followed him. They returned in split seconds with fresh magnums of the effervescent wine.

The good doctor continued. "Ve hit upon it a gubble of months ago. Zpace cafard, about which nobody knows nudding. Ve found it largely based on claustrophobia, *nicht?*"

"Nicht, yet," Sophia Anastasis murmured to Luciano, who ignored her.

Doctor Johannisberger said happily, "But how to induze claustrophobia, eh, how? Zurprisingly, it vas but a small broblem. Zum twenty years ago, a nonbrescriptive drug vas brought out on the American market. A cure for the gomman gold, *nicht?* It actually vas quite effective." He beamed again. "Undil they discovered zum of the zide-evects. Zoz who took it ver prone to claustrophobia. Nobody knew vy, zee? But sere it vas. Ze drug, named Gold-No-More, a dypical Yankee name, *nicht?,* vas vithdrawn from ze market."

The prince said, "Ah, Doctor, if you don't mind, let's get on with it."

"Of gorse," the other said hurriedly. "Vell, vot ve did vaz izolate the element—you zay element in English, eh?"

"Yeah," Achille Lauro told him.

"Very vell, ve izolated the element vhich gaused ze claustrophobia. Und now, all zat is reguired is zat it be introduced into ze drinking vater of ze Islands."

Achille Lauro leaned forward. "And vot, I mean what, will result?"

The doctor held both of his hands out, palms up, as though nothing could be more obvious. "At virst zmall numbers of Lagrangists, bardicularly zoze already prone to claustrophobia, will zuccumb to zpace cafard. It is very contagious, *nicht?* Berhabs zey will zpread it to udders before zey can be rushed back to ze Earth. Zen, as more of our drug is indroduced into ze water—only a microzcopic amount is needed for each colonist, zee?—more und more of the Lagrangists vill zuccumb undil it is a madhouse, *nicht?*"

The prince said, "Very well, Herr Doktor. That will be all. Your fee has been deposited to your Geneva account."

The good doctor beamed, bowed and hurried from the room.

The prince looked about, all but beaming himself. He said to the Westerners, "That is the point at which your organization steps in. You are in a better position to exercise influence on the news media. In fact, if I am correct, International Diversified Industries own a good many of the Tri-Di, TV, and radio networks."

Caesar Montini snorted, "Hah, we sure as Christ do."

The prince said, "A great campaign will be launched to bring all Lagrangists back to Earth. Space is not safe for man to live in. The whole Lagrange Five Project must be abandoned. If attempt is made to ignore this demand, we will simply continue to add our drug to the water of the Islands. As the doctor said, it is quite undetectable." He sipped at his wine. "In time, if they continue to be stubborn, all will go mad, both through the drug and the contagion."

Giovanni Luciano said softly, "Now, all we have to figure out is how to get the drug into the water."

The prince smiled at him. "That is our problem and we have already solved it."

The syndicate members looked at him.

He said, "Know that in the past the Arab Union made no efforts to take its turn supplying officials of the Reunited Nations Lagrange Five Staff. Moslems rejected the opportunity to go into space. Had Allah wished man to enter the heavens, undoubtedly he would have given him wings such as worn by angels . . . and the djinn. But the time is shortly coming when a new staff will be appointed. We shall insist that the new Administrator be selected from the Arab Union."

He turned and indicated one of the other Arabs who thus far hadn't spoken and who looked more or less like the junior member of the firm of Near Eastern notables. The prince said, "Our distinguished states-man, Abou Zaki, accompanied by four bodyguards, will take over the office. Needless to say, as the figure representing the Reunited Nations in Lagrangia, his luggage and that of his men, will not be overly searched upon entry. Even if it is, the drug will be disguised as packages of dried cous-cous, the national dish of his nation and unobtainable in the Islands. Needless to say, he will be free to journey about the Island un-restricted—including the water works."

Abou Zaki cleared his throat unhappily. He said, "Suppose I, and my men, contract this space cafard."

The prince brushed that off with impatience, saying, "Don't drink the water. Be sure that anything you drink has not been contaminated."

"But it can be contracted by contagion, simply see-ing a victim can . . ."

The prince was still impatient. "My dear Abou, take every measure to avoid coming in contact with victims of the mental disease. Then, when it begins to become epidemic, you, with all the Reunited Nations staff, will return to Earth, proclaiming loudly and often that space is impossible for man to live in."

Sophia Anastasis said slowly, "There is a problem here. The Reunited Nations Administration Building is located in Grissom, one of the cylinders of Island Three. I can see where our Administrator might have little difficulty in depositing our drug in its waters, but he'd be sticking his neck out if he tried to get it around to the other Islands as well."

The Arab prince nodded to that. "Yes, he will be able to operate only in Island Three, but that will be sufficient, since it is the largest of the Islands and by far the most highly populated. The Lagrangists living in Grissom are continually passing back and forth to the other cylinder that makes up Island Three, Komarov. Undoubtedly, the disease will spread to there also, both by contagion and when the residents of Komarov drink the water, on visits to Grissom."

He smiled his satisfaction. "Friends, we are in business, as you Americans say. A year-and-a-half from now, at most, and there will be no Lagrange Five Project."

TWELVE

Whip Ford had had no difficulty in finding the home of Washington Carver Smith, by simply following Susie Hawkins's directions. However, he was still irritated by the time he arrived at the black engineer's door. He was growing ever more intolerant in his contacts with Whitey these days. Happily, Earth-side he worked almost exclusively with fellow Blacks and could avoid contact with the enemy race. Besides that, he lived in an upper-middle class neighborhood devoted to fellow successful Negroes and to the extent possible patronized stores owned by his own people. But it was a white man's country, basically, and you couldn't ignore the fact that over eighty percent of the population was Whitey.

Whip Ford didn't know exactly why Doctor Susie Hawkins had rubbed him the wrong way, but she had. He was no fool. He was aware of the fact that as individuals many whites were good people. It was just that the whole race irritated him so much that if he ever did meet any of the good ones Whip didn't know it. The anger in him overflowed before he could find it out.

He shrugged it all off and looked about, before entering the building. As one who had been born in the deep South, some thirty years before, Whip Ford could appreciate the vicinity. Some mighty good architects and city planners must have really swung out in New Frisco. He sniffed the flower scented air appreciatively. Why couldn't his people live in an environment like this? Why couldn't they have the clean air, the gardens and parks, the beautiful homes? Why did it all go to Whitey? He had forgotten what Susie Hawkins had said about there being no ghettos in Lagrangia.

He turned into the building to find that Washington Carver Smith's apartment was on the ground floor. There was no identity screen, so he knocked.

The door was opened by a small, smiling Chinese girl. She couldn't have been more than five feet tall but you had to look twice to realize that. Her posture was so erect, her body so graceful, she looked taller. She wore a white traditional Chinese *cheongsam* dress, slit up to her thigh on each side, the collar tight around her throat, and tiny golden slippers on her feet. She had a gardenia in her very black hair and the merest touch of lipstick on her mouth. It came to Whip Ford that it was the first cosmetic he had seen in Grissom. The women here didn't seem to go for cosmetics.

She took Whip in, smiled again in appreciation of the handsome figure he cut, and said, "Yes?"

Whip Ford said, "Is this where Washington Carver Smith lives?"

"Yes, but I'm afraid he's not in now. Wash had to attend a meeting. Won't you come in? He might be returning shortly." Her voice had a lilting quality.

He hesitated when she stepped to one side but then entered. They were in a living room that had similarities to that of Professor Casey's. Inwardly, Ford had to congratulate his fellow Black. The taste in which it was furnished was impeccable.

He said, "You waiting for Mr. Smith, too?"

"Oh no," she told him, leading the way to chairs. "I live here. Do sit down."

He blinked at that, but, what the hell, it wasn't as though she was a Whitey. Off hand, he couldn't remember ever having met a Chinese girl before. He assumed she was Chinese; in actuality, he couldn't tell one Oriental from another.

"Are you a new colonist?" she said brightly. "Perhaps we should be speaking Interlingua. New Lagrangists usually like the practice."

"No," he told her. "I'm a tourist."

"Oh," she said, "that's nice. Quite a few are coming up these days. When Island Four is completed, we're going to make extended efforts to provide for tourism with resorts and everything and even have some retirement centers for the more elderly."

"I thought you couldn't be a permanent resident unless you filled all the requirements."

She smiled. "You can't be a full Lagrangist unless you fulfill them, but there are no objections to persons beyond the working years and beyond the point where children are to be expected coming and living here. We're proud of our Islands, Mr. . . ."

"Ford," he told her. "Whip Ford."

"My name's Li Song," she told him. "The Islands still have many expenses Earth-side, including the depositing of ten thousand pseudo-dollars a year in Earth banks, for every colonist. The income from tourism and retired folks will help. Besides, we sometimes feel a little isolated in Lagrangia and it's pleasant to hear about the developments Earth-side from the tourists from time to time."

He took her small body in again. "You know," he said, "you don't exactly look like a construction worker."

She trilled a laugh at that. "I'm not. But construction isn't the only endeavor in Grissom, Mr. Ford. There are things such as education, services, distribution, communications. I'm in entertainment."

"Entertainment? In a space Island?"

"Of course. Man does not live by bread alone, Mr. Ford. From the first, we had some entertainment, even when the early workers were living in the construction shack for Island One. But now, with the larger Islands, we can go all out. We have practically all the entertainments available on Earth and some that are not. You should see folk dancing troupes perform in half gravity, or less."

"I guess it makes a lot of sense," he admitted. "Are you an American?"

"No, Chinese. I was born in Hong Kong."

"I see. Uh, are there many Chinese up here?"

"Why, quite a few. Mostly from places like Hong Kong, Singapore, and Penang. Not so many from mainland China."

"And . . . Blacks?"

"Quite a few. I really don't know. I don't think that there are any statistics on the percentages of the different races."

"But mostly whites, eh?"

She didn't seem to know what he was getting at and looked at him strangely before saying, "It never occured to me to notice. But there are a good many Africans and Asians in Lagrangia. Sometimes it's difficult to tell where a, say, Afghan or Dravidian Indian lets off and a Black or Armenian begins. I'm afraid we don't care up here, and don't think much about it."

For some reason, that irritated him. He looked at his wrist chronometer and said, "I guess I better run along and get located at the hotel. I can come back tomorrow. When will Mr. Smith most likely be here?"

"Wash is almost always present in the morning."

He stood and said, "Wizard. I'll be here then. Thanks for everything, Mrs. . . . ."

"Miss," she smiled. "Miss Li Song. I hope you're here long enough to catch my act. I perform at the Space Ritz nightclub—among other things."

She saw him to the door and let him out. "Good-bye, Mr. Ford," she said.

Out on the sidewalk, he thought about it. So Washington Carver Smith was shacked up with a Chinese girl. Well, he supposed he could see no reason why not. He wondered vaguely what a child would look like with a Black father and a Chinese mother. Probably cute, by the looks of Li Song.

When he returned the following day, the Chinese girl wasn't there but Washington Carver Smith was.

He was a big man, darker of complexion than Whip Ford, but with the same Caucasian type features. He looked like the construction engineer he was, tough of face, big of hands, muscular, in top physical shape.

At the door, Whip Ford held out his hand and said, "Mr. Smith? I'm Whip Ford."

The other grinned in friendly fashion as he shook. "Wash," he said. "Everybody calls me Wash. Come on in. Li Song said you'd been looking for me yesterday. Come on in. Have a seat. Too early for a drink, I suppose."

Seated, Whip said sourly, "Doctor Hawkins said to give you her regards."

"I haven't seen Susie for weeks, in spite of the fact she lives just up the street. She's a damn good woman. One of the best."

Whip looked at him. "She's a Whitey."

Wash eyed him flatly. "Maybe you could say I am too. My father was half white."

"You know what I mean."

Wash looked at him in rejection, even as he sunk into a chair across from his guest, and said, "Holy Zen, man, get out of South Carolina, circa mid-19th century. Susie is no more racist than you are." He considered that and added, "In fact, probably less so."

"That's not the way I sized her up. She figures the average Black isn't up to the average white."

"That's what I figure too," the other said. "But it's a matter of opportunity, educational opportunities, employment opportunities, environment, not a matter of one race versus another. Actually, this race stuff is a lot of curd. Your race has nothing to do with it. For instance, you don't look as though you're exactly starving to death. And neither do I. I've seen one hell of a lot of Caucasians worse off than either of us. It's been the breaks with both of us. The important thing is to fight along for more breaks for the *average* man, Black, mongolian, or white. You don't build yourself up by tearing the next guy down. We've got to work together."

"Yeah, but somehow or other the Black usually gets the shitty end of the stick."

Wash Smith looked at him for a long moment, breathing deeply, before saying. "You know, I've been there. When I was a young fellow. But I finally came

to this conclusion. It's the old Roman adage. Divide and
Conquer. Pit whites against Blacks, youth against the
older generations, nation against nation, religion against
religion, one sex against the other. As long as they're
so occupied, they don't see the sources of their real
troubles. The last case is as good as any. As long as
they were supposedly fighting each other, the two sexes
didn't see who was really fucking them."

"Who is?" Whip said sourly, unaccepting.

"The socioeconomic system. Remember a few decades ago when they were having all the troubles in
the Near East? The princes, the emirs and the sheiks
spent millions in spreading the message: the Jews are
coming, the Jews are coming! Wizard. All the more
aggressive, progressive Arabs rose to the challenge and
for twenty or thirty years spent all their efforts fighting
the Jews. Meanwhile, those who owned and exploited
their own Arab countries, smiled softly and enjoyed
their loot."

Whip looked at him, still unaccepting the other's
message. "And the Jews?"

"Were doing the same thing. That is, those who were
really at the top in Israel. You didn't labor under the
illusion that all of the Israelis were living in kibbutzim
did you? There was a very strong power structure there,
a favored class. Socialism my ass. The cry was sent
up; the Arabs are coming, the Arabs are coming. And
the rank and file Jews put his shoulder to the wheel
and sacrificed, while the wealth and power boys back
in Tel Aviv and the other luxury towns took their
ease."

Whip shook his head. "Wizard," he said. "Maybe
you're right, at least to a point, but whatever the reason the Black gets the shitty end of the stick; he gets it
and some of us want out."

Wash Smith frowned. "What did you come to see
me for, Whip?"

"Doctor Hawkins sent me. I came to see Professor
Casey, but he wasn't around. At least she said he
wasn't and didn't seem to know when he'd be back. I
guess we kind of rubbed each other the wrong way . . ."

"Doesn't sound like Susie," Wash said.

". . . and she sent me to see you. She said you probably knew as much about the subject as anybody short of Professor Casey himself."

"What subject?"

"Constructing space Islands."

"Oh, you a writer, a reporter, or something?"

"No. I represent the Promised Land Society. We want to build a space colony."

"I'll be damned. You do? You're not kidding? How many of you are there?"

"About ten thousand, so far. And, before you ask, we aren't any of us on Negative Income Tax. We've got funds."

"I'll be damned," Wash repeated.

Whip Ford said, "Doctor Hawkins said that probably the best thing to do would be to have a construction shack built here and tow it out to the asteroid belt and go to work on a space colony about the same as your Original Island One."

"Yeah," Wash said thoughtfully. "That'd probably be the best idea."

Whip leaned forward, his eyes narrower now. "What do you think it would cost?"

"A damn sight less than you'd think. All the really big expenses are behind us."

"That's what Doc Hawkins said."

Wash Smith said, "Even a single fella with his family could probably swing it for about what it'd cost him to build a private airplane, back Earth-side, and people are doing that every day. The professor worked it out some time ago. He says that for about 50,000 to 100,000 pseudo-dollars the guy could build a small craft, strike out with his family and the necessities for basic agriculture and mining, and homestead an asteroid. To take off from Earth requires high thrusts and precise timing. Every second is critical and if anything goes wrong, you're in bad trouble. But if a guy started out from an Island and his engine quit a week out, he could just stop and fix it, or radio for help and wait for the 'Space Guard' to pick him up. His navigation instruments wouldn't have to be any more than a telescope and a sextant. In fact, it'd be easier to navigate from Island Three, here, to the asteroids than it would be to navigate across the Atlantic. There are few surprises in space where there's no atmosphere or gravitational stresses."

"That's one guy. How about ten thousand?"

"The more there were of you, the cheaper it'd be per capita, of course. Probably your best bet would be to go through your ten thousand society members and screen out the two thousand who'd be the most use in building your Island. They'd come up here and have the construction shack built and tow it out to the asteroids. There they'd go to work building your Island and when it was finished the balance of your colonists would come out."

"Wizard. When can we start?"

Wash Smith looked at him. "When you get the okay of the Lagrange Five Project Council."

"Why do we need their okay? This Island would be out in the asteroids, not in Lagrange Five."

"Because that single guy I was talking about, home-steading an asteroid, would have to be a highly-trained spaceman, possibly with years behind him working here in Lagrangia. He could do the work himself, with the help of his family. But you people will be green, and you'll be building a whole Island to house ten thou-sand. You'd need a lot of expert help and the only way you can get that help is through the Lagrange Five Council."

Whip Ford said, less than happily, "Doctor Hawkins said we'd need experts." He looked up. "She said there were a lot of highly trained Blacks up here."

Wash was impatient. "There are, but let's not get off on that track again. They aren't all necessarily the kind of men you'd need. And even if they were, they might be off on some kind of assignment they couldn't be pulled off of, just to help you out. For instance, I doubt if the Council would let me go, at this point. I'm needed for the work on Island Four."

Whip didn't like that. He said grudgingly, "Suppose

you let us have some white engineer and it turned out he was a redneck southern sonofabitch and he sabotaged our Island, just because he hated niggers?"

Wash looked at him levelly. "We don't have any redneck sonsofbitches, southern or otherwise, in Lagrangia. They're all sifted out before they leave Earth."

The other wasn't really convinced but for the moment he let it pass and said, "How do we go about getting the okay of this Lagrange Five Council?"

"Your best bet, just about your only bet, would be through Professor George Casey. On things like this, he's the one everybody looks to. If he says yes, the Council will probably vote it through unanimously. If he turns thumbs down, you've had it. It's a funny thing about the professor. In actuality, he doesn't hold any position in the Lagrange Five Project. He's not even on the payroll. He's officially a member of the faculty of New Princeton University. And that's the way he wants it. Nobody can point a finger at him and accuse him of profiteering on space colonization, or grafting, or whatever. He doesn't get a cent out of it. But he's the guy who first dreamed it up and he's our inspiration, kind of a catalyst who pulls everything together. I don't know a single person in Lagrangia who doesn't worship him."

Whip eyed him. "Including you?"

"Including me."

Whip Ford came to his feet. "So I've got to wait around until the professor shows up."

"That's about it," the other told him. "You could go up before the Council on your own and state your case, but they'd undoubtedly postpone a decision until they heard from him on it."

THIRTEEN

When Rex Bader awoke in the morning, it was to find Susie's dark hair aswirl on the pillow next to him. She was lying on her back, the bedsheet pulled up around her neck so that only her head showed, including one of the perfect coral ears and the classical nose. He took her in, wondering how such a beautiful woman could so project herself, during working hours, that she looked positively plain. How she could do it, and why.

She opened her eye and said accusingly, "Who do you think you're looking at, my good man?"

Rex said, "How did I get so lucky?"

Susie said, "I'm a sucker for men with sad eyes."

He grinned at her. "I'll practice looking like a bassett hound."

She took him in contemplatively. "You know, you're not so bad for a man of forty."

"I was just bragging last night. This morning my back aches, as a result."

"You're much too modest, my dear. Have you ever made love in free-fall?"

"I beg your pardon?"

"Sex in free-fall. There's nothing like it."

He closed his eyes in rejection. "Good God."

She laughed mockingly. "Actually, the Floating Island Hotel has a one-tenth gravity. It's up quite near the axis. Real fun. Nothing like it, Earth-side."

"I'd think not."

She said wickedly, "When this is all over, we'll have to go up for a few days."

"If it's ever all over," he said glumly.

She suddenly became brisk, threw back the sheet and swung her legs to the floor. She was wearing her shorty nightgown. He thought that he had taken it off the night before. It was so transparent, he could see her black thatch of pubic hair, nestled between her good legs.

She said, crisply, "I'll go on into the bathroom first."

Rex said, "I'll go back to my own room. You know, I forgot to tell you why I came to see you last night."

She looked back at him. "Forgot? Like hell you did. What are you talking about? You mean, you didn't come to seduce me? That I seduced you instead?"

"Seduced? It was more like rape."

"Why, you cad."

Rex said, "Seriously, I came here to tell you that my luggage had been searched. Nothing taken, but I could tell. It had been searched."

She scowled her puzzlement and said, "But what could anyone have been looking for?"

He shook his head. "There's nothing in it that would tell anybody anything."

She walked over to the door of the bathroom, still scowling. "I'll see you for breakfast, darling," she told him.

Rex got up, found his clothes and, not bothering about his nakedness, carried them back with him to his own room. There was an order box there, similar to the one in his mini-apartment Earth-side. He had no trouble figuring out how to dial for a new shirt, new undershorts and socks. He took the things he had worn the day before and threw them into the disposal chute in the bathroom. His expense account was unlimited. Besides, he had read somewhere that in the Islands they didn't resort to laundry. With automation what it was, they threw away any soiled clothing; it was re-cycled and used over and over again, but not by the same person.

He showered, shaved, dressed, and went on into the

kitchen where he found Susie whipping up an omelet and making toast.

She had been right, he discovered. She was an amateur chef. The omelet was perfect, possibly the best he had ever eaten. And he told her so.

"It's mostly the eggs," she said. "We never eat eggs for breakfast that are over a day old."

"Holy Zen," he said. "What do you do with them, just throw them away?"

"Don't be a dizzard. We're not wasteful in Lagrangia, we dote on efficiency. We use them in cakes and other cooking. Rex, what are you going to do about the professor?"

He took his final bite of the omelet, his final bite of toast with marmalade, and then a sip of coffee.

He said, disgust in his voice, "Damned if I know where to start. See here, what enemies could Casey have here in Grissom? Sure, I know, the energy people such as the sheiks, down Earth-side. Some of the politicians. Some of the businessmen, especially manufacturers, you're beginning to compete with. Some of the religious cranks who think you're flying in the face of God by penetrating the heavens. But they're all down below."

Susie finished her own coffee and poured another cup. "Let's go into the living room," she said, sliding from her chair. She threw the remnants of breakfast, including the dishes and utensils and the frying pan in which she'd cooked the eggs into the disposal chute.

Rex winced. "Even the frying pan?" he said.

"It's easier and more sanitary to recycle them all, than it is to wash them," she said. "It's all automated."

He shook his head, poured more coffee for himself and followed her.

When she was comfortably seated she said, "They could come up as tourists if they wanted to get at him."

He nodded at that and then something came to him and he said, "Or they could come up as part of the personnel of the Reunited Nations staff you were talk-

ing about. Didn't you say that the head man was an
Arab?"

"Yes, the administrator is from the Arab Union this
year. His name is Abou Zaki. A little weasel of a man."

"How does the professor get along with this Reunited Nations staff?"

Susie shrugged. "He hardly ever sees them. They
haven't the vaguest idea of what goes on here and
we're all more or less contemptuous of them."

"Doesn't that get them teed off?"

"They couldn't care less. All they want to do is have
as good a time as possible during their two-year tour
of duty, collect their astronomical pay and go back to
Earth. Most of them hate it here."

"Why should they hate it any more than the average
Lagrangist?"

She said, "The average Lagrangist came up to the
Islands because he had the dream. He wanted to come.
If it turns out that he was mistaken and he finds himself subject to space cafard, or Island Fever, or whatever, he returns. But the Reunited Nations personnel
come up for mercenary reasons, the pay, the prestige
when he returns Earth-side. They're earthworms at
heart, not Lagrangists."

"So, on an average, they possibly dislike the professor."

"Most of them hardly know him." She sipped at her
coffee and added, "Oh, sometimes they'll meet at a
particularly important banquet, when some high-rank-
ing visiting firemen come up on a junket, a chief of state
or something, and the professor condescends to attend.
But that's all on a pretty formal basis. You don't
usually get to either like or dislike a man you meet at
a formal banquet."

Rex said, "It wouldn't hurt for me to check them
out, I suppose. I can't think of anybody else to see.
What's my excuse to go and visit this Abou Zaki, or
whatever you said his name was?"

Susie thought about it and said, "You could tell him
that you're the professor's latest Research Aide and

flatter him by saying that you thought you should check in with him, since he's the Administrator of Lagrangia."

But it was then that a knock came at the door.

Rex got up and answered it and was surprised to find John Mickoff there.

The other entered without invitation and said, "Is Professor Casey here, younger brother?"

"No," Rex said, following the other into the living room.

The IABI troubleshooter looked at Susie and said, "Good morning, Doctor Hawkins."

"Good morning," she said crisply as usual during working hours.

Mickoff took a chair across from her and put his hands on his knees. He said, "Look, I've been waiting to see him for days. Where in the hell is he?"

"I truly don't know."

"Well, it's become more urgent. He's wanted at the Reunited Nations to answer some important questions. I was called this morning and instructed to bring him down."

"There's nothing I can do about that, Mr. Mickoff. He left for Island One almost two weeks ago."

"Is it possible for me to go over there?"

"We could arrange it very easily," she told him. "But there's no guarantee that he's still there. It's possible that's he's gone on to one of the Island Twos, or possibly even to the construction site of Island Four."

Rex came over and began to resume his chair but another knock came at the door.

"We seem to be popular this morning," he muttered, going to answer.

It was Whip Ford.

He scowled when he saw Rex. "What are you doing here?" he said.

"I work here," Rex told him.

The other continued to scowl, in memory. He said, "I thought you told me you'd applied for a job and they turned you down."

Rex said, "That was before, and in construction.

Now I've been taken on as a Research Aide to the professor. What can we do for you, Ford?"

But Susie, seeking a manner of getting away from Mickoff's questioning, said, "Come in, Mr. Ford. Did you see Wash Smith?"

He entered and looked at Mickoff questioningly.

Susie said, "Mr. John Mickoff, Mr. Whip Ford."

Mickoff stood and the two men shook hands, the Black making it quick.

When all were reseated, Whip looked over at Susie and said, almost as though grudgingly, "Yes, I saw him. He told me just about what you did. That it could be done and surprisingly cheaply. But he said that I'd have to get the okay of what he called the Council and he said to get their okay, I'd have to check it out with Professor Casey, who's evidently got this Council in the palm of his hand. So, is the professor here now?"

Susie bit her lower lip, shook her head and said, "Sorry, no he's not. We've just been telling that to Mr. Mickoff who also wants to see him."

Mickoff said, lemon in his voice, "I want to more than just see him. I want to take him down Earth-side to be interrogated."

"Interrogated?" Rex said. "That sounds a little tougher than just being asked some questions in the Reunited Nations?"

Mickoff looked at him, in irritation, and said, "He's got a lot of questions to answer. This whole project is going off in directions not originally in the plans. The Reunited Nations is seemingly losing control. This so-called Council is assuming responsibilities that should be in the hands of Abou Zaki and his staff."

Susie said, keeping impatience out of her tone to the extent possible, "Mr. Mickoff, from the first, when the Lagrange Five Project was handed over from NASA to the Reunited Nations, they sent up staffs of men, supposedly to administer it, who knew absolutely nothing about space colonization. Which is perhaps understandable. The RN is primarily a political organization, not a scientific one. We of the project were forced to assume responsibility if there was not to be chaos."

Whip Ford was looking at Rex strangely. He said, "You don't look like a scientist and you don't sound like one. Something funny's going on around here. What do you mean, a Research Aide?"

Rex Bader said smoothly, "I'm on Professor Casey's staff as a socioeconomist."

Mickoff snorted at that. "Socioeconomist yet, ha! You're nothing but a private eye."

And intuition hit Whip Ford. He said, very slowly, "Something's happened to Professor Casey."

All eyes were on him.

"Don't be ridiculous," Susie said crisply.

But John Mickoff said, "Holy Jumping Zen, you're right. I should have suspected it earlier, certainly as soon as Bader made the scene." He turned his eyes from Whip to Susie. "You've been telling me for over a week that he left for Island One and hasn't returned as yet. That doesn't make sense. There's immediate communication between the Islands and everything else in Lagrange Five, including spacecraft underway and the construction site of Island Four. You're his private secretary. You'd be in constant touch with him—if you knew where he was. You wouldn't even have to know where he might be. You could raise him on his transceiver wherever he was. Look, he hasn't gone down Earth-side, has he?"

"I don't know." Susie said. "I don't think so." She obviously didn't like this development at all.

Whip leaned forward. "Look, what happens to the Council giving me cooperation, if something happened to the professor?"

Susie was candid. "It would probably hold up any decisions of that type, Mr. Ford. There'd probably be quite a bit of confusion for quite awhile. George Casey is the heart and soul of the Lagrange Five Project."

Rex put in, trying to soothe troubled waters, "But nothing is going to happen to him."

Whip Ford came to his feet and said coldly, "Shut up, Whitey. You're lying."

Rex raised his eyebrows, but shrugged it off. This was no time to precipitate a fight. He assumed that he could take the other. Ford didn't look the type who would have studied karate or judo and probably hadn't had a fist fight since he was a kid. Few grown men did, particularly prosperous looking ones.

Ford, obviously inwardly boiling, strode over to the door, flung it open, and left, slamming the door behind him.

"Emphatic character," Rex said mildly.

But John Mickoff had stood too. His voice was as cold as had been that of the Black. He said, "Come on, Bader. We're going to the Reunited Nations offices to see the Administrator."

"Fine," Rex told him. "I was about to go see him to pay my respects when you showed up."

The IABI man turned to Susie. "You'd better come along too, Doctor Hawkins."

Susie shook her head. "I'd best stay here in case something comes in from the professor. I really don't know what's happened to him, you must realize."

He said stubbornly, "I think that you'd better come and we'll have a showdown about all this."

But she was just as stubborn. "You're being somewhat cavalier, Mr. Mickoff. You have no jurisdiction over me."

He looked at her angrily. "No, but the Administrator, Abou Zaki, has."

"But he hasn't summoned me. And, even if he did, I'm not sure that I'd come. My primary obligation is to Professor Casey, who is not even employed by the Reunited Nations, but by New Princeton University City, where the Lagrange Five Project first originated."

Mickoff stared at her in frustration, but gave up, at least for the time.

He turned back to Rex and said, "Come along, younger brother. I know that you're on the Reunited Nations payroll and it'll be interesting to see Abou Zaki's reaction to you misrepresenting yourself as a socioeconomist."

When the two men had gone, Susie sank back into her chair and let air out of her lungs.

Another entered the room from a different door. The

newcomer said, "Well, things are coming to a head, aren't they?"

"It looks that way," Susie said, tiredness in her voice. "I think that Rex, in particular, is beginning to smell a rat."

FOURTEEN

Out on the street, Rex noted the electro-hover-car parked before the building. They headed for it.

"No bikes?" he said.

"I never learned to ride one," the other growled. "Get in."

Rex got into the seat next to the driver's and they started off in the direction of the administration building.

Mickoff said, after a moment, sounding irritable, "How do you like it here?"

"I like it fine," Rex told him. "I always did want to become a Lagrangist. How about you?"

"I'm beginning to hate the damn place."

Rex looked over at him. "How do you mean? Only yesterday you were talking about the wild strawberries and the availability of the curves."

"I liked it when I first came up here, but it's wearing off fast. People were never meant to live in this kind of environment. It's not so bad when you're inside a building and can't look up to the sky. But when you're outside and can see right up to the other side of the cylinder and the other valleys there, it does something to your guts. I get the damnedest feeling that the whole thing might cave-in any minute. It's like living in a steel whale."

Rex looked over at him again, from the side of his eyes. "Submarine was the term that came to me," he said. "But you don't have to worry about the cave-in, they've figured out all the stresses. Island Four is going to be several times the size of this one, and it's not going to cave-in either. Have you been checked out for space cafard, Mickoff?"

"What's space cafard?"

"Evidently, something they get up here. Particularly people who don't like it."

"Never heard of it. Here's the damn administration building. You'd better start making up your speech, younger brother."

It was the same building in which Rex had met the Council the day before and, it turned out, the Reunited Nations Lagrange Five staff occupied the second floor. Evidently, the hiking up six flights of stairs was not for them.

All over again, Rex admired the artistic qualities of the lobby and, seemingly, they weren't beyond the notice of John Mickoff, who growled, "These Lagrangists do themselves up proud, don't they?"

Rex said, "Susie tells me that they're making so much money now that they plow some of it back by buying art objects and such from Earth."

Mickoff nodded. "Yeah," he said. "That's one of the things they want to question the professor about at the Reunited Nations. Some of them don't like the idea of the Lagrangists hanging onto the profits made by the sale of the solar power. Since the Reunited Nations ponied up the original investment, why shouldn't they get the returns, except for the necessary expenses, of course?"

"Don't ask me," Rex said. "I'd picked up the idea that the Lagrangists were already paying back those billions it took to build the first Island. Didn't I read somewhere that in ten years the whole sum would be returned?"

They were ascending the stairs to the second floor.

Mickoff said, "That's the point. What happens when the debt, if you can call it that, is all paid off? From then on, does Lagrangia feel it'll keep all subsequent money realized? Younger brother, by that time for all practical purposes these Islands will be supplying the world with all its power. Hundreds of billions of pseudo-dollars will be involved."

They reached the second floor and started down a corridor. The IABI man seemed to know the way. He had obviously been in contact with Abou Zaki before. Which made sense, of course. Theoretically, the Administrator, no matter how scorned by the Lagrangists, was the supreme official of the whole project.

The corridors of the second floor were all but empty in contrast to the building's areas which housed the Council and other Lagrangists devoted to the administration and planning of the project's efforts. Those that were to be seen didn't seem to have much in the way of things to do. They passed one office with an open door. It contained some twenty desks, but only four or five persons, none of whom seemed to be working.

"They don't look as though they're overstaffed," Rex said.

Mickoff growled, "Probably most of them are already in the bar. Or, better still, didn't bother to come to work. I get the impression that Zaki's staff is a little on the philosophical side. I don't know how they get their work done."

"They don't, according to what Susie says," Rex told him. "They don't have any work."

Mickoff eyed him and said, "I'd like to go into that but here we are." They had come up to a large door before which stood two uniformed dark complexioned soldiers. They bore sidearms and though the uniforms were natty enough, though of a type Rex Bader didn't recognize, managed to put over a slovenly effect.

Mickoff said, "John Mickoff, Inter-American Bureau of Investigation. The Administrator is expecting me."

One of them nodded, on the face of it, recognizing the IABI man, but then his eyes went to Rex Bader and up and down him, somewhat insolently. He came closer and gave Rex a quick frisking, ending up with the .22 pistol in his possession. He eyed Bader coldly.

He said, "You expected to go into the Administrator's presence with this?"

"I forgot I was carrying it," Rex said wearily.

"Just a moment," the soldier said to Mickoff. He turned, opened one side of the double portal and went through and closed the door behind him.

The other soldier watched Rex thoughtfully until his companion returned, without the gun.

He said to Mickoff, "Very well, pass." He gestured at the open door and Mickoff and Rex filed through.

The office beyond was luxurious. Overly so. Rex got the impression of a nouveau riche multimillionaire Earth-side trying to impress his associates.

There was but one desk, a quarter-of-an-acre in size and with little in the way of papers in view but a half-dozen gee-gaws, including a curved dagger in a golden sheath. Rex's pistol was there too.

Behind the desk was seated a small man in rich Arab dress, up to and including the white muslin head-gear. He was bearded in Semitic fashion, very dark of face, very dark of eye, and very bright of teeth. He was smiling welcome, though the smile didn't impress so far as sincerity was concerned. He also seemed on the wishy-washy side, without much get up and go in his make-up.

He said, *"As-salaam alaykum.* May your lives be as long and lustrous as the beard of the Prophet."

Mickoff said, "Good morning, Your Excellency, and thank you. This is the Rex Bader I mentioned to you."

Abou Zaki said, "Sit down, gentlemen."

When they had taken chairs, he gestured at the pistol and turned his smile to Rex Bader, saying, "My guard told me that you were carrying this. Being a guard, he thought that perhaps you had assassination in mind."

Rex said, "It belongs to Professor Casey. It's not really a weapon, just a small caliber gun for target shooting and very small game. I had planned to bicycle into the countryside later and thought I might have the opportunity to see a rabbit or squirrel. Or might even have to defend myself against a snake."

"Snake?" the Arab said. "There are no snakes in Grissom, Mr. Bader. There are no dangerous animals whatsoever." He added, "Save man, of course. Though the ultimate creation of Allah can hardly be thought of as an animal."

"I didn't know that," Rex lied. "I just arrived yesterday."

John Mickoff took over. "Bader came up on the request of Doctor Susie Hawkins, Professor Casey's closest associate. He met with the Council immediately and they signed him on as a Research Aide for the professor, supposedly as an expert in socioeconomics. In actuality, he hasn't even a bachelor's degree, in anything, not to speak of political economy. He's a private investigator."

Abou Zaki looked at him questioningly and said, "A private investigator?"

"A detective. He was employed by the professor once before in the capacity of a bodyguard."

"I don't comprehend."

John Mickoff said, "From what I understand, the professor has disappeared and Bader was sent for by the Council to try and find him. At least, that's my guess."

"That isn't the way I'd put it," Rex said. "Ten days or so ago, Professor Casey took off for Island One and thus far hasn't returned."

The Administrator looked puzzled and flicked a switch on his ornate desk TV phone. He spoke into it in Arabic, then leaned back, ignoring his two visitors. After a few moments, the screen hummed and he looked into it, listened, then switched the phone off and looked back at Rex and Mickoff again.

He said, "Professor George Casey does not respond to calls on his transceiver."

Rex could have explained that, but didn't.

The Administrator said, "Professor Casey had a Priority Two on his transceiver, for obvious reasons. Otherwise he would be bothered with calls twenty-four hours a day. He is very popular. However, we used a Priority One and he didn't respond, which is unbelievable. It might have been the President of the United

States of the Americas, or The Gaulle of Common Europe, or even Number One from Moscow."

"He hasn't answered any of my calls, either," Mickoff told him.

"This becomes quite a mystery," the Arab said, fiddling with his small beard in the best of Moslem tradition.

Mickoff said, "Especially in view of the fact that I've received orders from the Reunited Nations, Earthside, to bring the professor down for, ah, consultation. He has a lot to answer for."

"Umm," Abou Zaki said. He looked back to Rex Bader. "You are a trained detective?"

"That's right," Rex said. "I have had a license to practice as a private investigator for some fifteen years."

"And you've worked on similar assignments before?"

Rex decided to give up the pretense that he didn't know if Professor Casey was actually missing or not. He said, "I can't say. I arrived only yesterday morning and have hardly begun. I don't know what has happened to George Casey. It's possible he has been kidnapped, though by whom is a mystery. It's even possible he's been killed, though by whom we haven't the slightest idea. There's even a remote possibility that he has committed suicide, though that seems most unlikely according to Doctor Hawkins who has been with him from the very first days of the Lagrange Five Project. In my fifteen years as a private investigator I've had many different assignments, but never one like this."

The Arab accepted all that and said, "Very well, Mr. Bader. You shall continue your efforts to find the celebrated Professor Casey and will remain an employee of the Reunited Nations until you have either found him, or evidence that he is no longer with us. Professor Casey is dear to us all."

"Wait a minute, now," Mickoff blurted. "You mean that you aren't going to kick this cloddy out of Grissom?"

The Administrator turned his eyes to the IABI man and said, "I suggest, Mr. Mickoff, that since you and your men are highly trained police agents that you also throw your full efforts into finding the professor."

"What do you think we've been doing this past week?" Mickoff grumbled. "If these damn Lagrangists hadn't been so tightmouthed, we possibly would have had him by now. I didn't find out, for sure, until an hour ago that he had disappeared. I'd gained the impression that he was flitting around the different Islands on some sort of inspection tour."

He stood, saying, "I still think that you ought to throw Bader out. He hasn't told the whole story. There's something awfully wrong going on and younger brother, here, is probably up to his eyebrows in it."

Rex said mildly, "I have no more information than you have, Mickoff."

The other snorted at that but then looked back to the Arab. "Wizard," he said. "My men and I will immediately start looking for Professor Casey. Bader always has been half-assed; he won't get anywhere."

"Good day, Mr. Mickoff," Abou Zaki said.

When the IABI official was gone, the Administrator turned back to Rex. "Was there anything else, Mr. Bader?"

"Do you have any idea, whatsoever, who might have had it in for Casey to the point of pulling this romp?"

"Romp?"

"Crime."

The other shook his head. "I am completely bewildered. Professor Casey is the most popular man in Lagrangia. He is so busy that we of the Reunited Nations staff see little of him, but we, too, of course, share the affection borne him by his fellow Lagrangists."

Rex came to his feet. "Okay," he said. "I'll get about the job. If anything comes up, or occurs to you, please get in touch. I'm staying at the professor's apartment."

The Administrator took up the small calibered pistol and proffered it. He said, "Let us hope there will be

no need for this, but perhaps you should carry it."
He smiled slightly. "In case of snakes."

"Thanks," Rex said, taking it and stuffing it back into his belt, before turning and leaving.

When he was gone, the Arab stared at the door for long moments. Finally, he turned to the tightbeam phone screen on his desk and said, "I wish to call Prince Jabir Riad, in Riyadh, Saudi Arabia, on Earth. Scrambled."

A mechanical voice said, "Carried out."

When the call came through, Abou Zaki spoke in Arabic, in fact, in one of the more obscure dialects of Arabic.

When it was over, the Administrator looked thoughtful and even somewhat apprehensive, after he had flicked the communications device off. He touched a button on the desk top and the office door opened and the bodyguard who had taken Rex Bader's gun entered and stood to attention.

Abou Zaki spoke to him at some length, again in Arabic.

The guard saluted, turned and left, his dark eyes beady.

FIFTEEN

Down on the street, Rex Bader found that Mickoff and his car were gone. Well, he hadn't expected to be able to bum a ride with the other. The IABI man was furious with him. He went over to the bicycle rack and got himself a bike, straddled it, and started back for the professor's apartment.

Mickoff wasn't the only one who was going to be furious with him. Susie and the Council weren't going to be particularly happy about his blowing his cover only slightly more than twenty-four hours after he had taken their job. Not that it was his fault. Obviously, it was just a matter of time before it came out that Casey was missing. And he'd already been gone something like twelve days. And, financially speaking, his cover being blown wasn't going to make a great deal of difference to Rex Bader. He was still on the Reunited Nations payroll, whether the Council would want to fire him now or not.

He was in no particular hurry as he pedaled. He couldn't think of anything to do next. There wasn't a clue working on this whole deal. It was all mystery.

He took in the town as he rode along, more impressed than ever. What had Susie called it? An Eden. And that it was. There was no city Earth-side that remotely equalled this. He wondered how Mickoff could dislike it, especially so intently, especially after extolling Lagrangia so strongly the day before. And he wondered again if perhaps the IABI man had gotten

134

a touch of the mental disease Susie had told him about, space cafard.

He let his eyes go up and he could see the areas four miles beyond and had it borne into him again how foreign this all was, how infinitely different from the planet surface on which he had been born and raised. That was what it was, undoubtedly, with the IABI man. It was just too damn foreign, no matter the efforts Casey and his Lagrangists had gone to to make it Earth-like.

Even had he looked back, he probably wouldn't have spotted the bicycle that was tailing him. There were a good many bikes on the streets and Whip Ford kept at least a block behind his quarry.

Rex had no difficulty, once again, in finding the building in which Professor Casey and Susie lived. Already he was beginning to get the hang of New Frisco. Having been built to order, it could have a plan. Most of the cities he had ever been in Earth-side had grown helter-skelter; New York, Chicago, Los Angeles, all were madhouses when it came to their layout.

He racked the bike and headed into the building. Behind him, Whip Ford stopped at a small park, leaned his own bike against a tree, and sat down on a bench.

Rex didn't bother to knock, knowing the door to be unlocked. He entered the living room to find Susie at the desk.

She looked up and clipped, "Well, how did it go?"

He let air from his lungs and slumped into an easy chair. "Not exactly as expected. Mickoff spilled the beans, of course, evidently expecting the Administrator to order me out of Island Three."

Her eyes rounded slightly. "You mean he didn't?"

Rex gave a little rueful laugh and said, "No. It would seem that he's as anxious to find Casey as you and the Council are. He kept me on, much to Mickoff's disgust."

She thought about that, her face sceptical. "I had gathered that the Reunited Nations staff, including Abou Zaki, weren't exactly happy about the professor, that they thought he and the Council had appropriated too many prerogatives. Did he have any ideas about how to look for Professor Casey?"

"No, and I don't think that Mickoff has either. He and his men have entered into the search. But we at least know that he wants to find George Casey as much as we do. For other reasons, of course."

Susie sighed and said, "I doubt if we'll be able to do much thinking on empty stomachs. I'll go and get lunch. How would you like a wild squirrel pie?"

"Sounds wonderful," he told her, but his heart wasn't in it.

She departed for the kitchen and he sat there trying to come up with the faintest of ideas on where to start. He considered going over to Island One and checking out the dispatch station there. But to what end? The professor had simply not arrived. His four-seater had, but he hadn't.

The TV phone hummed and Susie called, "Will you get that, Rex? I'm right in the middle of rolling dough."

He went over and flicked the set on, but the screen didn't light up. He frowned at that. "Hello," he said, wondering if the phone was broken.

A voice said, "Bader?" Rex didn't recognize it.

"That's right," he said.

"Can you come out to Camelot this afternoon at two?"

"Where in the hell's Camelot?"

"It's a little town about three miles down the valley, right on the main road. You can't miss it."

"Why? I mean, why should I come?"

"Now, isn't it obvious that it concerns the reason why you came to Grissom?"

"If you say so, which brings us to the question, who are you?"

"You'll find that out when you get here, won't you?"

"If you say so. Wizard, I'll be there. Camelot at two. Where in Camelot?"

"There's an Old English type inn, complete with thatched roof. I'll be in the bar. Come alone."

The phone flicked off.

Rex walked out to the kitchen. Susie was rolling crust into a deep pie pan, flour up her arms nearly to the elbows.

She said, "Who was it?"

"I don't know. Somebody who wants me to come out to Camelot at two o'clock and meet him at the inn there."

"But what was his name?"

"He wouldn't tell me."

"What did he look like?"

"He didn't use the phone screen. Just his voice came through."

She had stopped her work to stare at him. She said, "Are you going?"

"He hinted that it was something to do with the professor's disappearance."

"I'll go with you."

"He said to come alone."

She looked her exasperation, her lower lip in her teeth. She gave up and said, "I won't have time for this meat pie, if you're to get there at two. We'll have to order something from the auto-kitchens. We can have the squirrel pie for supper tonight."

After lunch, Susie told him how to get out of town and onto the main road which wandered down the valley toward the other end of the cylinder which was Grissom. He could have taken public transportation, which would have gotten him there in minutes, but thus far he hadn't been out into the countryside and wanted to see more of the nature of Island Three.

As he pedaled out of the outskirts of New Frisco, he once again failed to realize that he was being followed. In the city proper, Whip Ford remained behind only a block, but as they got into the equivalent of suburbs and the traffic lightened, he dropped further back.

The suburbs of New Frisco were just that, Rex Bader found. Rather than the largely apartment buildings of the inner city, these were houses spaced well apart and usually single houses. They weren't all of a type, mercifully, but different not only in architecture, in size, and paint, but also in the grounds about them. Some went in for lawn, some extensive gardens, some had swimming pools, some not. There were even a certain number of duplex places, obviously containing two families.

The suburbs soon ran out and Rex Bader was into countryside, complete with farms. He had no idea to what extent farming was done in deep space, outside the cylinder, but there was considerable right here inside Grissom.

If anything, it was more Earth-like in the countryside than it had been in New Frisco. In many respects, the city was too perfect to look like anything on the mother planet. You were made aware of this strangeness. It was too well-planned, too clean, too lacking in automobile traffic, advertising signs, shops, and all the rest of it. Out here, bicycling along a meandering, rather narrow road, you had to go out of your way to find evidence that this was not a rural area of Earth—for instance, by looking up into the sky. And the road truly did meander. Rex had not been on such a charming road for as long as he could off-hand remember. Paved super- and what they were now calling ultrahighways were everywhere, both above and below ground, on the planet of his birth.

The lack of advertising signs came to him again. And, now that he thought about it, he realized that there had been no advertising whatsoever in New Frisco as well. Not even signs before restaurants or theatres. It would seem that the Lagrangists took it to the extreme, made a real principle of it. No advertising period. He assumed that it applied to their Tri-Di and radio programs as well. Come to think of it, there would be no need for advertising if you produced only the best quality of everything and everything amounted to being free. He could see where they might announce the availability of a new product when it appeared, but that would be more like a news item than an advertisement.

He passed through a village which looked remarkably like one of the small hill towns of central Italy, through which he had once traveled on a second-class bus. It was charming and complete with an Italian-type *piazza,* complete with a fountain in its center. Rex was amused to see that at least half of the people in the streets wore Italian peasant-type dress, both men and women. He pedaled past a sidewalk cafe before which men, women, and children were seated. The wine bottles on the tables were of the long-necked Italian variety. Obviously, the town's residents made quite a hobby of doing the atmosphere up as authentically as they could. Rex Bader made a mental note to come back here some day, if he possibly could. And preferably with a girl, such as Susie, along.

He pedaled on through the small town and beyond. Even if he had turned and looked back, he wouldn't have recognized Whip Ford at this distance. He might have noted that there was a Black man on a bicycle behind him, but there were quite a number of Blacks in Grissom.

He realized that he must be coming up on Camelot. His phone caller had said about three miles and surely he had come that far. He wondered how he'd recognize the town when he saw it. There had been no name sign anywhere before or in the Italian village.

However, he had no difficulty on that score. In the same manner that the last village had been Italian, Camelot was Old English, Elizabethan or before. Most of the houses—cottages would be the better word—had thatched roofs, all had gardens before and around them. And the Fox and Hounds Inn was spank in the middle of town, and took up one whole side of the village square.

There was a main entrance and another into the bar. Rex put the bike into the inevitable rack and went on in.

The bar, it turned out, was even more picturesque and authentic than had been the Pub in New Frisco. He could have expected Alfred Noyes' *Highwayman,* his boots up to the thigh, his pistol butt a-twinkle, his rapier hilt a-twinkle, to have come swaggering in through the opposite door. The roof beams, the bar, and the furniture were seemingly of heavy wood, as the furniture had been at The Pub and had to be looked at quite closely to find that they were of plastic.

Walt Hanse stood at the bar, his somewhat squarish face attempting a smile but not bringing it off overly well. He had a pewter mug before him.

When Rex came up, the member of the Council shook hands and said, "Glad you could make it. Would you like a drink before we go out to the house?"

"Wizard," Rex said. "The ride out dried me a bit." He looked at the mug. "What are you drinking?"

"Mead."

"What in the name of Zen is mead?"

"An old English drink, based on honey."

"I'll be damned. It sounds awful." Rex looked at the heavy-set bartender who wore the costume of a lower-class Elizabethan up to and including what looked like a leather apron around his belly. "I'll have a mead, please," Rex told him.

When the pewter mug came, he sipped at it carefully. It was something like a cross between beer and hard cider, not too strong, and he couldn't detect the presence of honey.

"Not bad," he said. "What's all the mystery? If you wanted to talk to me, why not do it on the phone, or come to the professor's apartment?"

The bartender had drifted down the bar a way to wait on another customer. Rex wondered if his job, too, was a hobby, as at The Pub.

Walt Hanse lowered his voice. "Because I didn't want to discuss the matter in the presence of Doctor Hawkins, or anyone else, and didn't want the computers to record it. Besides, I wanted you to meet some people."

Rex knocked back the greater part of the mead and put the pewter mug back down on the bar. "Wizard," he said. "Let's go and meet some people."

The big man finished his own drink and turned and led the way to the door. They selected bikes and started off.

"This is a beautiful town," Rex said. "You live here?"

"No, out aways," Hanse told him. "I like the country. There are a lot of these villages and towns in Grissom and all the rest of the Islands for that matter. The inhabitants will chose a theme and in the way of hobby build as authentically as they can, a Norwegian town, a French one, German, Greek, both modern and ancient, an American frontier town, a Mexican pueblo, and on and on. They even have a Polynesian village, up against the largest lake over in Komarov, including outrigger canoes on the beach. They make a point of going around in grass skirts and sarongs."

Rex laughed. "It must be fun at that."

Walt Hanse said, "A little on the frivolous side."

They'd left the Old English village behind and now Hanse led the way up a smaller path from the main road and, after a few hundred feet, a still smaller path.

"Here we are," he said, pulling up before a cottage.

To Rex, it seemed a bit more austere than most of the dwellings he'd seen today. However, that fit in with the appearance and personality of his companion.

They leaned the bicycles up against the side of the house and Hanse led the way to the front door. He opened it and gestured for Rex to enter, then followed him.

Immediately within was the livingroom cum library and study. Somewhat similar to Professor Casey's place, it had a bachelor decor, though evidently Hanse went in for the outdoor sports even more than the professor. There were several rifles and shotguns, and considerable fishing equipment and, rather strange for a living room, mountain climbing gear in a case against one wall. It would seem that Walt Hanse emphasized his hair-chest qualities.

There were three others in the room when Rex and Hanse entered, two of whom Rex vaguely recognized from the Council meeting the day before. He couldn't remember their names and what positions they held on the Council.

Walt Hanse made introductions and the two men stood to shake hands.

"Mr. Rex Bader, Ms. Shirley Ann Kneedler, Doctor Sal Sinatri, Mr. Herman Klein."

Rex Bader, wondering what it was all about, took the chair offered him, and decided inwardly that it was their rubber band and they could start stretching it any time they wanted.

Walt Hanse said, "If you don't mind, Mr. Bader, a few preliminary questions."

"Fire away," Rex said.

"You are a private detective. One of the last, so I understand. Why?"

"Why am I a private detective?" Rex said wryly. "Possibly because there was no other field I seemed to be able to get into. When I left school, I studied to become a pilot, but, by the time I got my various licenses, the airlines had become almost completely automated. I tried to get into other fields, but they were the same. Automation—they're beginning to call it ultramation—and computerization have thrown over ninety percent of the working force out of employment and onto Negative Income Tax. Most don't give a damn. I do. I *want* to hold down a job and earn more than just a poverty-level income. When I was younger, I used to like to read stories about the old private eyes, Philip Marlowe, Sam Spade, even Mike Hammer, and it occured to me that here was a profession I might be able to get into. I studied up on everything that seemed to apply and, sure enough, got my private investigator's license. That was some fifteen years ago."

Shirley Ann Kneedler, who Rex remembered now had been introduced as a representative on the Council from Distribution, and was a plain faced, rather short and dumpy woman of about forty, said, "And have successfully plied the trade ever since?"

He looked at her and shook his head. "Hardly successfully, Ms. Kneedler. It's no mistake that there are so few private eyes any more. There's practically no work for them to do. With the introduction of the pseudo-dollar and Universal Credit Cards, crime became largely meaningless. You can't spend another man's money, even if there was any way of stealing it, conning him out of it, or whatever. There aren't even many divorce cases, an old standby. Few bother to get married any more and even if they do, they're probably both on Negative Income Tax and have no property worth squabbling over. At any rate, I get few assignments and am usually on Negative Income Tax myself."

Hanse said, "But in fifteen years you've accumulated quite a bit of experience?"

"I suppose so," Rex said warily. He didn't know what they were building up to.

Hanse said, "Have you ever killed a man, Mr. Bader?"

Rex became more wary still, but he nodded reluctantly.

Hanse said, "How many?"

"I wouldn't remember," Rex lied.

"At least several, then?"

"I suppose so. What's all this about?"

"We wish to hire you, Mr. Bader."

Rex ogled him. "To kill somebody!"

The one who had been introduced as Herman Klein and who hadn't spoken thus far, chuckled. "Hardly," he said. His name came back to Rex now. Susie had said something about his making an anti-Earth speech.

Hanse said, "Let me, Herman." Then to Rex. "We four are the leaders, the Executive Committee, of the Radical wing of the Sons of Liberty. We are inexperienced in matters pertaining to violence. In fact, there must be very few in all Lagrangia who have seen much in the way of violence between persons. We are largely scientists, technicians, engineers. You are experienced, consequently, we wish to hire you. We are in good funds, all of our members have been accumulating their ten thousand pseudo-dollars per year, for lengthy periods."

Rex said cautiously, "You want to hire me to do what?"

The other couldn't have been more reasonable. "To participate in overthrowing the government of Lagrangia."

SIXTEEN

Rex sank back into his chair. "Oh," he said. "The Independence movement. Susie Hawkins mentioned it. You're the group that wants immediate independence from the Reunited Nations' administration, as opposed to the Conservative branch that wants to take things slower."

"That's correct."

"The trouble is, Ms. Kneedler and gentlemen, I've already got a job, even if I was interested in your proposition. I was hired by the Council to find Professor George Casey."

Doctor Sal Sinatri, who Rex vaguely remembered as being the head of manufacturing, or power, or something, said smoothly, "I'm sure that our offer would be considerably more lucrative, Mr. Bader."

Walt Hanse, who seemingly was impatient of anyone else speaking up, said, "In actuality, Bader, that's one of the aspects of this offer of employment. We are in no hurry to have the professor found."

Rex looked at him. "I beg your pardon?"

"Expelling the Reunited Nations staff will be comparatively simple. There are only a relatively few of them, only four of which, the Administrator's bodyguards, are armed. But that is only the beginning. During the excitement and confusion of returning the earthworms to Earth, we plan to make some basic improvements in the Council system of government and establish a more realistic one."

"What changes?" Rex said. "I had gathered the impression that most Lagrangists were pretty happy about this pseudo-syndicalism, or whatever you want to call it, that you've set up."

Hanse said hurriedly, "Oh, basically, few changes would be made. We simply desire more efficiency. Democracy, Mr. Bader, has never really worked. It's a farce. The very idea that inferior people should elect superior ones to direct them is ridiculous. They have always proven themselves incapable of doing it. Under the present system here in Lagrangia, the common workers elect their foremen, who in turn elect their supervisors, who in turn elect a representative to the Council. However, we have no guarantee that the workers elect the best foreman, nor that the foremen appoint the best supervisor, not to speak of the supervisors electing the superior representative to the Council. Sometimes indeed they do, but not necessarily."

"So how would you change it?" Rex said softly, suspecting what was coming.

"We would reverse the order. The Council, headed by a Chief Councilor, would appoint the supervisors of each function. That is, Sal Sinatri, in Manufacturing, would appoint the supervisors of each of his subdivisions. They in turn would appoint, from the ranks, the foremen below them. The advantage is obvious. Obvious that the men above are in a better position to know the most efficient below them, than those who are still further below."

Rex said, "I see. And how would the Councilors get to their top position? Suppose one of them died? Where would his successor come from?"

"Then the Chief Councilor would suggest a replacement and the balance of the Council would vote to elevate the nominee. If they voted him down, the Chief Councilor would nominate another, until one was found acceptable."

"I see," Rex said. "That Chief Councilor would have quite a bit of power."

"There should always be a head of every enterprise, Mr. Bader," Shirley Ann Kneedler told him. "You can't have a successfully operating body without a head."

Rex said, "In actuality, what you're advocating is similar to the program of Technocracy, Inc., back about the time of the Second World War and the depression that preceded it. They didn't get much of a hearing. Under your new set-up, would all Lagrangists still get all expenses and ten-thousand-a-year paid Earth-side?"

"Even more so," Klein said smiling. "Released from Reunited Nations domination, our resources would be almost incalculable. We could afford to purchase in abundance the luxuries of Earth. We could afford literally everything."

"And all Lagrangists would equally profit?"

Walt Hanse slightly twisted his often sulky mouth. "Well, of course, we believe that rank should have its privileges. For instance, it would help immeasurably if such as the Council members would be allowed personal servants, to give them more freedom to devote to matters of government. At present, no such exist in Lagrangia. There are other things, as well. Our methods of transport here in the Islands are somewhat primitive. Ranking officials, such as supervisors and members of the Council, should have limousines for the sake of efficiency."

"I see. Rank would have its privileges, as contrasted to the present system." Rex went on. "You said that my job would be more lucrative than it is now."

"Yes, certainly," Hanse said, attempting another of his sour smiles. "Mr. Bader, we have looked into you with care. It would seem that some time ago you studied up on the Lagrange Five Project in hopes of acquiring a position among the construction workers. The computers turned you down. Do you still have the Lagrangia dream?"

"Yes," Rex said emptily.

"Very well. If we are successful in our enterprise, you will be made a Lagrangist."

"I don't seem to have the qualifications, the I.Q., the Ability Quotient, the education."

The head of the Radical element of the Sons of Liberty said, very sincerely, "We are of the opinion that some exceptions should be made to those requirements. A man's true worth cannot always be so measured. For instance, Steinmetz, the electrical genius, was a cripple; Thomas Edison had only three years of grade school; Winston Churchill received very poor marks in school. Probably none of these outstanding men would have been selected by the computers to become colonists in Lagrangia."

"I see," Rex said. "Then, after your successful take-over, and I had become a Lagrangist, what would I do? Lacking technical training, I don't . . ."

Hanse said smugly, "You would become a member of the Council, our Minister of Defense."

"Your *what?*"

"Minister of Defense!" Herman Klein blurted. "Can't you see? Possibly the earthworms wouldn't take this sitting down. They might attempt to regain their position of dominating us, by force. We might have to defend ourselves. They would be fools, since we control their source of power, but we already know that they are fools. Beyond such an attempt, we must consider the further future. Sooner or later, we are going to have to take a hand in Earth-side activities. We can't afford a continuation of the chaos which applies today. They are continually on the verge of war. If war comes, Earth-side, one of the first steps to be taken by the belligerents will be to destroy those Satellite Solar Power Stations that send energy to the enemy nation. It would be far from difficult. A dozen nations now have nuclear weapons and the means to put them into orbit. They might also, especially if faced with defeat, in retaliation bomb the Lagrange Five Islands as well. No, sooner or later, we will have to take a hand, in sheer self defense."

"I think that will be sufficient, Herman," Hanse said. He looked at Bader, satisfaction in his expression. "Well, sir, you will come in with us?"

Rex Bader came to his feet. "No," he said. "I won't. In the first place, as I said, I already have a job, finding the professor, who I assume is against this plan of yours. Secondly, I'm against your program. What it amounts to is replacing a democratic socioeconomic system with a rule by an elite. The trouble with an elite is that it's up to those in power to decide just who is elite. Once a group gets into power they immediately declare themselves to be the most competent persons available to rule. For instance, when the Nazis double-dealt themselves into control in Germany they immediately let it be known that Hitler and his clique were the most competent persons to rule the Reich. Curd! Another thing about rule by an elite is that the ruling class invariably takes measures to perpetuate itself. Nepotism and favoritism immediately raise their heads. It would be up to you to decide who was to become a councilor and who were to become supervisors. I can see just how long it would be before your relatives and friends, no matter how comparatively incompetent, would be occupying such positions. No, thank you. Despite my desire to become a Lagrangist, it's not my cup of tea."

Walt Hanse was enraged. He shot to his feet. "Why, you fool! We've told you everything. We were certain that you would come in with us. We can't let you go now."

Rex Bader unbuttoned his jacket and began to say, "I'm afraid that I'm armed, folks. Perhaps some of you are too, but as has been pointed out, I'm the only experienced . . ." He broke off in mid-sentence and pointed. "We've got an eavesdropper!"

All eyes went to the window at which his finger was directed. A head quickly disappeared.

The men, including Rex Bader, made a dash for the door. By the time they got unscrambled getting out to the road, they could see a bike rider's back, disappearing around the nearest bend in the path.

"After him?" Herman Klein snapped to Hanse.

But his leader shook his head in disgust and said, "What could we do, even if we caught him? He'd simply call for help on his transceiver and then the fat would be in the fire and we're not quite ready to move."

Rex took up his bike and slung a leg over it.

"And with that, gentlemen," he said. "I shall bid you good day, but not good luck."

"Wait a minute," Hanse said urgently.

"Sorry, I've got a date," Rex told him and pushed off.

His trip back to New Frisco was uneventful although he'd half expected the overgrown Viking, Walt Hanse, and perhaps Herman Klein, who was also a young man who seemed to be in pretty good trim, to follow him. They didn't.

When he passed through the pretend Italian village, Whip Ford, who was seated at the sidewalk cafe, turned his back so that Rex wouldn't recognize him. When the other had passed, Whip got up, got his own bike, and started trailing again.

Rex wondered, as he pedaled, whether or not these towns with a theme were populated with elements from the nation they were copying. For instance, that Italian village he'd just passed through. Were the villagers Italians, perhaps with feelings of nostalgia? Well, perhaps some of them were, but he suspected that there was a lot of moving around in Lagrangia. It would be both fun and of interest to live in an Italian village for six months or so then perhaps move to the city, New Frisco, with its many restaurants, night spots, theatres, and other urban entertainment. When city life palled, you could, possibly, go on over to Komarov, the sister cylinder of Grissom and live in the tropical Polynesian village. Yes, that's the way he'd do it, if he ever became a Lagrangist.

He tried to wrench his mind away from that line of thinking. Perhaps he should have taken up Walt Hanse's offer. It was the best chance he'd ever had to get out of the Negative Income Tax rut in which he had spent his adult life, Earth-side. Since his father's death, when Rex had been a youngster, he had resided in a mini-apartment, on a subsistence level. It wasn't much of a life.

He entered the suburbs of New Frisco, admiring them all over again, and headed for the apartment area of town. These houses here were a far cry from the mini-apartments of New Princeton. A far cry. There were no poor in Lagrangia and evidently no unemployment, save for those who were retired and those who were too young to work. At the pace at which the construction of new Islands and new Satellite Solar Power Stations was going, there was no room for unemployment.

He wondered how long it could continue, this expansion. Always before, a new frontier was finite. Even one as vast as North America eventually came up upon the Pacific. But space? It was infinite. Beyond the solar system were billions of stars that could ultimately be orbited by colonists from Earth and from the earlier Islands. It was the biggest dream the human race had ever had.

He parked his bike before the professor's apartment building and entered, feeling weary, but not from the bike ride.

Susie was sprawled on the couch, her shoes kicked off and her feet up. She had a glass in hand and looked as though she'd been having a siege of worrying. However, she looked up with a weak smile of welcome.

"Well, who was your mysterious caller and what did he know about the professor?"

Rex went over to the bar and mixed some of the imitation Scotch with water and brought it back to the chair across from her.

He said, "It was Walt Hanse, and, among other things, he didn't want the professor found. He and his chum-pals, Shirely Ann Kneedler, Herman Klein, and Sal Sinatri."

"Oh, the executive committee of the Radicals, eh?"

"You know about them?"

"Oh yes," she said. "They're quite out in the open. Hanse is the chairman and theoretician, Klein is their outstanding speaker. What did they want?"

"They wanted me to drop trying to find Casey and to come in with them as a trouble-shooter. They don't seem to be very experienced as conspirators go. They told me their whole program. They want to kick the

Reunited Nations staff out soonest and then make some basic changes in the method of representation you've worked out."

"They've told everybody else too," Susie said, finishing her drink and swinging her long legs about to the floor. She got up on stockinged feet and went over to the bar to refresh her glass. "It's no big secret."

Rex was surprised. He said, "Look, just how big is this Sons of Liberty organization?"

"Oh, I'd say half of the Lagrangists, more or less, belong to it. Half Radicals, half Conservatives. Most of them aren't very active. They join up because it's the thing to do and everybody gets a kick out of running down the Reunited Nations staff and the earthworms in general."

"What chance have the Radicals of putting it over?"

"Probably better than you'd think," she said, as she mixed her fresh drink. "That is, unless the professor throws his weight completely behind the Conservatives. You see, he, too, wants eventual independence and so does practically everybody in Lagrangia. The Radicals want to put over a *coup d'état,* overwhelm Abou Zaki and his staff, and send them a'packing to Earth-side. It wouldn't be very difficult."

"He's got some armed bodyguards," Rex said mildly.

"Only four and no weapons beyond sidearms. Quite a few of Hanse's people have hunting guns. It's unlikely that there'd be much of a fight, if any. Then the Reunited Nations would be faced with a *fait accompli.* What did you tell Walt when he propositioned you?" She had returned to the couch and now resumed her reclined position.

"I told him I already had a job and that, besides, I didn't like dictatorships, even if they're headed by top scientists."

She looked over at him, eyebrows raised a bit.

Rex took a pull at his drink and said, "The fact that a man's got a phenomenal Ability Quotient, a doctor's degree or so, and a stupendous I.Q. doesn't mean that he has integrity. Some of them seem to think that their strength is the strength of ten because their hearts are pure. And why are their hearts pure? Because they've spent several thousand hours in classrooms, lecture halls, and laboratories. It doesn't prove out. Some of the most vicious people in history have had high I.Q.s and probably Ability Quotients had they been able to test them in those days. Look at Napoleon. Look at Hitler, Goering, Schacht, and Speer. For that matter, look at some of the top-notch criminals, those that had the ability to work out a system of robbing a bank or some outfit like Brinks for a take that added up to millions. They could hardly have been in the low I.Q. ranks."

"Quite a speech," Susie nodded. "So you turned him down. Didn't the Executive Committee offer some special inducements?"

"Yeah," Rex said. He finished his own drink, got up and went to the bar, made another and returned. He felt like getting drenched. "They offered to make me a Lagrangist and when they got into power I was to be on the Council as Minister of Defense."

"Holy Jumping Zen," Susie said in protest. "What do they mean by Minister of Defense?"

"They mean Minister of War," Rex told her. "Klein, in particular, seemingly wants to hit Earth before Earth has a chance to go to hell in its own way."

"Holy Jumping Zen," Susie repeated. "That's a new one, and it doesn't sound so good."

SEVENTEEN

The phone screen hummed and Susie went over to answer it. She came back shortly, her face wan.

"What's the matter?" Rex said.

"That was Doctor Garmisch, over at the hospital. There have been six more cases of space cafard already today."

"Six!"

"That's right. Four spontaneous cases and two from contagion. Two of the hospital orderlies collapsed while cleaning up in the contagion rooms."

"What are contagion rooms?" Rex said.

"You've got to completely isolate cafard victims. Unless you, yourself, are at least partially immune, the very sight of someone in space cafard can set you off. The way Poul Garmisch had been working it to this point was to immediately isolate a cafard patient until transportation to Earth-side was available. But spacecraft aren't leaving daily, not passenger vessels big enough to have sickbays with isolation wards."

Rex said, "Why don't they put through a crash program to convert some of your space tugs to hospital ships that could rush these victims to the safety of Earth?"

"And let the information out that such steps were necessary?" she clipped in irritation. "The news would be all over Earth in a matter of hours. Among other results would be a drying up of new colonists, and at this point of the Lagrange Five Project we need new colonists. Not to speak of giving the Lagrangist enemies

154

Earth-side a weapon. They'd claim the whole project too dangerous."

"Six in one day," Rex said blankly. "Maybe it is."

"Two of them from contagion," Susie said. "That's one of the prime difficulties. It spreads like wildfire once it gets out of hand. Those two hospital orderlies won't be the last and once the hospital goes, what can we possibly do?"

Rex Bader shifted his eyes sideways, in thought. He said, "Why not recruit the ten-year-olds?"

"What in Zen are you talking about?"

"You said that kid Virginia Dare Robbins was eleven years old, and the ten-year-olds coming after her were already taking their I.Q. and other Lagrangist tests. You also said that children born in space seemed immune to cafard. Okay. Recruit them to act as orderlies and hold down any other routine hospital jobs in the contagion areas."

"But ten-year-olds!"

He said, "You mentioned that these kids born in space were on the precocious side, very smart, very adult. Okay, a ten-year-old isn't as young as all that. They can mop floors, make beds, carry food trays, take out bedpans, and whatever else hospital orderlies have to do."

Without saying anything further to him, Susie returned to the phone screen. She flicked in on and said, "Hospital. Doctor Poul Garmisch."

He spoke first, as soon as he saw who it was. "Good God, Susie, two more. Two stretcher bearers. We thought that they were immune."

Susie said, "Look Poul, start getting volunteers from the ten-year-olds, even some among the nine-year-olds might be up to some duties. Both boys and girls."

"What are you talking about? Look here, Susie, have you been checked out for cafard recently yourself?"

"Yes, Poul. The space born children are immune. Put them to work in the isolation rooms."

His eyes widened. "Holy Zen, you're right!"

The doctor's face faded without a further word.

Susie turned back to Rex with a look compounded

of relief and perhaps a new respect. She sank down on the couch again.

She said, "That'll give the doctor some respite, if the children can do it, and there's no reason why they can't. It's not much more than playing house. Thank whatever powers there might be that the doctor himself seems to be immune. Several of the nurses, too."

"Is this happening in all the Islands?"

She frowned unhappily. "No, it isn't. That's one of the mysteries. We can't understand it. While all were still living in the construction shack, which was a comparatively tiny place to house almost two thousand workers, and later when we moved into Island One, the disease was practically unknown. Oh, we had some few mild cases, but we just shipped them back to Earth and forgot about it. We used to kid them, called them earthworms, and everybody usually called it Island Fever in those days. You've got to realize that space cafard is largely based on claustrophobia. Without the claustrophobia element, it wouldn't hit. The other elements can be contained with a little psychotherapy and that sort of thing."

"How about the Island Twos?" Rex said.

"Same thing there. Even less space cafard than in the construction shack, or in Island One. Which makes sense. They're considerably larger and hence would seemingly be less susceptible to claustrophobia."

He said, "How about your other cylinder that makes up Island Three?"

"Komarov? Why, they're having some cases of their own, but not as bad as here in Grissom. We're accounting for nine out of ten patients in Lagrangia and ours are usually the all-out, hopeless cases. We simply can't understand it. How can you get claustrophobia in an area as large as Grissom?"

Rex replenished his glass, once again, and, without asking, Susie's as well.

After he'd reseated himself, he said, "As a detective, I'm beginning to suspect something out of the way."

"How do you mean?"

"It doesn't make sense and when something doesn't make sense, I get premonitions."

"Oh, don't be silly, Rex. Medicine isn't your field, nor mine. This is up to medical research, not to physicists and private eyes."

"Forgive me for breathing."

"Oh, don't be silly. Are you up to squirrel pie for supper? I finished that one I was working on. All it needs is heating up."

"Squirrel pie it is. I ought to get something on my stomach. All my tendencies are to get drenched. And that's not going to do the professor any good."

He followed her into the kitchen and sat at the table there while she wound up the preparations for their meal. Thus far, he had never been in the dining room, and suspected that except when they had guests, Susie and George Casey made a practice of eating here.

She said, as she worked, "Any ideas at all about where Professor Casey might be?"

"None," he said gloomily. "I'm no further than I was yesterday, and yesterday I wasn't anywhere. He took a four-seater to Island One and never arrived. Period. That's all we know, for sure. For some unknown reason, he left his transceivers here, which doesn't make sense but does prevent us from getting a fix on him, if he's still alive."

She shot a quick look at him. "You don't think that he's alive, do you, Rex?"

He flipped a hand in rejection. "No, I don't, but we've got to proceed as though we believe he is."

The meal was good and again Susie Hawkins had proven herself an experienced amateur chef, but neither of their hearts were in food. Rex had never eaten squirrel before, in a pastry dish or in any other manner, and decided that the space colonists had been smart to stock their woods with the tree rodent. The meat was delicious. Nevertheless, he put his fork down before finishing more than half the portion she had served him.

She knew how he felt and didn't bother to ask him if he didn't like the dish. She put down her own utensil, stood, and began to gather up the balance of the meal to dispose of it.

She said, "I've got a meeting I'll have to attend this evening. I'll have to stand in for the professor. Zen only knows how long it will take for the word to get out that he's missing, now that both Mickoff and the Administrator know it."

"And that Whip Ford fellow as well," Rex said. "Between them, they've probably already spread the story."

"Are you going to stay here, while I'm gone?" she said.

He thought about it. "I don't think so. I'm getting tired of spending so much time cooped up in this apartment. I think I'll go down to The Pub and knock back a few more drinks. I can think as well there as here. Not that I have much to think about. If you want me, you can raise me on my transceiver."

"Wizard," she said. "Probably, it's just as well that it'll be out that Professor Casey has disappeared. Maybe somebody will come forward with some information that will help."

He said, "Look, you said that it was possible that a spacecraft of the type you use in construction could have come up beside the four-seater that Casey was in and removed him. Is there any manner in which you could check on the location of every vessel you have, at the time involved?"

Susie said, "Yes, the computers have a fix on every craft in Lagrangia at all times. In case of emergency, aid can be sent immediately. But we've already checked on that. There were no other spacecraft en route between Islands One and Three at the time of the professor's trip, not even automated freighters."

"Would there be any chance of fouling up the computers on this? You've got some pretty astute boys up here when it comes to electronics."

She was negative to that. "We considered every possibility and decided that it couldn't be done."

"Damn it," he complained. "I wish that you'd told me that sooner. That eliminates kidnapping. Or, at least, it eliminates kidnapping while he was still in space. He could have been snatched either at the dispatch station here in Grissom, or the one at Island Three."

She said in rejection, "That would have to involve the whole dispatch crew, at least ten men, on the shift involved. It seems unlikely. There might be a few in Lagrangia who dislike the professor, though I don't know of them, but I doubt if a whole dispatch crew could be corrupted."

"Wizard," he said. "I didn't take the possibility too seriously myself."

She finished cleaning up and headed back for the living room to get her attaché case.

"See you later," she told him.

"I'll probably be in bed, in preparation for a morning hangover," he said bitterly. "I simply don't know where to start on this damned thing."

He sat there awhile, after she had left, trying to think but decided shortly that his idea of crossing over to The Pub was a good one. He left the apartment and started for the stairs, but then pulled himself up. He usually made a policy, when entering a new building, to check it out, if he was going to stay awhile. He liked to have a possible route of retreat, if retreat was in order. Or he liked to know the layout, in case it came to his chasing someone.

So now he prowled down the hall. There was a window at either end of the corridor, but no fire escape at either. That probably made sense. There was precious little in the building that would burn, certainly none of the construction material. He was surprised to find only one other door in addition to the professor's own. Well, this wasn't a very large building. He stared out one of the windows for a moment, down at the ground. Directly below was a garden. Probably soft soil. It would be possible, in an emergency, to hang from the window and drop the three stories involved. Possible, but no fun, and could easily wind him up with a broken leg, or at least a sprained ankle, in spite of the fact that during his aviation training Rex Bader had practiced parachute jumps.

He started back for the stairs and, as he went, heard the sound of the door of the second apartment opening behind him. Involuntarily, he turned his head to look back over his shoulder. But the door closed quickly. He inwardly shrugged. Perhaps the professor's neighbor had remembered something at the last moment and had to return for it.

It was dark by now, and he automatically looked up for the stars. There weren't any, of course, that could be seen through the strips of windows of Grissom. What he could see were lights in the other valleys; individual lights, clusters of lights for small villages, larger clusters for towns of greater size. He shook his head. It was a strange sight, fascinating to him, and evidently frightening to John Mickoff.

Across the street was a small park. As he headed for The Pub he could see from the corner of his eye a figure detach itself from the shadows of a grouping of the larger trees.

Rex pretended not to notice, but as he went he checked out the fact that whoever the other was, he was being followed.

One of John Mickoff's three agents? Possibly, though if the IABI official was wasting his manpower trailing Rex Bader, he was a damn cloddy. For that matter, it might be one of Walt Hanse's half-assed, so-called Radicals, though he couldn't come up with any reason why Hanse would want to keep track of him.

He shrugged it off in irritation. It was a free world, this Lagrangia. If anyone wanted to walk on the street behind him, he didn't see why not.

The Pub was more crowded at this time of the evening than it had been the last occasion he was in. There were no empty tables and he had to find himself a narrow space at the bar. He was sorry now that he had come. He'd have his work cut out trying to think in this hub-bub.

There was a new bartender, a smaller, thinner man than the other hobbiest, but he, too, was done up in stereotype British bartender style, complete with the obviously phoney walrus mustache. It seemed to be sort of a standard badge. There was also a barmaid, a blonde, lusty-looking wench, on the face of it having the time of her life playing the part. Right now, she was chattering away with two of the customers.

Now that he was here anyway, Rex ordered a draft beer and began working away at it as soon as the rich head had gone down.

The more he thought about it, the more he was irritated by the fact that somebody was following him. And it came to him that whoever it was must have something to do with the professor. There could hardly be any other reason for following Rex Bader.

On a sudden impulse, he put the half-finished drink back on the bar, turned and made his way through the thronging drinkers. About a dozen of them were nosily playing darts at one end of the room.

He left the pub and started back up the street as though returning to the professor's apartment. As he went through the door, he could make out a figure fading back into the shadows a short way down the street. So his friend was still with him. Rex Bader's irritation was still growing. Just for luck, he checked with his hand the pistol in his belt. Grissom wasn't exactly the type place you expected to be mugged, but you never knew. Somebody in Island Three was playing for high stakes.

He didn't turn again, but he could hear footsteps on the sidewalk quite a ways behind him. Oh, his friend was still there, all right, all right.

Almost opposite the professor's building, Rex Bader did some fading himself. He stepped off the sidewalk into the park, increased his pace somewhat and made for the darkest clump of trees. He could hear the footsteps hurrying up. The other had obviously decided that Rex was trying to shake him.

He remained stock still until the tailer was nearly upon him and then stepped out and said, "Wizard. What spins, chum-pal?"

The other reacted in complete surprise, and immediately swung a punch.

Rex went into the 5th Kata, giving the Kiai cry,

"*SUT!*" even as he counteracted the enemy's blow with a left hand inside block. He moved in quickly, brutally, with a right forward kick to the groin, which, in compassion, he pulled at the last moment, and simultaneously his right hand, fingers held in spear fashion, was thrust forward to the left side of his opponent's lower rib, and the other groaned in agony and collapsed to the ground.

Rex Bader took him under the armpits and hauled him to the nearest bench, which was only a few feet away. He plunked the man down and stepped back a yard or so and put his hands on his hips.

It was Whip Ford.

Rex held his peace until the Black had recovered to the point where he could talk.

Talk he did. He rasped, "What was the big idea attacking me, Whitey?"

Rex said mildly, "I was only going to say boo. You tossed the first blow, friend."

"I told you once before that you're no friend of mine."

"Wizard. And you sure go out of your way to prove it. Why were you following me?"

For a moment, the other held silence, but then he said, "I figure you know where Professor Casey is. I thought that you might lead me to him."

"You could take a few lessons in tailing, chum-pal. And even more in street fighting. Never go up against a pro. You knew I was a detective. Did you think I hadn't been checked out in such goodies as karate? Besides, I haven't the vaguest idea of where Casey is. I'm looking for him myself."

"I think you do," Ford said sullenly. "And I've got to see him soonest. I've got to talk him into giving this Council outfit an upbeat report on our Promised Land Society's plans to build ourselves an all-Black Island."

"What's your hurry?"

Whip Ford took a deep breath. Seemingly, he was shaking the pain that had resulted from Rex practicing the 5th Kata on him. He said, grudgingly, "The Society's in kind of a turmoil. Some want to do this, some want to do that. Some even want to try and go ahead without the help of the Lagrange Five Project people, which is downright crazy. We couldn't begin to afford it. Others are getting disgusted and might drop out. If I can get back as soon as possible with an upbeat report, everything will be fine."

"It's okay with me," Rex told him. "But it's the professor you'll have to check it out with and he's still missing, whether or not you think I've got him stashed away somewhere."

"I don't trust you, Whitey," the other growled.

"Okay," Rex said. "I don't particularly like you any more than you do me, but you've still got the space colonization dream, haven't you?"

"I've got the dream, Whitey. It's the only answer for we Blacks to get out from under your damned discrimination."

"Personally, off-hand I don't remember ever having done any discriminating, Ford. But the thing is, so far as space colonization is concerned, somebody is trying to fuck it up. That puts you and me on the same side, at least for the time being. We both want to find the professor."

"You're not fooling me, Whitey. You and I'll never be on the same side of anything."

"Have it your own way," Rex said in disgust. "But get a little more practice in hand-to-hand combat before you tail me again. It makes me nervous and next time I might really hurt you."

He turned and walked off, leaving the Negro cursing quietly behind him.

EIGHTEEN

In the morning, Rex Bader awoke to find no Susie Hawkins in bed beside him. He had hit the hay fairly early, completely disgusted with all developments, and she had evidently come in late. He imagined that she'd had a rugged meeting. Without doubt, the rumors were spreading like a grassfire. Possibly, the Council had given up all attempts to keep the lid on and now actually admitted that something had happened to the father of the Lagrange Five Project.

He went through the usual morning routine of shower, shaving, and dialing fresh clothing to be donned and then went on into the livingroom.

By the looks of her, Susie Hawkins, Research Aide extraordinary, could have used some aid herself. She was on the phone screen and her voice seemed a little hoarse rather than maintaining the usual clipped quality she used during the work day.

He settled down quietly until she finished her call. From what little he could hear of the conversation, it was with Doctor Garmisch at the hospital.

She turned and without exchanging even good-mornings said, "It's getting worse. Every hospital in Island Three is overflowing with space cafard victims. Other patients are being moved out to whatever emergency quarters can be jerry-rigged so that all hospital rooms can be converted to isolation areas for the cafard victims. More than half of the medical doctors and the nurses are being devoted to the disease. More medics are being rushed in from the other Islands."

"It still hasn't hit them, eh?" Rex said softly. "Only Island Three."

She nodded to that. "Four-fifths of the cases are here in Grissom, almost all the rest in Komarov. Such victims as have turned up in the other three Islands are either Lagrangists who have recently been in Island Three, or local ones who have contracted it from contagion."

"Holy Zen," Rex said. "What's being done to get them Earth-side?"

She shook her head in despair. "The Council has decided that we can no longer try to hide the fact that space cafard is reaching epidemic proportions. We are quickly converting two of our passenger spacecraft into hospital ships. One patient to a stateroom. They'll be able to take a hundred apiece, if it reaches that point."

"Jesus," he said.

"Doctor Poul Garmisch and Doctor Hans Ober are calling for volunteers from among the known immunes," she told him.

"What's a known immune?"

"Just what it sounds like. Somebody who's been exposed to cafard and didn't react. Like the children. They're working like Trojans, by the way. I believe that I'm one, too. I've twice been exposed to victims. Once a mild case on Island One, the second a very bad case, one of the worst."

"What was it like?"

"It was horrible. He was a big construction engineer and had been in Lagrange Five for years. Out of a clear sky it hit him. I was there in the hospital when they brought him in. He was terrified, hysterical. I tried to comfort him. I took him in my arms. He was insane with fear and like a child. His bowels and bladder had come away in his clothes. He kept screaming to go home. He . . . he wanted his mother. However, the point is that it didn't hit me. A nurse present was effected but not me."

"Stop talking about it," Rex said. "It's beginning to get to me."

She looked at him. "I doubt it. When they checked you out at the hospital at the spaceport in Los Alamos, you showed little or no propensity for claustrophobia. That's one of the things they check on most carefully. Any would-be Lagrangist who shows more than a minimal tendency toward the disease is eliminated. By the way, that's something that Doctor Garmisch has turned up. The victims so far in this current rash of attacks are those that had the most tendency to claustrophobia to begin with. Not much, perhaps, because, as I say, they are weeded out, but even a small tendency seems enough to send you over the brink first."

She sank back in her chair as though exhausted. She said, "I still can't understand how this could be possible."

Rex said, "And I still smell a rat. Could Hanse and his group be behind it for some reason I can't even think about?"

Susie Hawkins was shocked. She said definitely, "Walt Hanse, Herman Klein and all the rest of the Radicals might have some differences of opinion with many of the rest of us, but they're all loyal Lagrangists. They all have the dream."

"That's wizard," Rex told her. "But, for instance, those old Romans in Caesar's time all had the Roman dream but they managed to butcher each other off until by the time of Nero there were no members of the Julian or Claudian gens left. Possibly Hanse has the dream so bad that he's willing to kill to bring off his version of it."

She brushed the idea off. "No, it's ridiculous, Rex."

She sat erect again and flicked on the phone and said, "Get me Administrator Abou Zaki. At this time of day, he's probably not in his office."

"Carried out," a robot voice said.

The Administrator's Semitic face faded in. As always, he affected his agalas headdress over the white muslin kaffiyeh. Susie wondered if the Arab wore it to bed.

"Doctor Hawkins," he said. "May you know grace. *In Sha'allah.*"

"Good morning, Your Excellency," Susie said. "We are clutching at straws. It occurs to me that on your staff are various medical doctors who, while they aren't trained in space medicine, might have some opinions on the current near-epidemic proportions of space cafard patients."

"My dear Doctor Hawkins, I am sure that the medical contingent of my staff are already cooperating to every extent with the Lagrangist medical department."

"Yes, of course," she sighed. "But, well, however, if anything does occur to any of your people, please let us know soonest."

"Certainly, my dear Doctor."

Her face was gone and Abou Zaki leaned back for a moment in thought. Finally, he turned to this tightbeam phone screen and said, "I wish to call Prince Jabir Riad, in Riyadh, Saudi Arabia, on Earth. Scrambled."

"Carried out."

When the Prince's face at length faded in, the Administrator again spoke in Arabic. He said, "Your Highness, there have been developments here."

Prince Jabir's face was even darker than usual. He said, "And here. I was about to call you. Has anything gone wrong?"

"Not as yet, Your Highness. The mental illness progresses as planned. The hospitals are now overflowing, but thus far the accursed Lagrangists have been able to contain the near-epidemic. How much longer they will be able to do so is in the hands of Allah."

"What else?"

"Two elements have been brought up from Earth, as I have already informed you: Rex Bader, the private investigator, and John Mickoff of the American IABI and three of his agents. They all seek Professor George Casey. I have pretended to encourage them."

The Prince waved a hand negatively. "Take measures to forestall them. As long as Casey is missing, the Lagrangists will be confused. He is their Prophet and they have never been in difficulties before when he was not there to guide them. By the way, do you know anything at all about his disappearance?"

"No," the other said. "I have been mystified. There must be something developing of which we are unaware. I do not like it, Your Highness."

"Well, here is something else you won't like."

The Administrator's scrawny face looked apprehensive.

The Prince said in disgust, "That son of Shaitan, Doctor Gerhard Johannisberger, has published a scientific paper on his extracting from the American Cold-No-More medicine the active ingredient that caused claustrophia symptoms. The fool! Undoubtedly, his incredible ego could not withstand the opportunity to shine before his medical colleagues. The paper will automatically go into the medical banks of the International Data Banks and be available to anyone with a scientific priority. It is just a matter of time before someone involved stumbles upon it and connects the new extract with the space cafard outbreaks in Island Three."

Abou Zaki was appalled. "Your Highness, what did you do?"

"There was nothing that could be done. Through our associates of International Diversified Industries, Johannisberger was, ah, liquidated, as the Soviets call it, before he could make some other foolish error that might connect us with the matter. But it was too late to recover the paper. It is now irrevocably in the data banks."

"But what can we do now?"

"We must speed up the operation. Place still larger quantities of the claustrophobia drug into the water system. We must precipitate such a number of cases that they will no longer be able to contain an all-out epidemic."

Abou Zaki said unhappily, "It is already near the epidemic stage, Your Highness. I was going to suggest that the next step be taken, that I and my staff return to Earth, declaring that space colonization is unsafe."

"Not yet!" the prince told him. "Just do as I tell you. Get more of the drug into the water. You will have ample time to make your retreat later. You must re-

main on the scene until we are certain that no unforeseen developments thwart us."

"But, Your Highness, one of my staff has already
been hospitalized. A common Europe woman in our
communications department. She went out onto the
street and was present when one of the Lagrangists
collapsed. She herself was effected immediately."

"She was a fool! Simply be sure that none of your
people leave the building you occupy and that none of
them use any water from the Grissom's ordinary supply."

"But, Your Higness," the prince's underling said in
alarm, "*I* will have to leave the building to put an
additional quantity of the drug in the water supply."

"May Allah guard you, as undoubtedly he will since
our cause is so necessary for his chosen people."

Abou Zaki swallowed and said, "*In Sha'allah,*" as
the Prince's face faded.

Prince Jabir Riad stared at the blank screen for a
long moment. His creature, Abou Zaki, was a tool not
to realize that he and all his staff were fated to die
with the Lagrangists when all went mad and began
destroying each other. Nothing else made sense. The
outcry against the Lagrange Five Project would be that
much the stronger if all the Reunited Nations staff
contracted the space cafard as well as the colonists. Besides, as verily all the wise know, dead men tell no
tales, and Abou Zaki was too weak to be trusted.

He turned to another phone screen and said into it,
"Sophia Anastasis, the International Diversified Industries Building in New York City, the United States of
the Americas. Scrambled."

The robot voice said, in Arabic, the equivalent of
"Carried out."

When the beauteous face of Sophia Anastasis came
on, she raised penciled eyebrows questioningly. "I
thought we were to avoid communicating as much as
possible."

"*As-salamm alaykum, Sitt,* Sophia Anastasis," he
said, touching forehead, lips, and heart in the traditional Moslem greeting. "It is of the utmost urgency."

"Very well, go ahead, Your Highness."

"We are reaching the climax of our project."

"So soon?" she frowned. "I thought we were to build up to it more slowly."

"There have been some unforeseen developments. Please put yourselves in full readiness to publicize the fact that the Lagrange Five Project is in turmoil, that thousands of the Lagrangists are down with a space disease that cannot be cured, save by return to Earth. Put your best writers on this immediately, but in full secrecy. Those that write the material should be isolated so that under no circumstances can they reveal that they wrote the broadcasts, articles, and news items before the event actually occurred."

"I'll isolate them, all right," Sophia Anastasis said grimly. "They'll be stashed away, under guard, for at least six months. By then, it'll all be over. If it came out now, we'd be sunk."

NINETEEN

Rex Bader was eyeing Susie Hawkins bleakly. She was on the phone screen getting the latest reports on the progress of the disease. Her face registered the fact that the reports were far from reassuring.

When she was done, Rex said, "Damn it, if Casey was here he'd figure out some way to lick this cafard thing."

But Susie shook her head wearily and said, "No, he wouldn't."

Rex looked at her in surprise. That didn't sound like the faithful Susie, for some fifteen years the professor's right hand. "How do you know he wouldn't?" Rex said.

"I just know," she said sadly, obviously weary to the point of exhaustion.

Rex stirred in his chair in rejection of the whole situation. "Possibly this is an indication that man was never meant to be in space," he said. "We've bit off more than we can chew in this Lagrange Five Project. We've failed. The only thing we can do now is pull an all-out evacuation."

She said angrily, "No, we haven't failed, or, at most, only for the time. Perhaps we will have to temporarily evacuate, which would present its problems. You see, there are over half-a-million persons in Island Three. There are insufficient spacecraft suitable for taking them Earth-side all at once. The best that we could do is temporarily ferry them over to the other Islands, un-

til they could take their turns at transport to Earth.
But even that wouldn't be the end of the dream, Rex.
Sooner or later, we'll lick this space cafard. Already,
the children are immune. Even if we have this set-back
now, when the children are grown they can return to
the Islands and take up the job. Tens of thousands of
kids have already been born in the Islands. They'll be
able to take up where we . . . earthworms couldn't
make it."

He said, just to be arguing, "If you return them to
Earth for a period of years, possibly they'll have lost
their immunity."

"I doubt it, particularly the older ones. But that will
have to remain to be seen."

Rex said, still argumentively, "But why colonize at
all? The Satellite Solar Power Stations are already
operative and being turned out wholesale through automation. Wizard. The other Islands haven't been particularly hit by cafard, so far. Discontinue the building of
this king-sized Island Four and concentrate on building
more SSPSs until we've got all we need to power the
Earth. Then pull all the colonists out and retreat Earth-
side. The SSPSs can be serviced from Earth by space-
men going up for limited periods, in conventional space
shuttles. The last time I asked you about the need for
going into space, you said because it was there. But
that answer is inadequate. There are some places man
simply can't colonize, the surface of the sun, for instance."

Susie nodded acceptance of part of what he had said,
but she rejected most of it.

She said, "One of the biologists on our staff explained it this way. In the evolutionary pattern, if there
is space and if any life form can adapt to it, internally
regulate utilizing the sources of energy at hand well
enough to insure their replication, organisms will fill
that space. On Earth, for instance, there are some sun-
requiring algae actually living inside carbonate rocks.
You'll find red and green microorganisms covering the
newly fallen Arctic snows and multiplying on its sur-

face. You find small blind arthopods scurrying at the rear of caves. And giant luminescent female fish inhabit the darkest depths of the ocean, carrying their tiny parasitic males. Such examples are endless. Where life *can* live, it will. And man can live in space and, eventually, in orbit about possibly billions of stars in this galaxy."

"It would seem that it remains to be seen whether or not we can live in space," he said glumly.

Rex Bader was frustrated. He had nothing to go on. He couldn't think of anybody to go and see, or anything to go and do. He might as well remain right here in the professor's apartment, which doubled as his office. If anything developed, Susie would immediately be informed. In George Casey's absence, she had taken over his duties, to the extent possible.

He prowled the apartment, reviewing everything that had thus far happened. And came up with nothing that seemed to lead to anything. He sprawled in a chair in the living room, and stared unseeingly out a window. And came up with nothing. He went into the professor's study and again went through his papers, including his date book, his appointment book. And came up with nothing.

He avoided bothering Susie, who remained at the desk in the living room, at tasks he didn't understand. From time to time, she'd phone or be phoned.

It wasn't until they were at a late lunch in the dining room that they communicated again. She had been too busy to cook and they had dialed food from the community automated kitchens.

Rex said, "I still can't get rid of the suspicion that someone is behind this whole thing. It's too much of a coincidence that Casey would disappear just when this space cafard epidemic started. And I also still don't like the smell of the fact that only Island Three has been hit. And, as somebody pointed out, it's the biggest Island of all. Why should somebody come down with a disease largely based on claustrophobia in a cylinder as large as Grissom? Hell, most of the time, particular-

ly when you're inside a building, or even in the countryside, you forget that you're in an Island."

Susie had no answer to that. She continued to force
herself to eat, though she had no appetite.

Rex pursued it. "Who else is against the Lagrange
Five Project besides the energy people? And besides
the politicians Earth-side who are astute enough to realize that the socioeconomic system developing here is
dangerous to them?"

She shrugged and said, "I'm afraid their names are
legion, Rex. Even the farmers are beginning to see the
handwriting on the wall. When Islands Four and Five
go into full production can you imagine the competition
they will be able to give to Earth-side agriculture? Year
around sunlight, year around perfect climate. No pests,
no parasites. Here in the Islands we can take from the
soil, or our hydroponic tanks, as many as four or five
crops a year."

"Who else, besides farmers?" Rex said. "Farmers, as
a rule, don't organize too well."

She thought about it, not overly interested, before
saying, "I would imagine that Earth manufacturers are
also getting the willies. Thus far, we've manufactured
comparatively little for shipment down to Earth markets. To this point, largely we Lagrangists have devoted
ourselves to building more Islands, constructing the
Satellite Solar Power Stations, additional spaceships, orbiting telescopes, and that sort of thing. All meant to
be utilized only in space. But I was talking to Sal Sinatri the other day and . . ."

"The member of the Radical executive committee?"

"That's right, but he's also on the Council as the
representative from Manufacturing and a good man. Sal
was of the opinion that it would be possible in Island
Four to build an automobile manufacturing industry
there with export to Earth in mind. The advantages
would be endless. Practically free power, inexhaustible
and easily extracted raw materials. The plant would be
located in zero-gravity and would utilize the very latest
in automated equipment. None of the machinery would
be obsolete, since we'd start from scratch, while on

Earth the car manufacturers have billions of pseudo-dollars tied up in equipment they can't afford to scrap.

"But one of the big advantages, as Sal pointed out, was delivery. On Earth, a car might be manufactured in Germany for export. They ship it over to New York where it is unloaded and trucked or otherwise freighted to, say, Los Angeles, where it is eventually sold. That car had to be shipped halfway around the world before finding its customer. But the Lagrangist cars could be sent down in automated, unpowered titanium space gliders, as they call them, and splashed down into the sea at the nearest point to their destination. The cars would be picked up and sold, the titanium would be recycled and marketed, since an unpowered space glider has no means of being returned to Lagrangia. Titanium, of course, is a very valuable metal, difficult to extract earth-side, since a great deal of power is involved, but plentiful up here, along with the energy to extract it."

"So farseeing manufacturers wouldn't mind seeing the Lagrange Five Project done in," Rex said. "Who else?"

Susie forced a rueful smile. "As I said, the number is legion. One somewhat far out grouping is organized religion. Shortly after we opened up Island Three, here, the so-called prophet of the United Fundamentalist Church, a man who calls himself Ezekiel, found out to his supposed horror that no temples, synagogues, mosques, or even churches had been built in Lagrangia. He immediately protested to the Reunited Nations and was given permission to build one of his missions, as he calls them, here in New Frisco. Wizard. He built it and came up himself for the initial service. The Lagrangists stayed away in droves. The handful that did show up came to gawk, or even snicker, not to worship. I'm afraid the type of person accepted as colonists are not prone to religion, or, even if they were, certainly not to fundamentalism. Not that the computers consider religion at all, any more than they do race or color. Obviously, Ezekiel was enraged, particularly when attendance at the mission fell off precipitately after that poorly attended opening ceremony. And he is intelligent enough to realize with what regard Lagrangists are looked upon, particularly by young people, Earth-side. And if Lagrangists scoff at organized religion, why shouldn't their admirers?"

Susie put down her fork. "I'm not up to dessert," she sighed. "I'd better get back to work."

Rex prowled the floor some more, stared out the window some more, irritated the hell out of himself some more, before he gave up.

He said to Susie, "I'm going to take a walk, before I go up the wall. Perhaps it'll help me get a slant on all this. If anything comes up here, while I'm gone, buzz me on my pocket transceiver, eh?"

"Wizard," she said, not looking up from a report she was reading.

Down on the street, Rex Bader looked at the bicycle rack for a moment, then decided the hell with it. He'd walk. For one thing, he could use the exercise. For another, he hadn't done much in the way of walking since his arrival in Grissom and you saw more when you walked than you did from any vehicle.

He looked up at the mountains which were at the end of the cylinder and which climbed thousands of feet toward the axis. New Frisco was in the foothills which developed into the mountains proper. Rex decided to head in that direction.

As he turned, someone jostled him.

"Sorry," the other apologized and grabbed Rex to keep him from stumbling.

"That's all right," Rex said. "I wasn't looking very carefully, myself."

The other hurried on. He had been a dark complexioned man, dressed in typically informal Lagrangist style. In no way unique. However, Rex looked after him, scowling. He got the damnedest impression that he had seen the man before. But, for that matter, possibly the fellow lived in this neighborhood and they had passed on the street.

He shrugged and started off.

The edge of town wasn't very far and there were no suburbs in this direction. There were winding paths but no roads that amounted to anything beyond the environs of the city. And after leavings its bounds, he saw few persons in his vicintiy. He got the impression that this was one of the wilderness areas someone had mentioned. That is, a section of the Island devoted to hiking, picnicking, camping, hunting, mountain climbing, that sort of thing. It was also evidently a bird and animal refuge, since right from the beginning he began to spot wildlife.

The day was already fairly well advanced by the time that the climbing got steeper. And the wilderness got wilder. There were quite a few trees now, and, unless one looked up, precious little evidence that you were inside a gigantic cylinder. A deer broke from cover and scampered for it. Rex watched in pleasure. He had never seen a wild deer before. What with the growing population, the exploitation of formerly wild areas, the pollution of even once remote areas, it had gotten to the point where wildlife was all but extinct in the States.

He had been wondering about John Mickoff and his three men, as he hiked. How were they doing? Rex had no illusions. All four of them had undoubtedly had considerably more training than he could boast. Besides that, Mickoff was obviously working in conjunction with Abou Zaki and the Reunited Nations staff and had their facilities at his command. No, it was much more likely that Mickoff would locate the professor than that Rex Bader would.

It occurred to him that he had covered three or four miles, all uphill, but that so far he wasn't particularly tired. Which was astonishing. He was in fairly good shape, physically, but not as good as all that. He should have been puffing by now. But then it came to him. He was climbing toward the axis of Grissom and the nearer he got to it, the less the gravity became. He wondered what he was actually in now. Two-thirds gravity? As little as one-half?

Well, whatever, he'd leave until another day a real assault on the mountains. He'd taken too late a start. It was getting dusk, as the mirrors without the space

Island slowly warped, reflecting less of the rays of the sun. He reversed his engines, and started back toward New Frisco, where lights were already beginning to appear.

Two rabbits popped from a bush and began running in wild zig-zag, rabbit style and he watched them as appreciatively as he had the deer earlier. It would seem that the Lagrangists did a thorough job of stocking their wildernesses. Next time he came up to this area he'd see if he couldn't bring a camera.

Just out of exuberance, he bent to pick up a pebble to throw at random.

And it was then that the first shot rang out.

TWENTY

The whiplike crack was characteristic of the Gyro-jet rocket pistol, but whoever was firing was either a lousy shot or was being thrown off by shooting uphill, or the fading light. Rex didn't even hear the whine of a passing rocket-propelled slug.

He had been bending when the attack came, he continued on, hitting the dirt and gravel of the narrow path that he had been following, and rolling desperately for the cover of a boulder twice his size to the right of the path.

The shot had come somewhere from below and, by the sound of it, from about a hundred and fifty feet away. By the crack, he would guess it was a 7.65 mm Gyro-jet, as compared to his own 9 mm back in his mini-apartment in New Princeton. Not a really heavy caliber but heavy enough, about like a .32. The Gyro-jet had enough punch that the slug didn't have to be very heavy to do its job. You could have killed an elephant or whale with a 7.65 mm Gyro-jet.

A hundred-and-fifty feet, over this type mountain terrain, meant it would take his unseen foe some time to get to him. Rex Bader fumbled desperately for his transceiver. He usually kept it in the right side pocket of his jacket. His intention was first to yell for help in general, and when that message had been sent, try and raise John Mickoff. Undoubtedly, whatever was going on had something to do with Professor Casey, and Mickoff would come a-running.

But his pocket communicator wasn't in his right jacket pocket. Nor the left. He sent his hands seeking through other pockets, then realized, in a sinking feeling, that he simply didn't have it with him. Holy Zen, could he have left it back at the apartment? But no. He never left to go out without automatically checking to see if he had his transceiver and his Universal Credit Card.

And then it came to him. The fellow who had jostled him outside the professor's apartment building, and then grabbed him so that Rex wouldn't fall. Among other things, the other had apologized in English. How could he have possibly known that Rex spoke English, but not Interlingua? Obviously, the man was a trained pickpocket and now had Rex's only means of summoning help.

He groaned and rolled a little to one side so that he could pluck the small target gun from his belt. It wasn't much, up against a Gyro-jet, but it was better than nothing and would make a noise. Perhaps the other didn't know just how small a caliber a .22 was, and that was all that Rex was armed with. On the other hand, perhaps he did. Rex didn't have any idea who it might be who was shooting at him, but the other was knowledgeable enough to have known his victim to be was in the professor's apartment and that he spoke English.

He heard a sound before him and slightly to the left. Someone coming through the brush, rather than up the path that Rex had ascended. Then Rex froze. There came another sound from forty or fifty feet to the right. There were two of them.

His position was untenable. Coming in on him from both sides, with several times his firepower, they had him.

He darted his head about, sizing up the surroundings. They were fairly well into the mountains now, and he was surprised and irritated with himself that he had come this far before turning back. Yes, he'd been wrapped up in his thoughts, but he must have walked for hours.

He was a sitting duck behind this boulder. He'd have to make a dash for it.

He jumped quickly to his feet, fired one shot at he who was to the left, and another quick one to the noises in the bushes to the right, then spun and, bent double, scurried, zig-zagging, toward an outcropping of rock, some fifty feet off.

He made it by the skin of his ass. Two cracks came, just as he flung himself around the outcropping and this time there was a bit more accuracy. He heard both slugs zang up against the rock, not a foot from his side, and then carom shrilly off into the mountain air.

He didn't stop to take breath but, keeping his rock outcropping between him and his assailants, he dashed on, heading higher into the mountains.

He tried to sort it out, even as he made the best time he could. There was no particular reason to believe that they were any more adept at playing hide-and-go-seek in this rugged terrain than he was. He was in fairly good shape, wasn't tired, and, to top it all, he had once, though some years ago, taken a mountain climbing course during one of the few vacations he had ever been able to afford, in Rosenlaui, Switzerland. He had been somewhat disappointed but the two weeks he had spent scrambling up and down the Kingspitz and other Alp peaks had been educational. Now perhaps it would pay off.

He could still hear the others behind but it seemed to him that he had put some distance between them. The gravity was little enough now that he bounced, rather than just climbed. And still he had no signs of exhaustion as a result of the exertion. He was beginning to consider the possibility of his flanking them, circling around and then trying to get back to New Frisco and safety.

In fact, he was starting the operation, trending over further to the right, rather than going directly up. Traversing, the instructor had called it in Switzerland. You seldom went straight up a rockface, more often it was a series of working your way sideways and up as hand and footholds allowed.

He was beginning to congratulate himself. Surely, he had worked his way far enough to the right of his pursuers that he could take a chance on starting down. It was getting increasingly darker. Perhaps they wouldn't spot him at all, if he could just keep from making more than a minimum of noise in all this rock, gravel and pebbles.

But it was then that there came another crack, from off to his right, another crack of a Gyro-jet and a *spang* as a slug hit near his right arm. It was a miss, still once again, but the closest yet. In fact, a sharp sliver of rock was knocked from the wall and buried itself painfully in the arm.

Had one of the two he thought quite a-ways behind managed to flake off to the right and catch up with him?

But no, he was just kidding himself. This was a third pursuer. He scurried back to his left after winging a quick .22 bullet in the general direction of the shooter who had nearly gotten him, just to keep the other honest.

He continued traversing, this time to the left and up. It was no longer hills now, they were definitely in the mountains proper. One man on approximately the same level he was, two behind and at a slightly lower altitude. Nobody was attempting to hide the sounds of their movement; he could hear all three of them. And, undoubtedly, they could hear him.

A voice called up from below. "You haven't got a chance, Bader. Give up and you'll be okay."

The words were in English and even used American idiom but there was a slight accent he couldn't put his finger on.

And I'm the Queen of Rumania, he thought.

However, for the moment, he was taking a breather and checking out his surroundings, planning out his way. He was in a good sheltered position, so he yelled back, "And what happens to me then?"

The other shouted, obviously trying to make his voice convincing, "We'll take you back to New Frisco and see that you're shipped back to Earth on the first available passenger ship."

Just for the hell of it, Rex yelled, "They're using all the available passenger ships to take space cafard victims back Earth-side. There's no room for me, and there's none for you either, chum-pals. When this epidemic really hits, we've all had it. I won't get out of Grissom and neither will you. Everybody goes crackers, when it really hits."

There was another long pause before the other yelled again, "You're full of shit, Bader."

It occurred to Rex suddenly that they were engaging him like this to draw his attention while one of them was trying to pull something. He hurriedly began traversing again to the left and upward, possibly he could still flank them and head for the safety of New Frisco. There had been a tremor in the spokesman's voice at the end there. Rex wondered if he had set them back with his prophesy of doom. Who in the hell were they, anyhow? Obviously, they wanted nothing short of his blood. But why?

His hopes of flanking them from the left went with the snows of yesteryear. From a hundred feet before him there came a flash from a gun's barrel, a crack, and a whoosh that passed over his head. The one following him, on the same level he was maintaining, cursed in some language Rex didn't recognize. It would seem that the rocket bullet had come nearer to him than it had to its target.

Zen! There were four of them and he was surrounded on all sides, save up.

He had only one immediate chance. His only break would be if none of them had any mountain climbing experience whatsoever. If they were still clumsier in these rocks, cliffs, gullies, and shifting, sliding gravel than he was.

He started up the cliff side, groaning at the possibility that he was in clear sight of any, or all of them. Dark it was certainly getting, but not so dark that they wouldn't be able to make him out and shoot.

He tried to bring the climbing instructions of the Swiss guide back. It had been a long time.

There are eight main handholds in mountain climbing, large, normal, small, steadying, pressure pull, pressure push, side-grip, and under-grip. There are six common footholds, large, normal, small, sloping, pressure, and wedge.

The feet of the rock climber, Rex had been told, must become sensitive. A sense of touch right through stocking, leather and nails, or rubber soles is the prime necessity. Your feet must be as though they have eyes, they must seek out elusive footholds.

Wizard. But Rex Bader was wearing ordinary shoes of the type utilized for city streets, not climbing cliffs. And his hands were comparatively soft. Already they were banged and bruised, with broken fingernails, and probably a few small cuts, if he could have seen them.

But up he went, seeking out handholds, footholds, standing on ledges when they were available, to get a breather. They must be, by now, at less-than-half-gravity but no matter how little the gravity, this was exertion. He was going practically straight up the cliff by now.

Behind him, the others were doing their best. He could still make out the sounds of their progress, occasional shouts back and forth to each other, occasional curses of frustration, though he still couldn't make out the language. They had one considerable advantage over him. There were four of them and they could help each other in the climb. They could boost each other over a bad spot, then the one above could reach down and pull the following up. When Rex came to a spot he couldn't navigate alone, he had to take the time to seek an easier alternative.

He thought they were falling behind somewhat in the chase, but he wasn't sure. He had to admit that they were game. Whatever their motivation for wanting to finish him, it must be a strong one. The bastards weren't giving up for a minute.

From time to time, one or the other of them would think he spotted Rex and wing off a shot. None of them came even remotely near. He held his own fire, not wanting to spot his location to them.

He came to a chimney and sweated out remembering how to ascend one. You put your back to one wall, feet to the other, and "walked" up it. This one must have been a good forty feet high and he was puffiing at the top.

But it was the top. That is, it was the top of *this* cliff. There were others beyond, how many he couldn't know.

He squirmed over to the edge and stared down. It was too dark. There was the very faintest of light that the mirrors still reflected into Grissom but, without moon or stars, it was far from bright. He couldn't make any of them out, but he could still hear them. He doubted if they could see his head.

Grinning wolfishly, he brought up the nearest small boulder he could find and heaved it over. It fell with a banging and crashing as it rolled and bounced down the cliff side, starting a miniature avalanche of minor stones and gravel.

The cursing from below intensified.

He laughed and crawled back away and began heaving over the cliff's edge every stone of any size that he could find. Whether or not he even glancingly hit any of them with even the smaller of the rocks, he never knew. But he was making life tough for them. They had no manner of knowing that the next boulder wouldn't crush in a skull and make mush of a brain.

They must have found some sort of goat or deer path that he had missed, because suddenly they were coming faster.

He swore, pushed himself to his feet, and ran on. For a time, it was comparatively level, only a slight rise, and he was even able to locate a very narrow path, probably utilized in its day by mountain climbers and mountain animals.

He was grateful, but it petered out after possibly a quarter of a mile and he was up against a nearly sheer cliff again. He considered looking for a cave or some other place where he could go to ground, but that wasn't it. They could hear him, stumbling and sometimes even falling, as well as he could hear them. If he hid, they'd simply come to the area where they'd heard him last and fan out and search.

He looked at the new cliff, wearily. Possibly fifteen feet up he could make out a ledge. What was beyond, he hadn't the slightest idea, but there was nothing for it. Taking several deep breaths, he bent his knees and jumped. The gravity now couldn't be more than possibly one quarter that of Earth-side. He soared up, grabbed the edge of the ledge and pulled himself over it without difficulty. There was certainly something to be said for lesser gravity, Rex decided inwardly.

The ledge was narrow. He pressed his hands and back against the cliff wall and mentally flipped a coin, heads to the right, tails to the left. He went left, edging himself along.

By the sounds, the foursome had seemingly reached the crest of the first cliff and now were coming at all speed they could muster down the path. They obviously assumed that he had taken the path. It was the only thing that made sense. He cursed his stupidity. That was the point at which he should have tried hiding. He could have ducked behind some larger boulder and when they had hurried up the path, could have started down the cliff again.

Now he was a sure target for them, a bull's-eye, if they came up on him before he could get off this ledge and higher up the cliff side.

He came to a fairly wide crevice, took his chances and started going up it, utilizing every iota of mountain lore he had accumulated in his inadequate two weeks in the Alps. As he went, it widened until it was almost like a chimney and for fifteen feet or so, he could "walk" up once again.

He could hear them chattering behind and below him and then suddenly he could hear them no more. Nor could he hear the noises that would have been forthcoming had they been climbing after him.

Oh, oh. Had they found another path? One that would take them to the top of the cliff before he arrived at his slower pace?

But it was then that he reached the top and, to his surprise, came out onto what looked like nothing so much as a very small airfield complete with a dozen or so of the strangest looking aircraft he had ever seen, if that's what they were.

Someone, hard to distinguish in the almost total dark, came around one of them and said, "Hello, Bader."

It was Whip Ford.

TWENTY-ONE

Rex jerked the .22 from his belt, leveled it and snapped, "What the hell are you doing here?"

"Following you, Whitey. I still think that sooner or later you'll lead me to the professor."

"Maybe I will, at that. How'd you get up here ahead of me?"

The Black said, "I followed you out of New Frisco. Before very long, I realized that there were four other guys following you, too. I decided to take a chance that you were going all the way up, possibly to meet Casey somewhere. So I went back to New Frisco and to one of the vehicle pools and got a pilot of a helio-jet to fly me up here. I've been waiting for you. What the hell was all that shooting about, down below? And what's that about maybe you'll take me to the professor?"

Rex said, "Something came to me while I was climbing. Possibly I know how to find him. But meanwhile, there's four gunmen after me. I haven't the vaguest idea of who they are. How do we get off this damn mountain top?"

"There's no further to run, Bader. This is the top of a peak. Everything's down from here. This is one of the play areas of Island Three. The pilot of the helio-jet was telling me about it. We're almost to zero-gravity. See those pedal-planes?" The Black pointed at the strange looking craft.

Now Rex could see that they were a type of aircraft all right. The wings were small and there were three of them, making it a triplane. There were two big propellers, almost as big as the wings. There was a bar which, he decided, was meant to be sat upon as you pedaled what looked like a bicycle arrangement. The landing gear was a light tripod of wheels.

"Think you could fly one?" Whip Ford said. "I've read about these things. They're meant for low-gravity flying. As long as you're near the axis, your pedaling powers it. If you get lower, you've hardly got more than a glider."

"How about you?" Rex said, straining his ears for his pursuers. "These cloddies are trigger-happy. If they saw you, they'd probably shoot first and find out they didn't know you afterwards."

"I'm a coach at a school, Earth-side," Whip said. "I've tried every sport going—including gliding."

"Let's go," Rex said, heading for one of the craft. The Black had been right. They were at almost zero-gravity and walking was a chore. "I used to study flying, got a pilot's license and all, but this gismo is something else again."

The pedal-plane was so rigged that it set the rider at an angle almost like lying down. There was a bar at waist-level to hold onto. When they began to pedal, the large propellers revolved in opposite directions.

They took off with surprising ease and reached for altitude.

Whip Ford yelled over to him, "We can't get too near the axis. There's no gravity at all there. There's no 'down' and these things are designed to fly at about five percent gravity, or more."

They could hear shouts behind them and then the crack of Gyro-jet pistols.

"Pedal, man!" Rex yelled to the other.

"What do you think I'm doing, coasting?" Whip called back.

The range was too great and it was too dark for accurate shooting.

Rex looked back. "Holy Jumping Zen," he said. "They're coming!"

Four of the pedal-planes were taking off after them.

Whip called over, in despair, "And they've probably flown these damned things before. Pedal, man!"

Rex edged over closer to him. "You said they were designed for five percent gravity, or more. What happens if you go so low that you're in normal gravity?"

"If I remember correctly, your pedaling becomes less and less effective and you're little more than a glider."

"Wizard, damn it. Let's head for New Frisco. We can duck them there."

Whip Ford looked over his shoulder and said, "They're catching up. Like I said, they've probably flown these things before and know the ropes. It's a popular sport here. Pedal, man. Where'd you say the professor was? If anything happens to you, but I get away, I still want to find him."

"My chum-pal," Rex said. The propellers made so little sound that an all but normal conversation could be carried on between the pedal-planes. "I didn't say. I just had a hunch that I can track him down."

He looked back. Whip Ford had been right. Their four pursuers were coming up and fairly fast at that. New Frisco was still miles away.

"We're going to have to fight," Rex called to the Negro.

"Oh, wizard. And they've got guns. So do you, for that matter, though it didn't look like much of a shooter when you pointed it at me."

"It's not," Rex groaned. "It's a twenty-two. They've got Gyro-jets. But they're going to have their work cut out operating one of these things and doing much in the way of target practice on us. We must be getting into more gravity. No matter how much I pedal, I don't seem to get much bite out of the propellers."

The four pursuers were only a matter of a score of yards behind them. A shot rang out.

"Dive!" Whip yelled.

Rex Bader, unfamiliar with his craft as he was, did a wing-over and dove. The pedal-plane, increasingly becoming no more than a glider, responded better than he had hoped for. The stubby wings gave it little more gliding-angle than that of a brick, but that wasn't of much importance. There was no reason for trying to soar. Their only bet was to get to the vicinity of New Frisco. There the hit men wouldn't dare fire and bring attention to the whole conflict.

Something came to Rex Bader. He yelled over to Whip, "Do you know what an Immelmann turn is?"

"Yeah, but in these things?"

"When we get up a little more speed and I yell, give it a try!"

"Wizard!"

There came another shot from behind and although Rex could hear its passage, once again the shot went wide. Nevertheless, the pursuers were closing in. Much nearer and they'd have a considerably better chance of scoring.

The diving and the rapidly increasing gravity had built up speed considerably.

Rex yelled, "Go!"

Simultaneously, the two fleeing craft nosed up into a half loop. At the top, when they were upside down, both did a half-roll and they were now heading in the opposite direction and were above the foe.

Whip called, anxiously, "I used up too much flying speed. I'm going to spin-in!"

"Try to come out of it," Rex called. "Stick your nose down!"

But the Black had lost flying speed. He tried desperately to get control, but, already spinning, he was nearing the level of the gunman furthest to the right of the line they maintained. He was going to be within gun range in moments.

Rex groaned, flipped over onto one wing in a hard turn and dove. He passed over the desperately fighting Whip Ford and began to come out immediately over the pedal-plane of the gunman below.

The pilot, his face startled, tried to avoid him, trying at the same time to snatch his gun from its holster under his left armpit. He was trying to do too much at once, in his flimsy craft.

Rex came in from one side, sheering off his own landing gear as he zoomed in low above the other and tore off his foe's twin propellers.

The propellers, though decreasingly efficient at this altitude, were still required to keep flying speed. The other craft dropped precipitately. Rex Bader winced at the idea of the splat it would make when it hit the mountain surface.

Whip came out of his spin and they were side-by-side again and heading for New Frisco once more.

"Damnedest dogfight in the history of aviation," Rex muttered.

"Thanks . . . Whitey," Whip called over.

"Don't mention it," Rex yelled back. "But we're not going to be able to pull that little trick again. I'm fresh out of landing gear."

But evidently their pursuers now had second thoughts. When they looked over their shoulders it was to see the three remaining pedaling violently in attempt to regain altitude and obviously with intent to return to the field from which they had all taken off so short a time before. If they made it, undoubtedly they'd be able to summon a helio-jet with their transceivers to take them off the mountain top.

"I'll be damned," Rex called. "We won. I feel like von Richtofen."

"We'll see if we won when you try to bring that wreck in," Whip called back, apprehension in his voice.

Rex called, "You have any idea where we can set these things down? With these stubby wings, we're going to have to have quite a runway."

"Yeah," Whip called back. "The vehicle pool where I got the helio-jet. It's on the outskirts of New Frisco."

They came in fast, faster than was safe, but there was nothing to do about that. The thing was, they weren't going to have the opportunity to make a second pass if the first one came a cropper. They no longer had power. Pump as they might, manpower was no longer sufficient to give flying speed, you had to dive.

At the very last moment, only feet off the runway,

Rex desperately slipped right, slipped left, right, left, to kill his speed. Whip looked over at him anxiously.

And crash, the ground came up with a bang.

Rex sat there for a long moment in the wreckage, leaning on his bar, his eyes closed.

Whip, whose own craft was still in one piece, came over. "You all right, Rex?" he said.

"I don't know."

"Well, let's get the hell out of here before somebody comes and starts asking questions. Zen only knows what kind of answers we could come up with. I doubt if one of these damn things has ever been landed at normal gravity before."

They were at the far end of the small airport's runway. Only a few yards of it remained. They'd taken the full length to set down. Hadn't they lost flying speed when they did, they would have crashed into the trees of the park that ended the runway.

They hurried for the shelter of the park and disappeared into it just as they heard the siren of the small airport's meat wagon.

Both chuckled simultaneously.

Whip Ford said, "They're going to be surprised boys when they find that wreckage and nobody around. What do we do now?"

"We liberate a couple of bicycles and check something out," Rex told him.

"Something about the professor?"

"That's right."

There was one of the everpresent bike racks in the center of the park. They chose two and started into town proper. It was fully night now and there were comparatively few pedestrians and fellow cyclists on the streets.

Rex said, just to be saying something, "After a few days here in Grissom, do you still want to live in an Island for the rest of your life?"

"Hell, yes," Whip told him. "I'd read up on it as much as I could, but it's even better than I thought. This is for me. Earth's become just one big slum, a garbage dump. Even the so-called affluent countries."

Rex sighed. "Me too," he said. "But it's evidently no go."

The other looked over at him. "Why not?"

"I don't meet the qualifications."

They rode to the Maglev Station, which Susie had taken Rex to before, and repeated his first trip. Side-by-side they racked their bikes and descended the stairs to the station. Rex asked one of the Lagrangists there how they went about locating an express to the dispatch terminal at the other end of the cylinder and was politely told.

When the streamlined underground vehicle came up before them they entered and settled into seats. Evidently, Whip Ford had ridden in one previously and it held no surprises for him.

Again, at their destination, they were in free fall and pulled themselves along the rails that led to the compartment from which the space craft utilized for inter-Island transport were actually launched. Whip hadn't been here before, but he held his peace, after looking questioningly at his companion.

One of the crew came jetting over, utilizing his Buck Rogers, and grinned a welcome at them.

After a three-way exchange of names and handshakes, Rex said, "Lon Karloff isn't around, is he?"

" 'Fraid not. Lon's on an earlier shift. Anything I can do for you?"

"Well, I suppose so," Rex told him. "Look, my friend and I are tourists and a lot of this, obviously, is new to us. We got into an argument, kind of a silly one. But we'd like to be straightened out."

"Fire away," the Lagrangist said.

"Well, Lon was telling me how the whole terminal here works. For instance, suppose you're dispatching one of those four-seaters to another Island. Wizard. The passenger gets in, the crew chief goes over to the control room for the exact moment to fire, or whatever you call it, and the rest of the crew makes themselves scarce to get out of the way."

"That's about it."

"What I wanted to know is, would it be possible

for that passenger to leave the four-seater, in between the time he got into it, and the time the crew chief fires, without anybody seeing him?"

The other looked at him strangely. "Why?"

"Just for the sake of argument."

"I suppose he could."

"Without the crew chief, or anybody else, seeing him leave?"

"As a matter of fact, they couldn't see him even if they wanted to. He wouldn't be in sight range. But it's kind of silly . . ."

"Wizard," Rex said. "Thanks a lot, chum-pal."

The other made a gesture with his two hands. "Nothing at all."

Rex and Whip retraced their way, pulling themselves along the zero-gravity rails.

Whip looked over at him. "Find out what you want?"

"I think so."

In silence, they waited for another express returning to New Frisco. In the largest city of Grissom they again got bikes and Rex led the way.

Whip said, as they pedaled. "What now?"

"You'll see."

They arrived at the professor's apartment building, dismounted, racked their bikes, and headed up the stairs.

Rex didn't bother to knock, in view of the fact that he was living here, but opened the door and preceded Whip Ford into the living room.

Susie, even more wan than earlier, looked up from the desk and said, "Rex! Where in the world have you been? What's happened to your clothes? Hello, Mr. Ford. I'm afraid I still have nothing for you."

Rex said, "Susie, where is the professor?"

TWENTY-TWO

She frowned at him. "What are you talking about, Rex?"

Rex Bader waved Whip Ford to a chair and took one himself. He said, "You hired a detective. All right, then you've got to expect me to detect. I finally came up with two clues. One, this morning when you were so definite about the professor not being able to solve this cafard problem even if he was here. There's only one reason for you saying what you did. You *knew* Casey was working on it, and was being unsuccessful. Which means that you were in touch with him."

She looked thoughtful. "You misunderstood me," she said.

He shook his head in rejection. "The other things came to me when I mentioned the possibility of his being kidnapped either at the dispatch terminal here at Island Three, or the one at Island One. You didn't seem to think that likely either but later it came to me that possibly he could kidnap *himself* here at Island Three's dispatch terminal. So I went out there again and asked and was told that it was quite possible for him to have left the four-seater, before it was dispatched, and quite unseen. So, I ask again, Susie, where is the professor?"

She sighed and said, "He's right here. To be exact, in the other apartment on this floor. The usual occupant is on a lengthy vacation, down Earth-side, so it was quite easy for Professor Casey to just move in."

She looked over at Whip Ford but shrugged and came to her feet. She went to one of the walls of the living room and knocked on it with her knuckles, three knocks, a pause, then three more. Then she went over to the bar.

"Drink, anybody?" she said.

"Holy Zen, yes," Rex said. "Whip and I have just been saving each other's lives. It's thirsty work. Make it strong."

Whip said, "Anything will do. Like Rex said, make it strong."

She was still mixing when the professor entered.

He began to say, somewhat excitedly, "Susie, I think I've got . . ." but then his eyes took in the other two, and his brows went up.

In his mid-fifties, Professor George Casey was a bit more heavyset than when Rex had seen him last. However, he was still a trim, conservatively dapper man, still affected his modified shag haircut. And he still radiated his boyish enthusiasm.

"Why, hello, Rex," he said. "What spins?"

Rex stood and came over to shake. "Hello, Professor," he said. "Damned if I know. I can't figure it all out." He turned and introduced Whip Ford.

Whip had also stood and now he too shook hands.

Casey said to him, "Susie told me about you and what you had in mind. Sorry I couldn't see you sooner, there are various irons in the fire."

Whip nodded and said, "Obviously. But I'd like to talk it over with you as soon as it's practical."

"Of course."

Susie said, "Scotch, Professor?"

"Fine."

When all had drinks and were reseated, Susie said, "I told you I thought Rex was having second thoughts. He figured out how you pretended to take the four-seater to Island One but then left it before it was dispatched. He didn't know where you were in hiding, but assumed that I was in on the secret."

Rex said, unhappy with them both, "Why'd you send for me, if you didn't want to be found?"

The professor accepted the reasonableness of that question. "The Council wasn't in on the disappearance. They were keen for a search. Susie and I decided to suggest you. From past experience, we trusted you and felt that we could convince you to maintain the secret if, by any chance, you did locate me."

"Wizard," Rex said, taking a lengthy pull at his glass. "So what's the secret? Why did you go into hiding?"

"For a couple of reasons, one of which was probably a mistake. Things are coming to a crisis point. The Reunited Nations, down Earth-side, have been demanding I return to face various charges, among them in regard to the brain drain that is resulting increasingly in the best minds of Earth, from all countries, applying to become Lagrangists. They've also undoubtedly heard rumors that Lagrangia is considering severing its connections with the Reunited Nations and declaring independence, which is true, though personally I am not as yet in favor of the move. At any rate, I wanted to avoid testifying."

"What else?" Rex said, taking another pull at the drink.

"As you've undoubtedly already discovered, Walt Hanse's Radical wing of the Sons of Liberty is in favor of immediate independence. I'm not, as I've said, but I was of the opinion that if I wasn't present they would make no steps in that direction. I was evidently vain enough to think that neither Hanse nor his associates would do anything precipitate if I wasn't on the scene."

"You were mistaken, all right," Rex said. "Walt Hanse and his executive committee wanted to hire me *not* to find you. They've decided to pull off their coup without you and didn't want you to be in the way."

"So Susie tells me. I suspect that the only thing that's holding them back is this space cafard epidemic. Things are confused enough as it is."

The professor turned from Rex to his Research Aide and enthusiasm came back into his voice. He said, "Susie, I think I've got it. The reason for the space cafard explosion."

Her eyes widened. "You have!"

"Yes, I think so. In an attempt to track it down, I went into the International Data Banks and looked up everything on hand involving claustrophobia. It's not the only factor pertaining to space cafard, of course, but it's the most important and it seemed to me the least likely to be contracted in an Island as large as Island Three. To my surprise I found a recent scientific paper by a Doctor Gerhard Johannisberger, telling of his extraction of the active ingredient which induced claustrophobia in a now banned drug called Cold-No-More. According to Johannisberger's report, an incredibly minute dosage of his extract will induce claustrophobia in just about anyone not absolutely immune to the mental illness."

The other three were bug-eyeing him.

Whip said, "But who'd want to do anything like that? I've been hearing about this space cafard. There's a lot of people in Grissom coming down with it."

Susie said, "Never fear. Rex and I have been talking about that. There are plenty who'd do it if they had the chance. Religious crackpots, reactionary politicians, Arab sheiks, some manufacturers . . ."

"Wait a minute," Rex said. "Arabs. Now I remember where I saw that guy on the street who picked my pocket and swiped my transceiver."

The professor frowned and said, "What in the world are you talking about, Rex?"

"It's a long story," Rex told him. "But my transceiver was stolen so I wouldn't be able to call for help when four characters tried to gun me down, up in the hills where I'd taken a walk. The one who picked my pocket was one of Administrator Abou Zaki's bodyguards. Didn't somebody say he had four bodyguards? Well, four men jumped me. If it hadn't been for Whip, here, I never would have gotten off the top of that mountain peak."

Whip said, "Now that you mention it, Rex, I got a pretty good look at one of them when we were fluttering around in those pedal-planes. He could have been an Arab."

"Pedal-planes?" Susie said blankly.

"It's a long story," Rex said again. "At any rate, doesn't the Administrator come from the Arab Union?"

"Why, yes," Casey said.

"And the Arab countries are feeling the squeeze from your cheap solar energy?"

There didn't seem to be any reason to answer that.

Susie said, "But surely the Administrator wouldn't order his men to eliminate you, Rex."

"He's a sneaky-looking type and John Mickoff told him I was here looking for Professor Casey. He pretended, at least, to want to cooperate but it occurs to me that if he's pulling a fast one with this space cafard he wouldn't want the professor found. With the professor's reputation as an authority on space, he might just come up with some solution to the control of cafard. Which, of course, he has." Rex turned back to George Casey. "How could the stuff be administered?"

The other frowned. "I don't know. Possibly through our food, if the poisoner had access to our automated kitchens. But even though he did, it would take a considerable amount of the drug to be effective on the over half-a-million Lagrangists in Island Three. Only a minute amount is needed, true, but when you consider half-a-million persons . . ."

Susie said slowly, "It might be possible to smuggle in a small amount, though even that would be difficult. Remember how careful they are, first at the Los Alamos spaceport Earth-side, to search every last item that goes into space, and to sterilize it all? And then, the second search and sterilization of all your things at the Goddard space station where you transfer from Earth orbit to a passenger ship to bring you to Lagrange Five. And then the final search when you dock at one of the Islands. I'm of the opinion that you couldn't smuggle an aspirin tablet in without it being detected, not to speak of enough of a drug to poison half-a-million people. So far, we've been able to keep out even undesirable bacteria."

Rex said definitely, "Nevertheless, space cafard is

being induced in some manner in Island Three. It must be deliberate, since it hasn't shown up in the other Islands. I say, let's go over to the Administration building and confront our boy. He lives there, doesn't he?"

The professor nodded. "All of the Reunited Nations staff have their quarters there. But it would mean my coming out of hiding."

"You'll be doing that, anyway," Rex said. "This crisis is getting too big for you not to be openly participating."

Susie said, "He has four armed bodyguards."

"Three," Whip said. "One came to a bad end."

Rex said, "We'll have to face that problem when it comes. Are you with us, Whip? We could use the manpower.

Whip Ford stood. "I'm with you. I came to ask a favor, so I can hardly not return one. Let's go."

The others began to rise.

A voice from the door said, "None of you are going anywhere—except where I take you. Professor Casey, you're under arrest."

All heads turned.

John Mickoff stood there in the doorway, a sardonic smirk on his square features.

George Casey had met the IABI official years ago. He said, "Here in Island Three, I don't come under your jurisdiction, Mr. Mickoff."

"I'm afraid you do, Professor," the other said. "I've received a special authorization from the Reunited Nations to return you to Earth, no matter what steps might have to be taken. You've got a lot to answer for, Mr. Father of the Lagrange Five Project."

Rex said, in disgust, "How'd you find him?"

Mickoff grinned at the other. "I didn't, younger brother. You evidently did. I was staked out across the street, not being able to think of what else to do and just keeping my eyes on things in general. When I saw you enter the building, I thought about it for awhile and decided I might as well check you out, find out what you'd hit upon, if anything. So I came after you, and, surprise, surprise, who do we find? Professor George R. Casey."

"Where the hell're the rest of your goons?"

"I sent each of them to one of the other three Islands, to see if they could find any trace of the professor. But we don't need them. The Reunited Nations staff has assigned me a special spacecraft with which to return our boy, here, Earth-side to face the music. It's going to be quite a tune. We leave immediately. You'll go as well, Doctor Hawkins. I'm not even going to give you time to pack a bag. There are four of you, only one of me. And I'm taking no chances. Not that I think you've got enough on the ball to cause me any trouble."

"Why, you bastard," Rex rapped out, starting for the other.

John Mickoff flicked a Gyro-jet from under his jacket. He said, softly, "That'll be all, younger brother. My orders are to play as rough as I have to. Hand over that peashooter of a gun you've got. And move awfully slowly as you bring it to me."

Rex Bader's shoulders slumped. He had no doubt whatsoever that the other would act. John Mickoff had made it very clear that he was all-out to thwart the Lagrange Five Project. Rex took the twenty-two from his belt and handed it over.

Mickoff grinned again and tucked the target pistol into his side pocket. He said, "Let's go, Professor, Doctor Hawkins. Our spacecraft awaits us."

Shaking his head in rejection but hopeless to resist, the professor headed for the door.

Rex said, "I'm coming too, Mickoff. I don't want to run any chances that you're gung-ho enough to shoot him while he's, ah, trying to escape."

"Balls," Mickoff grunted. "But come along, if you want. As far as the spaceship, at least."

"Me too," Whip said. "I don't like the way this thing looks."

They headed down the steps, Mickoff, gun in hand, bringing up the rear.

On the sidewalk, before the apartment building, the IABI man said, "My car's parked down the street a-ways."

He looked up into the sky where the lights from the other valleys of Grissom could be seen and involuntarily shivered. He said, "It grows on you. This is the goddamnedest place to live anybody's ever devised. I'd go around the bend if I had to stay here."

Rex shot a look at the other. And then it suddenly came to him.

He too pretended to look upward and alarm came into his expression.

"Mickoff!" he yelled. "You were right! It's closing in. Can't you feel it! You're right. It's collapsing. It's not natural for us to be in here, in this environment. We've got to get back to Earth!"

The IABI mans' face was going slack. "No," he whispered. "No, no."

"Nonsense," the professor blurted. He, Susie and Whip were staring at Rex as though he'd gone out of his mind.

Rex shouted, still in extreme alarm, "The shell is caving in. You were right. It's collapsing."

Mickoff's eyes had taken on a blank quality. His body was sagging. The gun dropped from his hand to the sidewalk. He staggered, muttering something the others didn't get.

The professor snapped at Rex, "You complete fool! It's space cafard. He must have immediate sedation, and we have none!"

Rex moved forward, toward the IABI man. He said, "Here's his sedation," and he slugged Mickoff brutally on the jaw, catching him as he fell forward.

"Holy smog," Whip Ford got out.

"Take his feet, Whip," Rex said. "We've got to get him up to the car." He scooped up Mickoff's Gyro-jet and stuck it into his belt.

Susie and the professor, both aghast, followed after as Rex and Whip carried the unconscious IABI man toward the four-place electro-hover.

TWENTY-THREE

Rex and Whip manhandled the unconscious Mickoff into the back of the small vehicle and then Rex climbed in beside him. Whip squeezed in too, though it was a tight fit. Susie got behind the wheel and the professor took his place beside her.

"The hospital!" Casey said unnecessarily.

Vehicles in Grissom evidently had no horns. As Susie drove desperately at full speed, the professor took out his white handkerchief and held it out the window on high and waved it vigorously as a warning signal to other traffic.

They swooped up to the hospital entry and Susie and George Casey got out hurriedly. Whip squeezed out and turned to help Rex with the police official.

They didn't take the time to summon stretcher bearers. Susie led the way, calling, "Gangway, gangway! Cafard victim. Shield your eyes. Gangway!"

They made their way through the lobby and up the stairs to the offices of Doctor Garmisch.

"I hope the doctor's still here," Casey said anxiously. "He's the best man on space cafard in Lagrangia."

"He's here," Susie told him. "He hasn't left the hospital for days. Sleeps on a cot."

Susie was correct, Garmisch was in his office and so was Nurse Edith Gribbin. Both were red-eyed with exhaustion, and both came to their feet wearily. They seemed to have no doubt about diagnosis.

Rex and Whip dumped the unconscious man onto the operating table.

The professor took over. "He's not had any sedation, Poul. Mr. Bader knocked him unconscious when the cafard hit. Now this is it, Doctor. This man must be returned immediately to Earth. He told me that the Reunited Nations staff has placed a spacecraft at his disposal. As honorary chairman of Grissom's Council, I commandeer it. I don't know the size of the craft, however, put him into it, along with as many other cafard victims as it will hold and have it blast off for Earth immediately."

Nurse Gribbin was already injecting Mickoff with something more orthodox in the way of sedation than Rex's sock on the jaw.

The doctor pressed a button on his desk, summoning help.

He looked at Professor Casey, and said, "Glad to see you, George. I've been busy but I heard somewhere that you'd mysteriously disappeared."

"I've reappeared now," the professor told him. "We've got to go, Doctor. I'll call you later to see if this works out. By the way, I think I've found the cause of the claustrophobia."

"You have! Holy Zen, George, what is it?"

"A drug that causes it. Only a minute amount is needed. Somebody is administering it, in some manner, to we Lagrangists."

The doctor looked at him blankly. "Administering it? You mean putting it into the water system or something?"

"Holy smog," Whip ejaculated.

Rex, Susie and the professor stared at each other.

"That's it," Rex said. "Who's got access to the drinking water system?"

"Among others, the Administrator," Casey said grimly. "Let's get going."

While in the car, Rex had fished his pistol out of John Mickoff's side pocket. When they got out into the hall, he handed it over to Whip. He said, "Do you know how to handle this? I'll keep the Gyro-jet."

Whip took the gun, flicked the magazine from the butt, checked it, returned it to its place and jacked a cartridge into the firing chamber and flicked on the safety. "I told you I was a coach," he said. "Among other things, I coached the small arms team. Do you have any more ammo for this?"

"No," Rex said.

They hurried down the stairs and out onto the street and got back into Mickoff's car. Susie took the wheel again.

Rex said, "What's the deal with water in Grissom?"

"It was one of the big problems," the professor told him, over his shoulder. "When we first started, we had ample oxygen, it's a by-product of our processing oxide ores which we lob up from the Luna base with the mass driver. But, for all practical purposes, the moon has no hydrogen, so we had to bring it up from Earth-side, in liquid form, of course. For every ton of hydrogen brought up we could make nine tons of water. But that was in the old days. Now that we're mining the asteroids, we can bring our hydrogen from there and are no longer dependent on Earth."

Rex said impatiently, "I mean, how is it distributed here in the Island?"

"Oh. Well, obviously, it's a very important division of the project in all the Islands. When they are being built, the pipes are laid underground. There's one big pumping station. In this case, Grissom, it's underground, near the town of Hanford. In fact, the whole town is devoted to it. The water is pumped out, not only to every building, including homes, but also to pseudo-springs and brooklets, in the hills and elsewhere. The springs and brooklets feed larger streams which in turn flow into small rivers and eventually into our lakes. For instance, Lake New Bomoseen is the largest lake in Grissom. Obviously, in an Island it has no outlet so from the lake it is pumped back to Hanford, repurified and then sent on its way again. There are other features of the Hanford station, of course, such as humidifying the air, and also extracting the water from waste and recycling it."

Whip said, "You really go in for this recyling bit, don't you?"

"Why yes. An Island is a vivarium. And everything is recycled. Everything. For instance, we never cremate our dead. We bury them out in the fields, without a marker. In this manner, the bodies are 'recycled' by enriching the soil. We don't have graveyards since, aside from taking up valuable space, they're a leftover from superstition. You know, until Mao's communists took over, a sizeable percentage of China's land was devoted to graveyards, going back for centuries, even millennia. The communists plowed them under."

Rex said, impatiently again, "You mentioned that the Administrator has access to the water system. Why and how?"

"In actuality," Casey said, "Abou Zaki is little more than a figurehead, but he has one value. He keeps off our necks the visiting firemen from Earth-side. Hardly a week goes by but that some delegation or other comes up. When you realize that there's some 150 countries in the Reunited Nations, each with politicians not adverse to free vacations, you can imagine how we're deluged. Very well, the Administrator, in all his glory as titular head of the Lagrange Five Project, greets them. According to their importance, he banquets them, wines them, possibly gets them laid by some of his Reunited Nations staff, if you'll pardon the term, Susie."

"Ha," Susie said. "By the looks of them some of that staff was sent up for no other reason."

Casey went on. "But, above all, he gives them the guided tour. Takes them to see the fleshpots of New Frisco. Takes them to see the hydroponic tanks. Takes them to the zero-gravity areas up near the axis."

"Gives them a ride in the pedal-planes?" Whip murmured.

"Why, yes, of course, if they're up to it. At any rate, one of the most popular sights is the water works of Hanford. I imagine that Abou Zaki must have to go through the routine of seeing them at least once a week, sometimes more."

"And he'd have the chance to drop something into the drinking water being distributed?" Rex said grimly.

"He'd have many opportunities. So would any members of his staff accompanying him on the tour."

"That's all I wanted to know," Rex said. "But I doubt if he leaves it to anyone else. One man can keep a secret. If you have two, it becomes twice as hard and from there on it's a geometric progression. If he can do it all alone, and there's no reason why he can't, he wouldn't have anybody else in on it. He could easily hide the stuff in those robes of his. The rest of the operation takes place on Earth, where the extraction of the drug has to be made, in complete secrecy, and somehow gotten up here and delivered to the Administrator."

"Makes sense," Whip said.

Susie pulled up before the Administration Building. It was getting late and most of the ediface was dark, but there were quite a few lights on the second floor.

"Living quarters for the Reunited Nations staff," Susie explained.

As they got out of the car, Whip said, "Is there any plan of action?"

"No," the professor said unhappily. "Actually, we have no proof of our suspicions. Abou Zaki might be completely innocent."

"Play it by ear," Rex said. "But he's not innocent. It all adds up too well."

They headed up the stairs of the building and into the lobby. At this time of night, there were only three or four late workers there. Two of them looked surprised at seeing the professor, but the small party was passed and heading up the stairway to the second floor before they could say anything.

Susie said, "The Administrator's office is part of his apartment."

They headed for it.

There was one guard posted at the door, leaning against the wall indolently. He stood straight when he saw the four approaching, and his eyes narrowed at the sight of Rex Bader. He also tried to hide his surprise at seeing George Casey.

The professor said, "I wish to see the Administrator. It is of utmost importance."

The other hesitated only momentarily. He knew perfectly well who Professor Casey was and it wasn't up to him.

He said, "Just a moment, sir. I'll inform him."

He opened the door, went through it, closed it behind him. They waited a full ten minutes before he issued forth again.

Susie had muttered, "He's probably in his harem, at this time of night."

But the guard returned and said to Casey, "His Excellency will receive you, Professor."

"Wizard," Rex muttered. "You're damn right he will."

He half-expected the guard to try and search him and Whip, in which case it would have been necessary to take him, but the man merely held the door open for them and they filed through.

Abou Zaki was seated behind the desk, dressed as always in full Arab garb. At their entry he stood and smiled unctuously.

"Professor!" he gushed, flashing his brilliant teeth, their whiteness emphasized by his black beard and dark complexion. "How pleasant to have you back. All were worried." He looked at Rex Bader as though in congratulation. "Help was even summoned from Earthside to seek you."

"So I understand," the professor said crisply. "Shall we get to pressing matters?"

He and Susie took chairs before the desk but Rex and Whip stayed in the background, leaning against the wall near the door, as though they were junior members of the firm and not to be bothering their betters.

"Pressing matters?" the Arab said in oily surprise.

Casey said, "The fact that a dangerous drug which causes claustrophobia is being administered into the drinking water of Grissom."

The Arab registered surprised disbelief. "Surely you jest!"

The professor was grim now. "Hardly," he said. "Hundreds have already been affected. Thus far, it has been possible to contain the epidemic, through the heroic efforts of Doctor Garmisch and his staff, but it is accelerating." He turned to Susie, "Doctor, call Communications on your transceiver and put out an emergency warning to all Lagrangists in Island Three not to drink water."

From her shoulder bag, Susie brought forth the communications device, activated it and said crisply, "Communications. Let me speak to Doctor Karl Kessinger, soonest." There was an answer and she said impatiently, "Yes, I would assume that he has left his office by now, but this is crash priority. Get him!"

The Arab was bug-eyed. "See here, Professor," he got out. "As Administrator of the Lagrange Five Project, I can't allow this. There must be water to drink and with which to cook."

"Let them drink beer," Casey said grimly. "Or possibly wine would be safer still. Guzzle might get them drenched but it won't give them cafard."

"I shall protest this high-handed affair to the Reunited Nations."

"You'll have your opportunity to give your side of it."

Susie said, "Karl? This is Susie Hawkins. I'm with the professor in the office of the Administrator. Professor Casey has discovered the derivation of the space cafard. Poison causing claustrophobia has been introduced into our drinking water. The professor requests that you put out continuing emergency broadcasts informing every Lagrangist in Grissom not to drink water nor use it in any form."

She listened for a moment and then said, "Certainly, Karl." She handed the transceiver to George Casey, saying, "He wishes to double check it with you."

The professor took the instrument and said into it, "Karl, follow out Doctor Hawkins's request absolutely soonest. I doubt if we have more than hours at our disposal before Grissom explodes in madness."

Abou Zaki blanched.

Casey deactivated the transceiver and handed it back to Susie.

The administrator blurted, "Hours! I didn't know it had progressed that far. We must flee. There is a Reunited Nations spacecraft . . ."

"It has already been commandeered to transport space cafard patients Earth-side," the professor said. "The rest of us will wait it out. Without the drinking water, the only way it can spread is through contagion and Doctor Garmisch isolates each victim until transport is available to Earth."

The Arab breathed deeply for long moments. Finally, he got out, "What did you mean, I'd have my opportunity to give my side of it?"

The other said flatly, "I doubt very much that any Lagrangist would subject himself to the possibility of contracting space cafard. That leaves only tourists, who wouldn't have the opportunity to plant the poison . . . or members of the Reunited Nations staff, and very few of them go into the Hanford water system buildings. The few that do go usually do so in your company when you guide VIPs about the Island."

"Professor George Casey! Are you suggesting that I know anything whatsoever about this scandalous matter? I warn you, sir! I am the duly appointed head of this Reunited Nations project!"

The professor was on thin ice now, and knew it. He had no proof whatsoever.

But it was then that Rex Bader spotted something. He crossed over to a steel file, set against the wall, and, frowning, picked up a sealed cardboard box, one of two which sat there. They seemed out of place in the office of the highest executive in Island Three.

He read the label, which was in both French and Arabic. At least he read the French part of it, moving his lips slightly in recalling his college studies of the language.

"Cous-cous," he said aloud. "What in the hell's couscous?"

To the surprise of the others, the Administrator hurriedly answered him, though, on the face of it, Rex

Bader was being on the boorish side, in prowling the office.

"It's a cereal food," Abou Zaki said. "The national dish of my country and of most Arab lands. It is the equivalent to the rice of China and Japan, the pasta of Italy, the potatoes of Northern Europe and America. It is our staff of life and since it is not available here in Grissom, I bring it up with me from Earth-side when I make trips below."

Rex intuitively smelled a rat. And the rat was Abou Zaki. What in the hell would a box of cereal food be doing in a swank office? Why wasn't it back in the apartment's kitchen? He pried the cardboard lid off and stared down.

"It looks like rice," he admitted.

"It's based on semolina wheat," the Arab said testily. However, there was a strange element in his voice.

Rex, carrying the box of cous-cous, came over to the desk, took up the water carafe there and poured half a glass of water. While the other four stared at him, he took a pinch of the alleged cous-cous and dropped it into the glass.

He proffered the mixture to the Administrator, saying, "If it's only cereal, then certainly you won't hesitate to take a sip. Though it looks to me as though it's already dissolving. That doesn't seem likely with a cereal."

Abou Zaki was less than either brave or a collected man, particularly when under pressure. Dark as his face was, he blanched as he cowered back in his seat.

"No," he said hoarsely.

Rex turned and handed the box to the Professor Casey. "Your proof," he said simply.

"Wild, man," Whip Ford chuckled.

But the Arab must have touched a button with his foot. The door sprang open and three of his bodyguards came charging through, the first one, gun in hand, the other two clawing their weapons from their holsters.

Rex, caught by surprise, snatched for his own gun, the Gyro-jet confiscated from John Mickoff.

But there was an overly loud crack of a shot and the pistol of the lead guard went flying from his hand. He grabbed his fingers from which blood was spurting.

"Naughty, naughty," Whip said, menacing the other two with his .22 target pistol.

They came to a quick halt and held their hands away from their holsters. Rex covered them as well, stepped closer and relieved them of their weapons.

He looked over at Whip Ford, "Holy Jumping Zen," he complained. "Who the hell do you think you are, Wyatt Earp?"

Whip said modestly, "I didn't mention the fact that I was university champion in the pistol team."

"Up against the wall," Rex said to the three guards. "Face first."

Professor Casey, as soon as he had recovered from his shocked surprise at the action, looked at the shaken Abou Zaki.

He said, "After this, it's obvious that you cannot remain in Grissom. I don't know whether or not you've had assistance in your attempted sabotage of Lagrangia. However, you and your staff will pack your possessions immediately. You will be confined to this building until returned to Earth as soon as transport is possible. There, of course, we will prepare criminal charges against you."

Abou Zaki was too far gone even to answer.

Rex Bader stepped closer to one of the three bodyguards, recognizing him. "Hand over my transceiver, you cheap crook," he growled.

The Arab eyed him apprehensively. "I don't know what you're talking about," he got out.

"My transceiver, you sonofabitch," Rex said. "Or should I say, you son of a sacred camel, or some such. At any rate, hand it over or I'll break that beak nose of yours with this pistol barrel."

The other, glaring hatred, reached into his side pocket and brought forth the communications device in question.

TWENTY-FOUR

The four of them left the Administrator's office, Rex and Whip still with guns in hand, the latter now with a Gyro-jet confiscated from the bodyguards. They didn't expect more trouble, but you never knew. The professor carried the two boxes of the drug, as though they were treasures. This was the ultimate evidence.

Rex said, shaking his head, "Imagine the stupid bastard having the stuff right there in open view. He must have been planning to give the water another dose tomorrow and had it ready. In the confusion of us busting in and confronting him, he failed to hide it."

Susie said, "It was a clever way of smuggling it into Grissom. As Administrator, they wouldn't have searched his things overly much, and the fact that it actually looked like cous-cous must have confused the searchers. There is such a thing as cous-cous, of course. I ate some of it in an Algerian restaurant in Paris once. It was terrible stuff."

Professor Casey said, "Let's go up to the Council conference hall."

Susie looked at him in surprise. "Why?"

"The night's not over yet," he told her. "In fact, it has hardly begun."

The four of them made their way up the remaining four stories to the Council's conference room on the Sixth Floor. Once there, Professor Casey slumped into the chairman's heavy seat and took a deep breath.

He said, "You all might as well make yourselves

comfortable. We'll probably be here for awhile." He looked at Susie Hawkins. "My dear, will you get in touch with all members of the Council and request that they come here immediately for an emergency meeting?"

She looked at him questioningly but he said nothing more, so she reached into her bag for her transceiver. She took it to the other end of the table and began talking into it in her usual clipped voice.

Casey said to Rex and Whip, who had taken chairs flanking him, "It'll take time for them to assemble." He sent his eyes to the Black. "You might as well give me your story. Perhaps I'll be able to state my opinion to them tonight. They should be in a receptive mood. Everything seems to be going well, at least potentially, for a change."

Whip cleared his throat and said, "I imagine Doctor Hawkins has given you the general idea. Our Promised Land Society wishes to build an Island of its own to colonize, probably in the asteroids."

"So I understand. And you're all Blacks?"

"That's correct. Our society has come to the conclusion that the final solution to the Negro problem is for us to start a world of our own, free from discrimination." His voice held some of the old sour quality that Rex Bader had come in contact with the first few times he had met the other.

The professor said, unhappily, "My own hope, so far as racial problems are concerned, has been that the races would slowly blend until we were all one. The process has long been underway and of recent decades, with developing transportation and shifts of population, has been accelerating, particularly here in space where no one cares what your race is. For instance, how many Blacks do you know in the States who are one hundred percent Africans? Very few. Most so-called Blacks are probably as much as fifty percent white, American Indian, Mexican, Puerto Rican, or whatever. You, yourself, Mr. Ford, I would take for at least fifty percent Caucasian."

"But I'm still a Black by the laws of the state in

which I was born. Do you realized that in some of the states where such laws are still on the books the definition of a Black is a person who has any percentage of Negro blood whatsoever?"

Rex laughed. "I'm afraid that would take in just about every white in America as well."

Whip said, not sure how to take that, "How do you mean?"

"Consider it," Rex said. "The Romans drew no color line whatsoever. Actually, some of their later emperors were African. For two thousand years they bred with Blacks without a second thought. So did the Carthaginians before them. The Romans took over by far the greater part of Europe as well as the Mediterranean shore. They were in England for centuries and, of course, where man goes he breeds, leaving his genes behind, be they white, black or yellow. Following the Romans, the Arabs took over much of their former empire, including parts of Southern France and all of Spain and Portugal, not to mention all of the Balkans to as far as Vienna, and such islands as Sicily and Crete. The Moslems to this day draw no color line." Rex laughed again. "Consider it, gentlemen, in view of the fact that the Europeans have been breeding with Blacks or partial Blacks for thousands of years, what chance is there that any of us doesn't have *some* Negro blood?"

"The point's well taken," Casey said. But he looked back to Whip and there was still an unhappy quality there. He said, "Mr. Ford, frankly there has been one aspect of space colonization that many Earth-side people have not known about. You see, we Lagrangists have not in mind *colonizing* space from Earth. We wish to *seed* space from Earth, using only the best seed. We wish to leave, to the extent possible, our genetic failures behind us."

Whip Ford returned to his old coldness. He said, "And we Blacks are genetic failures?"

Casey shook his head, quite emphatically. "That I didn't say. There are many Blacks in Lagrangia, Mr. Ford. I understand that you have met Washington

Carver Smith, for instance. One of our most valued colonists."

He thought for a moment before going on. Then, "You see, on Earth the human race is probably actually deteriorating. Cro-Magnon man probably averaged a higher intelligence than we boast today. Do not, obviously, confuse accumulated knowledge with intelligence. We have more accumulated knowledge than did our cave-dwelling ancestors, though Cro-Magnon had a larger brain pan. But in those days Nature winnowed out the unfit, the less intelligent, the less strong and healthy. Only the best elements of a Cro-Magnon clan survived. But as man continued he began to succor his weak and mentally unfit, though the Greeks and Romans, among others, exposed their children who weren't up to standards. For a time, famines, earthquakes, floods, plagues, and other disasters kept a curb on the unfit. They were the first to starve in a famine; their jerry-built homes were the first to collapse in an earthquake; they were the first to contract the plagues, since they were weak with malnutrition and since they had no means to flee the cities and retire to the more healthy hills."

Both Rex and Whip were giving him their utmost attention.

He said, "But with the coming of the modern age, steps were taken to combat famines, plagues, earthquakes, and all the rest. Millions of the unfit were preserved with our improving medicine, and our charities, to continue breeding and perpetuating their genes. In space, Mr. Ford, we have wished to continue man's progress, not to slip backward."

Whip cleared his throat again. "What's that got to do with our Promised Land—the name of the Island we want to build?"

The professor looked at him levelly. "What are the requirements of your colonists, besides that they be Blacks?"

"Roughly, the same as yours."

That set Casey back. "You mean . . . ?" he let the question dribble away.

Whip Ford was scornful. "Of course. We're not stupid. The Promised Land Society is composed of successful, progressive, highly-trained individuals. We may be race conscious, but we're not stupid. We realize that nine blacks out of ten aren't suitable for the Promised Land, they've been ground down too long. A Hottentot in South Africa may be black but he's not material for space. We decided to make the same requirements as you Lagrangists do. An I.Q. of at least 130, near physical perfection, and all the rest of it."

"I'll be damned," Casey said, leaning back in his chair in surprise.

Whip said, "Well, what kind of a report will you make to this Council of yours?"

"An upbeat one, obviously. I have one suggestion to make, Mr. Ford."

"Call me Whip. What is it? We of the Society could only think highly of your suggestions, Professor."

"I suggest that learning Interlingua become one of your requirements. Once you are in full operation, we will all wish to cooperate in trade, mutual safety in our development of space, that sort of thing. Surely in space we will be able to leave many of the sins of Earth behind."

"I'll take it up with the society. We're a democratic organization."

Susie looked up from her transceiver and called, "Professor?"

Casey got up and went down to her.

Rex looked at Whip Ford. "Congratulations," he said, smiling. "You made it."

Whip looked at him for a long moment. "It looks that way," he said. "Listen, Rex. Why don't you come in with us?"

"How do you mean?"

"Join the Promised Land. I'll swing all the weight I've got to bulldoze it through. Like you said, somewhere in your remote ancestory there's probably some Black blood. Okay, we'll make you an honorary nigger, or something." He grinned ruefully at that last.

Rex shook his head. "Thanks, Whip," he said. "But it's no go. The Radicals already have offered to lower the requirements in my case if I'd go along with them. But you see what it means? If you lower your standards once, you'll do it again. And again. And pretty soon every incompetent earthworm Tom, Dick, and Harry will be streaming up here. And you'd soon have the old story—breeding dumb clucks, degrading the race."

Whip looked at him. "Man, you're not easy on yourself."

The door opened and the lumpy Doctor Karl Kessinger came hurrying in. "George!" he said exuberantly.

Professor Casey, who had been talking in a low voice to Susie, turned and smiled. "Hi, Karl," he said. "What spins?"

"It would seem everything," the Communications Councilor said. "Where in the name of Zen have you been?"

"The rest of the Council will be showing up," George Casey told him, responding to the other's hearty handshake. "I'll cover it all. Did you get those no-water-drinking announcements out?"

"A thousand times over. This solves all of our problems, George. I thought that we'd had it."

"Not quite, to both statements," Casey said, rubbing the back of his left hand over his lips.

Shirley Ann Kneedler, Walt Hanse, and Sal Sinatri entered together, hesitated for a moment, but didn't approach the professor. They took three chairs at the table, side-by-side.

Within the next few minutes, most of the Council had turned up, all except the three Radicals, to press around Casey, shaking hands, all talking at once, all demanding to know what had happened. The professor grinned through it all as best he could, but avoided their questions for the time.

The last few stragglers entered and all took places at the long table. There wasn't even a raised eyebrow when Professor George Casey took the chairman's position at the table's head. Rex and Susie flanked him, Whip sat next to Rex. Susie had notebook and stylo in hand, a data screen before her.

George Casey looked about the table, taking them in one at a time. Finally, he said, "It's getting late and we have a great deal of work to do. Following this meeting, with your approval, I propose to have Doctor Hawkins get in touch with our fellow Islands and call for an emergency convening of the Grand Council. We'll also have to begin formulating our manifesto."

"Manifesto?" Doctor Fredric Economou said.

The professor looked over to him. "Yes, our Declaration of Independence. My principle reason for, ah, disappearing was to avoid the necessity of testifying before the Reunited Nations Earth-side. But now that is meaningless. Frankly, I am of the opinion that it is somewhat premature but circumstances have given us such a favorable opportunity to cut all governmental ties with Earth that we can't ignore it. Such a weight of right is on our side at this time that few could honestly deny it."

"Hear, hear!" Walt Hanse called.

Doctor Hans Ober said, "How do you mean, George?"

Professor Casey took the two boxes of supposed cous-cous from his pockets and put them on the table. "We have overwhelming, uncontestable proof that Administrator Abou Zaki has been poisoning our water supply with a drug that causes claustrophobia. When we release this information, Earth-side, there will be few to demur when we demand independence."

"Can we swing it yet, George?" Franz Zeigler, of Research, said.

The professor nodded. "I believe so. We are at present earning more from our sales of solar power Earth-side than we are expending there. And the figure is increasing monthly as more SSPSs are turned out."

For a time, there was a buzzing about the table, and Casey remained standing, but held silence until it subsided.

When it did, he said, "There is another matter that I would like to see passed tonight and recommended to the Grand Council tomorrow. It pertains to Mr. Whip Ford, here." The professor indicated the Black seated next to Rex Bader. "Mr. Ford undoubtedly saved the day, at the risk of his own life, when we confronted Abou Zaki and the Administrator called in his armed bodyguards."

"What does he want?" Hanse said.

The professor summed up the Promised Land project and highly recommended that the Lagrange Five Islands fully cooperate with all their resources.

Hanse said, "What kind of control would we maintain over them after their Island was completed?"

"None whatsoever," the professor said. "Our relationship would be strictly fraternal."

"Then I'm against it," Hanse said definitely. "We Lagrangists should maintain control over the colonization of space. A strong control."

"Do I hear a motion?" Casey said.

Doctor Dorothy Weiss said, "I make a motion that the Lagrange Five Project support to its utmost the building of the Promised Land."

"Second," Kessinger said.

With the exception of the three members of the Radicals, the vote carried unanimously.

Whip Ford's voice was shaky when he said, "Thank you."

Professor Casey went on again. "There is one other matter. During my absence, the Executive Committee of the Radical wing of the Sons of Liberty made plans to subvert our institutions, to seize power from the Reunited Nations by force and violence, to plan subversive and even military action against Earth, and to declare themselves what amounts to a dictatorship."

"That's a lie," Hanse shouted indignantly.

"I'm afraid not," the professor said. "You told the whole story to Mr. Bader here and tried to entice him into your ranks by offering to make him not only a Lagrangist, for which he does not have the qualifications, but a member of this Council, to which he had not been elected, nor is it possible, under our institutions, for him to be so elected, since he is not employed in any of our functions."

"He lies," Hanse said defiantly. "And it's his word against ours." He indicated Shirley Ann Kneedler and Sal Sinatri. Sinatri, at least, had the grace to look embarrassed, but said nothing.

Whip Ford said softly, "I'm afraid that there's another witness. During your meeting with Bader, I was posted outside the window of your cottage. I'd been following Rex." He looked directly into Hanse's face. "So I back everything the professor has accused you of." He looked over at Rex and said, "By the way, that's when I started having second thoughts about you. You stood up to those cloddies pretty well, considering all they offered."

Casey looked at Hanse and his two confederates again and said, "Doctor Hanse, in your advocating a change from our democratic to a more autocratic form of managing Lagrangia, you contended that democracy was too slow, too confused, to act quickly in an emergency. A dictatorship, though you didn't use that term, is supposedly faster. Very well, we shall see. We have few set rules in this Council but one of them is that a two-thirds majority can expel any Councilor from the body. Another is that the Council, by two-thirds vote, can expel any Lagrangist from the Islands, returning them to Earth."

"Why you . . . !" The enraged Hanse blurted.

Doctor Karl Kessinger said calmly, "I make a motion that Councilors Hanse, Kneedler, and Sinatri be ejected from the Council and I make a further motion that they be expelled from Lagrangia and returned to Earth."

"Second both motions," Hans Ober said.

The vote was unanimous, save for the three.

Hanse was on his feet, trembling with rage. "I won't accept this. I'll take it to the Lagrangists as a whole. We'll fight!"

The professor said, "I shall go on the air tomorrow and give a complete report to Lagrangia and ask for a referrendum. After I have spoken, you will have your opportunity to state what case you have."

"Why, you're nothing but a goddamned ,dictator! This Council is nothing but a rubber stamp for you."

Casey said in negation, "Doctor Hanse, as honorary chairman of the Council I have a voice but not a vote. I cannot coerce anyone, even if I so wished. Now, will you please leave? Some of the other things to be said tonight are not for your ears."

"No! I refuse. I demand my rights!"

Rex said, "Hanse, old chum-pal, you once offered your services to me in case I needed someone to be socked. You said you were up on pugilism and wrestling. Wizard, what do you say we go out in the hall and go round and round a little?"

Hanse stared at him.

Whip said, "He's more my size, Rex. Maybe I'm not up on karate, as you proved, but I was college boxing champ."

Rex looked at him in exasperation and said, "What in the hell weren't you in sports? Glider pilot, small arms champion, now you're a boxer. How in the hell are you at bullfighting?"

The table, save for the three so-called Radicals, chuckled or even laughed aloud.

Hanse flushed angrily, turned, motioned to his followers, and headed for the door.

When they were gone, the professor turned back to the others, tiredness in his face. He said, after a deep sigh, "Hanse was right, you know. This is unhealthy, the position I hold in Lagrangia. As a result, I intend to abdicate my title, father of the Lagrange Five Project."

"Oh, no," Susie blurted.

He shook his head. "After tomorrow, as soon as I can arrange it, I plan to return to New Princeton University and resume my teaching duties. Lagrangia has come of age. You should lean on me as a crutch no longer. After tomorrow, you will be independent and must stand on your own legs."

"George!" Kessinger faltered.

There were other shocked murmurs of dissent.

He shook his head again. "Look what you have done this evening. No one spoke a word when I urged the manifesto declaring independence. No one asked a single question, save Hanse, when I recommended that Whip Ford's society be aided. No one spoke a word when I asked for the expulsion of Hanse and his followers. It isn't healthy, dear friends."

Fredric Economou said in protest, "But George, some of us here have spent our adult lives in the Lagrange Five Project dream. And you have always been there."

Casey said sadly, "Fred, it's no longer a dream. It is reality and you must awaken to it. However, I would like to say one last thing."

They leaned forward.

Professor George R. Casey said, "In spite of the strict qualifications you have before an Earthling can become a Lagrangist, you are not, must not be, anti-Earth. We must devote all of our abilities to helping the sick planet of our origins. Human knowledge is doubling every eight years. With the concentration of scientific minds here in Lagrangia, even that might be sped up. You must continue to release your breakthroughs to your brothers Earth-side. Undoubtedly, you will be able to aid them immeasurably in the efforts to end pollution, depletion of raw materials, war, and all the other plagues that beset Earth. Experimentation is going on in regards to the upgrading of Intelligence Quotients. One day, undoubtedly, these will prove successful, so that more and more persons Earth-side will become qualified to emigrate to Lagrangia. At the same time, as Earth is rebeautified and made safe and progressive, there will be fewer who desire to colonize in space. Earth, again, will be beautiful, as once she was beautiful, and many will prefer to remain there."

After the meeting broke up, they stood around for an hour or more, in spite of the time and the hard work facing them on the morrow. They formed in groups, questioned, argued. Usually there were half a dozen around the professor, but Rex Bader finally had an opportunity to speak to him alone.

Casey said, "Yes, Rex?"

Rex said, "It occurs to me that Whip and I ought to move into your apartment for at least the next few days. It wouldn't hurt for you to have a couple of bodyguards, until those Arabs and Hanse and his stooges are out of Grissom."

The professor scowled. "I hate the idea, but I suppose that you're right. Yes, please do stay." He smiled and added, "At least until after I've fired Susie. Her destiny is here in Lagrangia, not returning with me to Earth-side to be an earthworm. But she might put up a fight."

One of the Council members was heading for them.

"Was there anything else, Rex?" Casey said.

"Well, yes. There's one last thing about this whole mix-up that I haven't figured out."

George Casey looked at him. "Well, what?"

"Was it you who searched my bag, there in the apartment?"

The professor laughed. "I wanted to be sure there was nothing to indicate that you already might be up on the real reason for my making myself scarce."

AFTERMATH

Susie Hawkins and Rex Bader lay side by side in her bed, watching the first flush of artificial dawn come through the window. It had been a strenuous night.

She said lowly, "So you leave today. You and Whip."

"That's right. Frankly, it all cleared up sooner than I had expected."

"Yes. But there was no alternative. In view of the evidence, particularly after Abou Zaki cracked and implicated the Arab Union and International Diversified Industries, there was practically no opposition in the Reunited Nations to Lagrangia becoming independent. It was more or less of an open secret how inept the so-called Reunited Nations staff were."

Rex put his hands behind his head and stared up at the ceiling. "So back we go. I understand that the professor is going to be on the same spacecraft. He knows very well he couldn't remain here without slipping into his old position. Frankly, I hate to leave. I'm afraid I still have the Lagrange Five dream."

She said suddenly, "Rex, you could retire."

"Retire?" He didn't get it.

"Yes. You don't have the requirements to become a Lagrangia . . . well, citizen, I guess you'd call it. But we've been planning for some time to take in retirees, once we had the room. For one thing, it would be fabulously healthy for elderly Earthlings. You'd have no vote, no say in our programs, but you could live here."

He had to laugh. "Retire? Aside from the fact that

I'm only a little over forty, what would I retire on? The United States of the Americas certainly isn't going to continue keeping me on Negative Income Tax if I remain up here."

She said softly, "I've been on the project some fifteen years, Rex. I've never touched the ten thousand pseudo-dollars a year that has accrued to my Earth-side banking account."

Rex Bader looked over at the woman he loved. "I'll be damned," he said. "But I thought one of the requirements of retirees was that they be beyond the child-bearing age."

She said, lowly, "You could have a vasectomy."

"Holy Zen," he said. And then, "Look, Susie, everybody and his cousin seems ready to smuggle me into space. Walt Hanse offered to make me a Lagrangist if I'd go along with him. Whip Ford offered to make me an honorary nigger, as he put it. And now you want to make me a kept man."

"That's not exactly the way to put it," she said in irritation. "I'm in love with you."

He held silence for a long time before saying, "It's no go, Susie. I might be out of my mind, but I'm actually in favor of the requirements to be a Lagrangist, or one of Whip's Promised Land Society. Ultimately, it makes sense. I'll go back to Earth and take up where I left off. Maybe I'll hit the jackpot on one of my private eye assignments and by the time I reach retirement age can come up here, hoping you'll still be around."

She didn't say anything.

He tried to give it a lighter approach. "Meanwhile, what the professor said might come true. There'll be a breakthrough in Biology and I can take a mental-stimulation-pill and, Wizard, I've got an I.Q. of 130. In which case, I'll be seeing you, darling."

ABOUT THE AUTHOR

MACK REYNOLDS was born in California in 1917 of Gold Rush stock. Following school graduation he went into journalism and edited several publications in the Catskill Mountain area of New York. During the Second World War he attended the U.S. Army Marine Officer's Cadet School and was later assigned to Army transport class ships as a navigator in the South Pacific. Following the war he sold his first story to *Esquire* in 1946 and soon became a full-time freelance writer. To gather material for both fiction and articles he moved to Europe where he based himself for eleven years. In all, he traveled in over seventy-five countries and sold his articles to publications ranging from *Playboy* to *The New York Times*. In addition to his travel pieces, he has written more than sixty books, most but not all of them science fiction, and perhaps 200 shorter stories. At present he resides in the art colony of San Miguel de Allende, Mexico, in a Spanish Colonial house which was originally built before the landing of the Pilgrims in New England. He lives with his wife, Jeanette, two Hungarian dogs, two parrots, two turtles and eight Siamese cats.

OUT OF THIS WORLD!

That's the only way to describe Bantam's great series of science fiction classics. These space-age thrillers are filled with terror, fancy and adventure and written by America's most renowned writers of science fiction. Welcome to outer space and have a good trip!

Buy them at your local bookstore or use this handy coupon for ordering:

FANTASY AND SCIENCE FICTION FAVORITES

Bantam brings you the recognized classics as well as the current favorites in fantasy and science fantasy. Here you will find the beloved Conan books along with recent titles by the most respected authors in the genre.